Connie

SHE STOOD UNCERTAINLY AS THE HANDSOME BLACK SLAVE CAME TOWARD HER.

He was going to violate his master's daughter; the penalty, if he were discovered, would be a hundred lashes and banishment to the fields . . . or a summary execution. Yet the sight of her white perfection had fired his desire to a fever pitch, blinding him to possible consequences. Her gray eyes widened and she could scarcely breathe as he took her by the shoulders and pulled her toward him. His hands moved over her body until she was shivering in ecstasy, all apprehensions forgotten. Then they fell to the soft white sand in a transport of desire. . . .

The sun was high in the eastern sky when she left him.

He held her horse's bridle. "You come back come mornin'?" he demanded, the old status of slave and young mistress forgotten.

She nodded. "Yes . . . I'll come back . . . tomorrow."

He watched her go, a deep welling satisfaction flooding his being: at last he'd had her, the arrogant little white bitch.

Weep In The Sun

Jeanne Wilson

A KANGAROO BOOK
PUBLISHED BY POCKET BOOKS NEW YORK

WEEP IN THE SUN

M. Evans edition published 1976

POCKET BOOK edition published November, 1976
2nd printing.................December, 1976

This POCKET BOOK edition includes every word contained in the original, higher-priced edition. It is printed from brand-new plates made from completely reset, clear, easy-to-read type.
POCKET BOOK editions are published by
POCKET BOOKS,
a division of Simon & Schuster, Inc.,
A GULF+WESTERN COMPANY
630 Fifth Avenue,
New York, N.Y. 10020.
Trademarks registered in the United States
and other countries.

ISBN: 0-671-80763-3.
Library of Congress Catalog Card Number: 75-46603.
Cover illustration by James Avati.

Printed in the U.S.A.

For Jeffrey
MY HUSBAND

Part One

~~~~~~~~~~~~~~~~~~~~~~

1662-1667

One

The sun blazed down on the backs of the Negro slaves and the white indentured bond servants. A waving sea of cane stretched for acres, bounded to the north by blue hills, to the south and east by the far-off glimmer of blue-green sea, and to the west by dense underbrush and woodland. The hot still air carried the sickly stench of cut cane, mingled with the acridity of sweating bodies.

Robert Vane straightened slowly, easing the taut muscles, and leaned the curved point of his heavy cutting machete into the hard ground. He squinted up at the sun: it would soon be noon. After two months in the field he could gauge the time fairly well. His eyes watered with the action and he shut them, trying not to remember that softer sun of his English homeland, where one could usually gaze at the sun with ease, so unlike this Jamaican sun, which encouraged the growth of plants ten times more quickly than the one Robert knew.

The sting of the overseer's lash cut across Robert's bare shoulders, bruising anew the tender sunburnt flesh. He looked up to meet the bloodshot eyes of Jez Davies. Robert's dropped as Jez sneered:

"You want to be strung up an' beaten? Y'asking for it."

He cracked his whip again. Robert made no move. Jez Davies had been an indentured bond servant once in Barbados. He had come from humble, oppressed stock living in the warrens of Bristol, then later had been deported to Barbados for some petty crime, and bonded for five years. He redeemed his bond by answering Penn's and Venables' cry for men to further Cromwell's plan to wrest the Indies from Spain and had become one among the thousands of riffraff that passed as an army—an army that later took only one island from the Spanish, Jamaica. He hated Robert Vane. As an educated man, Robert represented the class that had once oppressed him, and he was determined to prove that, for the moment at least, he was in command.

Robert felt again the stinging lash, and the pain triggered off an intense misery and homesickness. His blue eyes filled with tears and Jez, seeing them, shouted with coarse triumphant laughter:

"So you cry, boy, eh? Look at the sun, and weep . . . weep for what you were and what you *are.*"

He wheeled his horse and cantered off.

Robert stood there, ashamed of his tears . . . a man of sixteen did not weep. . . .

"Think of what you *were* and what you *are* . . ."

To think back caused more pain than shutting his eyes to the present, even with its misery, filth and back-breaking work . . . yet the past returned with an insistence that in his weakened state he was powerless to banish. . . .

Cambridge, England in 1658, even under the harsh yoke of Old Noll, as the people called the iron-fisted Protector, had the calm and peace of an academic backwater, and Robert Vane, aged twelve, a quiet gifted boy, was lapped in the same atmosphere. The intrigues of politics and divided loyalties to the regime of Cromwell or to the deposed monarchy meant nothing to the boy. The fact that his father, Richard Vane, had been

4

an ardent Cromwellian made no impression on him, for the memory of the father he had rarely seen was fading fast. He lived in the ancestral home, spending long hours over Greek, Latin, French, and mathematics with his tutor who came in each day from the nearby university. . . .

Then came a day in 1662. The intervening years since Cromwell's death and the Restoration had passed him by, the ebb and flow of politics had scarcely caused a ripple on the surface of his young life . . . until that day . . .

The early morning sun cast soft shafts of shadow across the walled gardens, drying the heavy dew on the close-cut turf and warming the shoulders of Robert Vane as he sat on a stone bench, a pile of books beside him, idly attempting to absorb Tacitus' biography of Agricola. But the air was too soft and balmy, the bird song too joyous for concentration, so that he abandoned the effort and let his thoughts roam. He was startled out of his daydreams by his tutor's voice:

"Come, come, Rob lad, this won't get you to the Inns of Court."

Robert looked up guiltily, quickly reassured that there was no real rebuke in Matthew Ormsby's burred Norfolk voice, though there was worry behind his calm gray eyes, and the lines about his mouth were more sharply etched. His long black scholar's gown was wet at the hem from the dew, and he lifted it away from the grass as he sat down beside his pupil.

"Is anything wrong, sir?" Robert asked.

The older man was silent for a full minute before he said heavily:

"Yes, boy, something very wrong; and how to tell you fills my heart and mind with deep misgiving."

He paused again and glanced around at the peaceful garden and at the mellowed brick of the house, originally built in the middle of the fifteenth century in the Gothic style, with later additions and alterations. The great hall was churchlike in a modified perpendicular fashion, while the buttery and pantry regions retained their original structure. A house lived in by many generations of Vanes, now owned by this young Robert, sole survivor of the Cambridge branch of the family, his father and two older brothers having been killed in Cromwell's ill-fated expedition to attach the Spanish West Indies in 1655. Since then the boy had led a lonely life in the care of his dead mother's sister, a maiden lady of uncertain age and temper, who cared admirably for his creature comforts, but offered no companionship or gestures of affection.

Matthew Ormsby sighed deeply and brought his gaze back to the earnest inquiring regard of his youthful pupil.

"Your kinsman Sir Henry Vane was taken eighteen months ago by the Convention Parliament, and charged with treason . . . and regicide."

Robert said quickly: "My kinsman, yes, but distant. I grieve for the matter, but only in a way that I would for any man so charged; to my knowledge we have never met."

"No, boy. But even so, this affects you and your life deeply."

"How so, sir?"

"Any one bearing the name of Vane is suspect to the present parliament. You will have to leave Vane Court . . . and change your name."

"But, sir," Robert protested. "I was but a child in the Civil War. . . ."

"It's the *name,* boy . . . *and* the fact that your father

6

fought in Cromwell's army in the New World. I have it on good authority that you are to be apprehended. You must leave quickly. . . . By this nightfall, you must be far from Cambridge."

Robert stood up, his face solemn in its perplexity.

"But . . . where will I go?"

"To London. In the teeming crowds of that city you can lose yourself. I will give you a letter of introduction and you will become a junior student at Gray's Inn of Court."

"And change my name, you say, sir?"

"Yes, take mine. . . . I will say you are my son."

"But what if . . ." Robert began dazedly, then broke off. The swiftness of events had clouded his normally astute mind, yet he could appreciate the danger in claiming to be Matthew Ormsby's son. "If I am sought here? What will you say?"

"That I sent you to the colony of Barbados these six months back."

"Won't the servants admit to my being here?"

"They are loyal, I firmly believe, and would say anything to save your life."

"And my aunt . . .?"

"Ah, yes, the good Mistress Ann. I fear that much breath will be expended in persuading her to agree to the deception—her deeply religious convictions forbid such tricks—but between us we must make her agree."

They found Mistress Ann Darby in the buttery supervising the potting of dried herbs. She was a short woman, plump and generally amiable, but with no imagination and no sense of humor. She was soberly dressed in the Puritan fashion, a plain dark gray gown of wool, with a high-necked deep collar that spread over her shoulders, the points in front nearly touching the full white apron that was tied about her practically nonexistent waist. Her still black and luxuriant hair was hidden by a plain white linen coif.

"Good morrow, Mistress Ann," Matthew Ormsby greeted her gravely. "I'm sorry to disturb your house-wifely duties, but I have a matter of some importance to discuss with you."

Ann Darby dusted her plump ringless hands together and murmured:

"A matter of importance. To whom, Master Orms-by?"

"May we speak privately, mistress?"

Ann Darby took one look at his face and led the way through to the principal staircase, a magnificent example of Elizabethan carving, and up to the solar. She seated herself on one of the few chairs and waved Matthew to another. Robert sat on a stool and gazed apprehensively at his aunt as Matthew unfolded his plan. Her pale eyes lit with mild annoyance.

"To encourage the boy in deceit, Master Ormsby, and to expect *me* to be a party to such a deception . . ." she exclaimed.

"It is to save Robert's liberty . . . perhaps his very life," Matthew persisted.

"The Lord will safeguard him."

"I'm afraid the Lord will have no say against the King's troops," Matthew said grimly, then went on, over more exclamations of outrage at such levity. "Believe me, Mistress Ann, I would not urge this course unless I were convinced of the necessity."

To Robert's surprise, there were sudden tears in his aunt's eyes.

"I cannot agree with your plan, but I have no option but to countenance it."

The next few hours passed like a muddled dream for Robert. Matthew Ormsby coached him in the story he would have to tell at the Inns of Court, and how he must live and *believe* that he was now Robert *Ormsby,* son of an obscure Cambridge don.

" 'Twill not be easy, lad, but you have a quick wit and an active brain. Don't be led into exchanges of confidences with anyone whom you may befriend . . . however great the temptation. Mayhap in a few months this newfound zeal for impeaching all those connected with regicides will have died down. I will keep eyes open and ears alert and will endeavor to acquaint you with what passes." He clapped Robert lightly on the shoulder. "Now, here is a letter of introduction to my old colleague, Christopher Wainwright. Only he must know your identity. He will place you in one of the Inns of Court and find you lodgings. Here is a pouch of a hundred gold angels. Guard it well, boy. Christopher Wainwright will arrange letters of credit. . . . Don't fritter away your money, Robert, but live well enough to ease the pains of banishment."

They talked until dinner time. In the great hall Ann Darby sat at her accustomed place at the foot of the table and gestured Robert to the head, not on her right, as was usual.

"You've been too young to take your rightful place, before," she said. "But just once, ere you go."

Robert nodded and gazed around at the evidence of wealth and opulence that belonged to him, hitherto taken so much for granted, never questioned, all soon to become but a memory. His aunt poured a golden liquid into one of the fluted Venetian glasses and said:

"This mead I put down these dozen years past, intending it for your coming to man's estate, but 'tis aged enough, I warrant."

He took the first sip of the crystal-clear brew: as its delicate nutlike aroma tickled his nostrils, his appetite returned with all the urgency of his boy's state.

After the meal was finished, Matthew said with a heavy sigh:

"A meal fit for the King's Majesty, one not to be forgotten. Now, lad, up and pack your belongings . . . but travel light, for the first stage of your journey must be by horse. Then . . . but of this later; just before you leave I'll give you your route."

Suddenly, as he packed, his bewilderment and depression fell from him and he was possessed of a mounting excitement at the unknown prospect ahead. He hefted the valise to his shoulder and ran down the stairs with a light step and a lighter heart.

Ann Darby had packed a basket of food for the journey; together with his valise, it was strapped across the broad flanks of Brown Boy, his chestnut gelding, whom he had ridden since he was a child of seven summers. He thrust the letter and paper with instructions for the route he must take into the bosom of his jacket, then with a hug and a kiss for Ann Darby and a hard handclasp for Matthew Ormsby, he was off.

He had over fifty miles to cover and hoped to make the first stop at the coach house at Ipswich by nightfall. He was lengthening his journey by many miles by going this way, but better that than going direct through the town of Cambridge, latterly Cromwellian headquarters and therefore still suspect by the King's men. He cantered past a group of pack horses laden with produce for the city, and once he overtook a cumbersome private coach, with its leather door hanging down, concealing the occupants. He entered the busy little market town of Sudbury at about three in the afternoon and stopped off at an alehouse to quench his thirst and to give Brown Boy a drink at the stone horse trough. Then on again, wending his way through carrier carts and pedestrians, panniered oxen and laden shoppers,

10

piled market stalls and urgent tradesmen, until he left
the little town behind and came once more to the open
highway, flanked by green fields, the occasional farm
or country house nestling far back in fragrant gardens,
filled with spring flowers, fruit trees heavy with blossom
or the soft green of young corn, until at last, tired by
the day's revelations and exertions, he reached the Bell
Inn, the coaching station at Ipswich.

He stabled Brown Boy with some emotion, winding
his fingers in farewell in the silky brown mane. "Master
Matt will fetch you tomorrow, boy. Eat at your oats and
rest. I'll miss our early morning canters together." He
patted the horse's sleek rump, then strode away to the
beamed taproom, resolutely pushing down this woman-
ish grieving.

He was on his own now.

After a pewter tankard brimming with Northdown
ale, Robert was shown by the hostess of the Bell to his
room under the eaves that shadowed the small unglazed
windows. He had left the taproom with some relief,
conscious of his youth and inexperience among a group
of soldiers, loud with their jests and laughter, their
sly appraisal of his sober but good quality clothes.

Mistress Bridget was panting somewhat with the
exertion of climbing the steep narrow wooden staircase, her full bosom swelling compellingly over the new-
fashioned low-cut gown. She cast a critical eye over the
small but neat and clean-looking room.

"You'll be comfortable enough here, young sir," she
said, then viewed his flushed face and avoiding eyes
with a crinkle of amusement in her own. "I'll send up
young Charity with a nice capon and some good white
bread. With a nice pasty to follow?"

"Thank you, Ma'am. That will do well enough,"
Robert murmured, conscious of her fingers on his arm.
She laughed at his gravity and moved closer: he caught

11

the strong woman smell of her, a compound of fresh and stale sweat, and a new exciting odor that repelled even as it fascinated him.

"Charity might be willing to give more than the supper I send . . . or . . . if you like to wait . . . *I'll* come to you later."

It was a blatant enough offer. Robert felt his throat constrict, and his cheeks burned. She laughed again and said softly:

"I reckon you've not yet had maid or wife. There . . . not to let that worry you, though I'll not press you . . . but if you *do* . . ." she paused for a moment. "Leave your door off the latch when you're ready to bed down."

After the alewife had left, Robert let out a sigh of relief. He removed his leather cassock and sluiced his hot face with cold water, then turned apprehensively at the sound of the door opening again. It was the young girl, Charity, bearing a wooden trencher laden with the promised capon and a hunk of good white bread and rich yellow butter, and another tankard of ale. Robert felt light-headed enough from the last draught but accepted the offering with a smile at the girl. She was young, younger than himself . . . but she held a worldly invitation in her light brown eyes and gave a provocative thrust of her budding breasts.

Robert took the trencher from her and rested it on the broad window seat.

"Thank you, Charity," he said with commendable firmness, despite a quickening of his pulse. "I shall need nothing further."

"Yes, sir," she said meekly but with an air of disappointment.

Robert fumbled for a penny in the pouch at his waist and presented it with some embarrassment. "My thanks for your trouble," he said.

She gave a little bob as she took the coin and went softly from the room.

Robert crossed deliberately to the door and latched it firmly.

$\mathcal{T}wo$

Matthew Ormsby was a worried man, sick with anxiety as to what might have happened to his pupil. The militia had clattered into the forecourt of Vane Court only hours after Robert had left. In answer to their demands for "one Robert Vane, kin to the regicide Henry Vane, now in close custody and awaiting his Majesty's pleasure," Matthew had stated that Robert Vane had been sent to the colony of Barbados many months before.

The young captain swore.

"A likely story. There's been talk of a youth about these parts, I made inquiries in the hamlet and was told of the young master of Vane Court."

"Ah, of course," Matthew said smoothly. "A youth indeed, my own son. A few months older than Robert Vane; these simple villagers would as like mistake one for the other."

"Fetch him."

"My humble apologies, Captain, but the youth has left my care."

"For what destination?"

Matthew spread his thin, blue-veined hands.

"York . . . so he said. He has ambitions to be a silversmith and hopes to get into the Guild as an apprentice." That will keep them from the Inns of Court, he thought.

The captain slapped his sword against his high leather jackboots.

"For your sake, master, I hope it's truth you tell. Be thankful your own name is not Vane. Who else lives here?"

"An elderly lady, aunt to young Robert . . . on his mother's side," he added quickly. "I will fetch her."

Ann Darby arrived in her usual tranquil somber manner. She answered the captain's questions coolly and asked: "You would like to search the house, Captain?"

He hesitated, then: "That will not be necessary, Ma'am."

"A stoup of wine, then? And ale for your men."

She waited tensely for his reply; any delay at all to make Robert's escape more certain. Why didn't he want to search the house? She could have made it take an hour or more. . . .

"Thank you, Ma'am. Most kind."

The wine was brought and dispensed with much slow ceremony by Mistress Darby, calmly ignoring the chafing impatience of the captain. Finally, with a curt "Good morrow" and an irate exhortation to his men to finish quickly with their drinking, the captain moved his cavalcade on.

The captain hesitated at the gates, then to Matthew's relief turned his horse's head in the direction that led to the north. One of the company spurred his horse to the captain's side and murmured a few low words; the cavalcade drew rein and at a signal wheeled about and moved off at a trot toward the road that led south . . . and the coaching station. The captain slowed as he passed the gates and shouted to the distant figure of Matthew, "This will go hard with you, Master Ormsby. Look to yourself on my return."

Matthew's heart grew heavy, not for his own safety,

15

but for the boy he had taught and tended these last years. The captain had only half believed his story in the first place. What had the trooper said that changed his mind from half belief to complete disbelief of his account of Robert's whereabouts?

There was a commotion from the pantry, and Ann Darby returned, dragging a weeping and frightened serving girl.

"This wretch . . ." panted Ann Darby, "has . . . ruined all . . . Let out to the trooper that Robert was here but *today*. After all the warning I gave her."

The girl sniveled. "La, Mistress Ann, I dursen't do it with thought to hurting the young master. The man spoke kind an' I let the day drop afore I can stop my mouth."

Ann turned hopelessly to Matthew. "A hundred swingeings won't undo the damage. What can we do?"

"I doubt the troop of horse will reach the coaching station until tomorrow morning. We can but pray that the coach tomorrow arrives betimes and he is on his way before they get there."

They spent a sleepless night, and before it was light Matthew was up and astride his handsome black mare, a stable boy perched behind him.

"I'm off to retrieve Brown Boy," he told Mistress Darby with a significant glance.

"God be with you," she replied quietly.

Robert woke the next morning to the sound of the steady drip of rain from the overhanging thatch outside his windows. He lay on his bed, gazing in a befuddled way at the dark beams and cracking plaster above his head. The unaccustomed quantity of ale he had imbibed the night before left his senses impaired and his head aching. Then remembrance returned with a jolt, and he sprang from his bed. He sluiced his face and head and dressed hurriedly. Then, securing his belongings, he hastened down the stairway, cracking his head on a low beam as he did so. The taproom was deserted and stank of spilled ale, unwashed bodies, and worse. He went through to a little parlor and so to the kitchen at the back. Here he found the alewife kneading dough; she turned with a smile, no rancor for his fast-latched door.

"You're up betimes, young master."

"I was not sure of the time . . . the skies are dark."

" 'Tis barely six of the clock and the stage not sighted yet. You've time enough for a hearty breakfast."

She sliced bacon with the efficiency of long practice from a flitch that hung by the great stove and tossed the slices into an iron pan which rested above the glowing coals. "And how come you learn your manners and fine way of speaking?" she asked.

Robert kept as close to the truth as possible. "My father is a scholar and taught me all I know."

"You're over young, young master, to travel afar."

"Not so young," Robert retorted, stung more by her maternal tone than by her proposition of the night before. Then, amazed by his reaction, he went on more mildly. "I go to London to study law at the Inns of Court." Then he bit his lip at his lapse in giving such information so near to home.

She nodded, then placed a trencher piled with crisp sizzling bacon before him and poured foaming ale and placed it at his side. She watched him in silence for a moment, then returned to her bread making.

Having breakfasted well and settled his board and lodging, he bade his hostess good-bye and wandered out to the courtyard to await the coach. It was not until nearly eight o'clock that it rumbled into the cobbled courtyard. The coachman, red-faced and gruff, his many-layered cape glistening with rain drops, said they

17

should reach the Swan with Two Necks in Lad Lane, London, in a day and a half, but added gloomily: "But with this plaguing rain and the roads fast becoming rivers of mud, I doubt that the journey'll take less than two an' a half days or more."

An hour later there was a clatter of hooves in the courtyard, a jangle of harness and a splatter of assorted oaths.

"Alewife? Ho . . . within."

She hurried in a flurry of indignation to the tap-room.

"I'll not be summoned in like manner," she began hotly, then subsided on seeing a posse of the militia in control of the tap and swarming in the courtyard. It was still too soon after the days of the Interregnum and the sudden swoops of Cromwell's New Model Army soldiers not to feel apprehensive at the arrival of spurred troops. "A stoup of ale?"

"Yes, but quickly, and for my men. They have ridden long and hard these many hours. You had a young man, no more than a boy, stay here last night?"

The alewife lowered her eyes and her hand paused briefly in drawing the ale, then she completed the task deliberately.

"A young man? What of him?"

"He is here yet?"

"No, he left by the stage, these hours past. He took the coach north, to Durham."

"To *Durham?* God 'a mercy, a fine chase we'll have. Right men, to horse."

The militia clattered out, spurs striking sparks from the cobbles, and amid a flurry of jangling harness and slipping hooves the cavalcade made off—to the north. Audrey Stapler watched them go, hoping that the boy would not be caught, fearing the outcome of the deception at the captain's hands when it was discovered, as no doubt it would be.

When Matthew Ormsby arrived at the sign of the Bell Inn, it was with a lightening of worry that he discovered that the coach had departed south some hours ago and that the captain and his men had been directed to the north.

" 'Twas the least I could do," the alewife panted, bosom again in danger of escaping its scanty confines. "The young gentleman, just a boy with the prettiest manners you ever saw, what could the lad have done to be under suspicion?"

She drew Matthew a generous tankard of ale; he accepted gratefully and paid her with a gold coin.

"You may have saved the boy long years' imprisonment . . . his only crime being in possession of the name he was born with. A blessing on you, Mistress."

She took the coin with gratified cluckings as Matthew finished his ale, then made his way homeward, Brown Boy and the black mare nuzzling each other with velvet noses.

After only one night stop, the coach approached the outskirts of London by late afternoon. Now the wheels rattled over cobbles. They went more slowly through the narrow streets, the high roof of the coach just clearing the myriad signs that hung from the shops and taverns. Robert gazed about in wonderment which increased as they neared the center of the city. The air was foul with heaps of muck and refuse that was piled everywhere, the way obstructed by numerous hackney coaches, private chariots, mounted horsemen, and swarms of pedestrians, and children darting in and out of traffic—sometimes, it seemed, under the very wheels of the coach.

His amazement at the changing scene grew with

every yard traversed, and when the coach finally lumbered to a halt, he could barely bid the coachman a coherent farewell. It was too late in the day to set off to look for Christopher Wainwright, and Robert decided to spend the night at the Swan with Two Necks.

He was roused by the noise of the waking city. He dressed in his gray wool doublet and breeches, with lighter gray hose and a pair of square-toed black shoes. The garret boasted no mirror, but he squinted down at this somberly clad body, certain by what little he had glimpsed on the coach ride into the city that he was sadly out of fashion.

He breakfasted off a piece of beef and bread, then summoning his courage, he stepped out into the pale sunlight on his first voyage of discovery in the big city. The inn's yard was crowded with a jostle of would-be passengers; ostlers, porters tossing baggage with careless abandon into the basket of the coach, and an assortment of idlers, peddlers, and beggars. Robert kept his hand tight on his money pouch, fearful of pickpockets, and edged his way out of the yard into the street. A shop owner was standing at the door of a draper's shop, and Robert asked him: "Could you direct me to Gray's Inn in the village of Holborn?"

"Holborn? Well, yes." The draper proceeded to give directions with many references to "pass the Boar Tavern at the corner of Little Lane" and "by my Lord Harwell's town house." Then he laughed at the expression on Robert's face.

"You'm just from the country, eh, young master? Best be you'd take a hackney coach, won't cost you much more than a silver shilling. But be careful, young sir, they circling boys will soon spot you're a green boy and try to catch you."

Robert thanked the man with relief, then looked about helplessly for a hackney coach; they all seemed to be occupied and clattering by at a great rate. The shopkeeper called out again in between his continuous trade patter:

"You won't get one by *looking*, young sir. S'life, you've got a lot to learn." He gave a piercing whistle, followed by a resounding cry of:

"Coach. *Coach*. A fare."

Almost immediately a passing hackney detached itself from the stream of traffic and lurched to a stop, the horse's hooves slipping on the slimy cobbles.

"Remember," the draper said firmly. "Not more than a shilling a mile or one and six an hour."

"Thank you, sir," Robert said gratefully. "Your humble servant."

The hackney went at what seemed breakneck speed through the narrow streets, the cobbles worn into deep ruts by the constant passage of coach wheels, until at last they arrived at the quiet village of Holborn and the gray stones and timbered pile of Gray's Inn. Groups of students strolled, gossiping or discussing points of law with a lively air; their voices and laughter followed Robert as he was conducted by a steward to where Christopher Wainwright sat working in a paneled room, one wall lined from floor to ceiling with books, their heavy leather bindings scenting the air. He greeted Robert courteously but with an abstracted air and a slight frown at the interruption. His manner changed as he read Matthew Ormsby's letter and he said warmly:

"Welcome, lad. I grieve for the cause for your leaving home, but I agree with Master Ormsby's decision. A fine man and a good scholar. We had many a romp at Cambridge as students together." His keen gray eyes clouded as he thought back to those far-off student days, then he shook off the memory and said briskly: "I will take you to the Master of the Bench.

He also will have to know the facts, but rest assured, no other will. He will decide if you can be accepted as a student and accommodated with lodgings in the Inn."

Robert followed the older man through many large rooms and long corridors, the ceilings beamed and black with age. Wainwright rapped softly on a heavy carved wood door. A brief command reached them:

"Enter."

The Master of the Bench seemed formidable to Robert: richly gowned in a dark green velvet cassock tipped at neck and wrists with fur; piercing eyes above hollow cheeks; trimmed beard, grizzled with gray. He listened in still silence to Christopher Wainwright's introductory speech, then read Matthew Ormsby's letter. At length he said in a clipped dry voice:

"You'll be safe here, if you're careful. From what Master Ormsby writes of your academic qualities you'll do well enough . . . but I want no trouble . . . no expression of political views of the rights or wrongs of the past few years."

"The views of my kinsman Sir Henry Vane I know only by hearsay, sir," Robert replied with spirit. "I was but a child during the Interregnum."

"Humph. We have many students who merely play at study, young gentlemen who come to the Inn with no further thought than leading a gay social life and acting in masques. I want no fripperies in dress or fine feathers on hats. No rapiers or swords to be worn in Commons; you'll be fined three shillings and four pence on a first offence . . . and keep clean-shaven." He allowed his stern features to relax in a semblance of a smile. "The latter injunction you won't have to worry about for a while, I wager. Well, boy, you have your belongings here?"

"No, sir, I left them at the coaching inn."

22

"Well, haste and collect them and return at all speed. Put him in the dormitory with young Lonsdale and Russell," the Master said to Christopher Wainwright. "They're high-spirited, but not over much and not likely to lead the lad astray or encourage him in cards or dice."

Later that day Robert made the journey back to Gray's Inn, paying off the coachman with a new assurance, disclaiming the man's demand for two shillings by saying firmly:

"The fare is a shilling a mile, or one shilling and sixpence for an hour. An' though I cannot be sure as to the exact mileage, 'tis less than an hour we have traveled. One shilling and sixpence."

The coachman grumbled but accepted the coins, mentally lamenting how quickly these young country greenhorns learned city ways, then drove off with a fine flourish of his whip and a clatter of wheels.

Robert stood for a moment contemplating his new home—the home in which he confidently expected to spend the next few years of his young life. Then he took a deep breath and crossed the courtyard to meet the other students.

Three

The days passed in a haze of strangeness, but Robert was settling into his new way of life quickly, beginning to enjoy both the work and the play. He had been lodged in a long narrow dormitory, severe with high bare rafters and simple oriel windows, shared by seven other boys. The two to whom he had been given in charge were Philip Lonsdale, eldest son of Sir Allen Lonsdale, a wealthy landowner who had managed to stay on the winning side during the last few years, so keeping his land and his head, continuing to do so by a judicious switch to the monarchic cause when the Restoration seemed inevitable. Philip was tall and fair, with drooping ringlets of natural hair that fell to his shoulders, pale blue eyes and a delicate skin. He was dressed in the height of the new fashion that was sweeping London after the austerity of the Interregnum, and yet he managed to avoid any degree of femininity, for his voice was deep with a slow drawl, and his shoulders, under the pale blue velvet and the wide lace collar, were powerful enough.

Hugh Russell was quite the opposite in looks, though from the same social background, somewhat higher in the scale. He was a distant cousin to the powerful Duke of Bedford, the Russells of Bloomsbury and of Woburn in Bedfordshire. His dress was every bit as fashionable as Philip's, but of a deep russet velvet, with cream lace at neck and wrists, which admirably set off his short sturdiness and dark brown lightly curling hair. They were both older than Robert, nearly seventeen, and had been at the Inns of Court for two years. They greeted Robert enthusiastically, but with raised eyebrows at his somber Puritan dress.

"S'life, man," Philip exclaimed. "You look like a reincarnation of Old Noll. We must take him in hand, eh, Hugh? Turn this young boor into a proper trig."

There was much more talk and good-natured ribbing in like vein, but Robert didn't mind . . . so might his elder brothers have treated him had Roger and Michael not lost their lives in the far off Indies.

At the first opportunity to escape the intricacies of law, the three young men took a hackney coach and set off toward the center of the city.

"Now," Philip said briskly. "First we must buy materials for our young trig here and get him out of these dull and sober garments, then to find a tailor worthy of turning out a fashionable rig."

They crossed the cobbled street, threading a perilous way through the many equipages that made a constant stream of traffic, to the long building of the Royal Exchange, its open courtyard thronged with merchants, buyers, sellers, visitors, and just plain idlers. They went up to the first floor and there bought such a profusion of silks, velvets, satins, fine laces and fine lawn for under-linen that Robert felt dizzy with the sheer delight of so much finery.

At length Philip and Hugh seemed satisfied with the purchases, and they left the crowded Exchange, laden with parcels. They made their way by side lanes and alleys to a quiet street where Philip declared that the garments would be best made.

The tailor was Flemish with little enough of the English tongue, but he understood Philip's precise instructions well enough, and measured and cut, throwing the material about Robert and snipping and slashing with such quick nonchalance that Robert was afraid his money was wasted. Philip, still pouring out a steady stream of instructions to the tailor on how this detail or that must be, how the doublet must be short with sleeves only just below the shoulder, and how the frill on the petticoat breeches must be so deep, broke off to say soothingly: "No need for concern, Rob, M'sieu Abrue's the best in town, even the Court gallants come to him."

After declaring that they would return in a week for the finished work, the three young men left the dusty little room and made their way back toward the Strand.

"I vow I'm exhausted after all that," Philip declared.

"What about *me?*" Robert asked indignantly. "I'm the one that had those scissors flashing perilous close to my ears at times."

"All in the cause of fashion," Philip said airily.

"Let us repair to the Rainbow," Hugh suggested. "A dish of coffee will revive us all."

"The Rainbow?" Robert asked.

"A coffeehouse . . . yet another step in your education."

"I have never yet tasted coffee, my aunt would never . . ." Robert bit back the words, conscious that he had nearly let slip some information about his former life. If he mentioned any of his family, then questions would be asked. He had grown to like Philip and Hugh in the few days that he had known them, and he felt a need to confide in them and reveal his true identity. He resisted the impulse, knowing it was foolish and a threat to his very safety. He went on quickly: "A coffee*house?* A place where you just drink coffee?"

"More than that, my lad. A place where one hears

26

the latest news; what runs through the galleries this morning is current in the coffeehouses by the noon hour. Where a cuckold can learn of his state, a jilted lover meets his successor. Then there's a good fire in winter, a dish of coffee that costs no more than a penny, you can meet your old friends or make new ones. Let us go."

The Rainbow was indeed a comfortable place to while away an hour or so. It was packed from wall to wall by both the fashionable and the unconventional.

Robert's senses were immediately assailed by the strange aroma that hung in the air like a tangible presence; the warm enveloping smell of roasting coffee beans that he was to smell again all too soon, but in another land under vastly different conditions.

The three sought for accommodation with little success, but at length, after much pushing and jostling, they found a small table for two and crowded onto a bench.

"Look," Philip said in a low voice. "Over by the fire. Sir Roger L'Estrange . . . a man vastly to beware of."

"Why?"

"Because, my innocent country bumpkin, he is a pamphleteer . . . let us say, *the* pamphleteer to end all of the breed . . . a wizard with words, and out to hound all others who write anything even approaching the seditious. His informers are prodigious, and anyone may earn a dishonest penny by taking information to his office at The Gun, in Ivy Lane."

Robert gazed across the smoky room at the man who, though he did not know it, was to have a profound effect on his life. He saw a man of about forty-five or so, dark ringlets of natural hair falling to his shoulders, fashionably clothed, yet not dandified. A lean hawk's face, dark hooded eyes that flashed pierc-

27

ingly when he lifted heavy lids, a thin mobile mouth that proclaimed implacability.

"Well," Hugh said with calm reason. *"You're* not a pamphleteer, so you've nothing to fear."

"No," Philip said slowly. "Not at the moment. But there are many issues I *would* like to write about that would not be to m'lord's liking."

Hugh looked at his friend in surprise. "I find hidden currents after all these years. Our elegant Philip at heart a rebel, yearning to set right the wrongs of the world."

Philip laughed, "Not enough energy, I'm afraid. Just the odd thought now and again."

The next few days passed in stern application to work. Both Philip and Hugh studied hard, not like many of the gayer, more frivolous students.

One night after an excellent supper, when the three were strolling around the courtyard, Philip said:

"There is a masque and a play to be performed next month, and I've been asked to write the play. But, s'life, I've no capacity for such, not fiction, give me facts to write about. Any ideas, Rob?"

Robert thought a moment, an idea beginning to form. "Yes," he said at last. "I believe I have. How long must this play be?"

"Oh, short enough, the masque is the main offering. Half an hour . . . perhaps as long as an hour. No more."

Robert nodded; the idea was taking hold rapidly and resolving into some form of coherence. He left the other two and returned to the dormitory, anxious to get a few notes down before the nebulous plot evaded him. For the next few evenings he worked on his play, discovering that an idea in the head appears vastly different transferred to paper. But he kept at it, and gradually it began to assume a likeness to his first inspired imaginings. By Saturday, when they were all to sally forth again for an afternoon of freedom, he had finished and had the sheets of close writing safe in his doublet. He planned to surprise Philip and Hugh over the dish of coffee at the Rainbow.

They went as rapidly as the crowds would allow to the little tailor's shop in Bantam Lane. To Robert's delight, all his new clothes were finished and fitted to perfection. Philip wanted him to change then and there, but for once Robert was adamant and not to be overruled.

"No, not with the dust of the city about my person. I shall need a good scrub with soap and water before I step into them."

Philip shrugged. "You'll wash yourself into the grave . . . why, only last week you bathed from tip to toe, 'taint natural."

They each carried a parcel, the finery carefully wrapped in clean old calico, and by three in the afternoon they were sitting in the same corner as last week at the Rainbow over a steaming dish of coffee. As soon as they were settled, Robert, with some pride tinged now with embarrassment, handed his play to Philip and Hugh. He watched their faces, anxious for the success of his first efforts at creative writing, waiting for words of acclaim: to his dismay he saw growing concern on each face, and before they had read even half way, Philip threw him an agonized look and burst out:

"S'life, Rob, what could you be thinking of? This could land you in Newgate for life . . . or worse."

Robert felt a tremor of fear at the words: but all that he had done in the play was to put down the true facts of his own flight, changing names all the way through.

29

"But, Philip . . . who's to know . . . the students only . . ."

"Many people in high places attend the masques. L'Estrange's men are everywhere . . ." he broke off and his eyes narrowed. "And L'Estrange is here right now, looking in our direction. Hide this, Rob, fast in your doublet. Talk and laugh, tell a joke . . . anything to act naturally, we've been too solemn over these papers. We'll leave as soon as is decently possible."

They tried to follow his commands, but their jokes were flat and their laughter forced, attracting the attention they wished to avoid. They willed themselves not to glance across the room to where Sir Roger L'Estrange held his usual court and not to look back when once at the door. So they failed to observe L'Estrange's quiet signal to an unobtrusive little man in an old faded doublet and wrinkled hose or notice that this same little man got up and followed them into the street.

They hurried along not speaking at first, Robert's mind a turmoil of incomprehension at the distress caused by what he had written. Then Philip said urgently:

"You must burn that play, Rob. It's a danger to us all."

"But . . . I only . . ." Robert began, but Philip cut in:

"No explanations *here* . . . later."

In their worried haste they had taken the wrong turning and now found themselves in a mean little alley, its narrow confines piled with rotting refuse, when without warning they were set upon by three hooligans, intent on seizing their purses and belongings. The surprise was complete, but Robert, who had had some boxing lessons in his quiet Cambridge backwater, was the first to recover, landing a swing to the jaw of his assailant, then, dropping his precious parcels, followed that up by a left to the stomach. Philip, for all his languid good looks, had taken equally good care of his attacker, who now lay groaning amid the filth, and had gone to help Hugh, who had been set upon by the burliest of the footpads.

"Quick," Philip commanded as soon as Hugh was safe, and grabbing up their bundles of Robert's new wardrobe, they ran for the opening of the alley that led to safer streets. None of them noticed that Robert's play had fallen from his ripped open doublet or that the quiet little man, who had witnessed the scuffle from a safe distance, now picked his way through the stinking, slimy rubbish and picked up the document.

The loss of the play was only discovered after they had reached the safety of Gray's Inn. At first Philip was worried, then he said:

"No matter, there is nothing on the paper to connect the writing with Robert." He glanced shrewdly at Robert. "Never criticize like that on paper, not in these days. A man has been hung for less. That was not a work of fiction, I'll be bound. Eh, young Robert?"

Robert was silent, and Hugh said quickly:

"Nay, Philip, don't press him. 'Twould seem the best counsel to keep silent."

Robert smiled at him in grateful relief. "One day, perhaps, the matter may be talked about."

"And till then . . . no more plays. A pity, for it was well written."

The days passed in their usual uneventful way, and gradually their fears and apprehensions subsided. It was on the following Thursday that Philip had occasion to leave the Inn to meet his father, who had arrived in town and was staying at the George, hard by Holborn Bridge. When nightfall came and he had not returned,

31

both Hugh and Robert became anxious, but Hugh remarked with all his usual stolid reasonableness:

"Mayhap he is to lodge with his father for the night."

"With no pass to sleep out?"

"When did such a minor point stop Philip from doing what he wants?"

When they repaired to the dormitory for the night, both felt convinced that Hugh's suggestion must be right, but just after the night watch had called "Two of the clock and a warm May night," there was a fumbling at the latch and Philip staggered in, bruised, battered, and bloody. . . .

Robert woke immediately and roused Hugh, and together they helped Philip to the anteroom, where they stripped his torn clothes from him and washed the blood and dust from his body. When at last Philip could speak, he said:

"It was . . . L'Estrange's men. . . . I was on my way back here and set on by four . . . I had no chance. They took me to L'Estrange. . . ."

"Did you write this?" Sir Roger had demanded and thrust under Philip's eyes the somewhat muddied but still recognizable copy of Robert's play.

Philip's heart lurched.

"Write that? I did not."

"But you know who did?"

"Indeed I do not, sir. I've never seen those papers before."

Sir Roger frowned.

"Don't play games with me, boy. I've seen you at the Rainbow in the company of two other youths. *One* of you wrote this . . . this scurrilous work, and it was seen to fall during a scuffle you had in an alley. Your name?"

"Philip Lonsdale."

"Sir Allen's son?"

"The same."

"What are the names of the other two?"

"Hugh Russell and Robert Ormsby."

There was no point in giving false names, Philip thought miserably. L'Estrange would quickly discover their true identity. And Hugh would be safe enough under the protection of his powerful kinsman, the Duke of Bedford.

Sir Roger said sharply: "Robert *Ormsby?* Don't you mean Robert *Vane?*"

Philip shook his head. "I know him only as Robert Ormsby."

Sir Roger rose from behind the littered table and paced the room. "It must be the same boy. The description fits from what little I saw of him at the Rainbow." He swung around and faced Philip. "Where does he lodge?"

Philip folded his lips.

Sir Roger nodded to one of the men who had abducted him. A stinging blow across his face brought tears to Philip's eyes and he began to tremble.

Another buffet cut open his eyebrow, and as he felt the warm blood trickle down his face and tasted its stickiness on his tongue, he tried to marshall his thoughts and his wits. . . .

If he could hold out for one more blow, then false information might be believed.

He shut his eyes and waited, trying to still his jerking limbs. Then it came, a vicious punch to his midriff. He gasped for breath and tried to nod.

"Enough." Sir Roger's voice seemed to come from a long way off. "I think he will tell us."

As the pain subsided and his breath returned, Philip

33

tried to raise his head, but was unable to do so and his voice came out muffled when at last he spoke.

"He . . . lodges . . . at one of the Inns of . . . Chancery. Staple Inn . . . I believe. Nay, I am sure, I . . ." His voice trailed off.

"Ah," Sir Roger breathed with satisfaction. "And you, boy?"

"At . . . Gray's Inn."

Philip held his breath, one thought uppermost: if Sir Roger believed his answer, maybe he could get away and warn Robert, and they could both be away before Sir Roger could discover his deception. Even *he* wouldn't risk a raid on one of the Inns of Chancery at night.

"That cub," L'Estrange said grimly. "A fine dance he's led us. Captain Powell has been scouring the countryside these last three weeks. You know who you've been consorting with, boy? A kinsman of Sir Harry Vane, a known regicide, Cromwell's close companion." He nodded curtly to the man who still held Philip by the arm. "See him back to the gates of Gray's Inn, and see that he makes no move to Staple Inn. . . . I'll not have the Vane brat warned."

"And so," Philip concluded, "I was brought back. The only piece of luck in the whole venture. He might have kept me till morning or let me find my way alone. My father's name carried more weight yet than I believed." He shut his eyes for a moment, then said: "We must now make all haste to be gone by daybreak."

"Where'll you go?" Hugh asked practically.

"France is still too risky, as are the Netherlands. Best be we make for Bristol and take a boat to Barbados," Philip said despairingly. "Our lives are not worth a penny piece now. When L'Estrange knows I tricked him, he'll be after me also."

At last Robert found his voice; it rang strangely in

his ears, hoarse and fearful. "I alone am to blame for what happened. I will go, and you must stay . . . surely your father will see to your safety."

Philip made a grimace. "I doubt he holds power enough . . . he was somewhat suspect himself at one time." He looked at Robert searchingly. "It was truth Sir Roger spoke? You are Robert *Vane?*"

Robert nodded. "Yes, but all that I have in common with my kinsman is the name of Vane. My play was but a work of fiction based on the facts of my own experience. But by Sir Roger's actions toward you and by the treatment that has been meted out to me, my views are being rapidly formed," he finished bitterly.

"Come, let us prepare." Philip got up from the low stool on which he had been sitting, recovered somewhat from his ordeal. "We'll take only what we can carry in one hand. A stage leaves the George by Holborn Bridge at dawn. If we go the long way across the fields, we should be able to get there without observation."

Hugh asked: "Have you gold enough for the journey?"

Philip nodded. "My father advanced me a handful of angels against my birthday next week. Rob?"

"Yes, I presented a letter of credit only today. I have about fifty gold pieces."

"Take this as well," Hugh said and handed across a small pouch that was comfortably heavy. He waved aside their protests. "You'll be away but a few months, and who knows, you may return with a hatful of Spanish pieces of eight. Meanwhile, I'll work at getting my kinsman the Duke of Bedford to sponsor you both. I doubt if even Sir Roger will go against *him* . . . and I will endeavor to get word across to you when all this has blown over."

The three clasped hands, their eyes wet with the unexpected separation. Then the two fugitives stole down the creaking wooden steps to the great hall below and out by a roundabout way into the soft darkness of an English May night and, they hoped, to a banishment of only a few months.

Four

After a weary, jolting, rumbling two and a half days on the road, the stage coach halted at the Bristol Maid, and the stiff-jointed travelers disembarked.

After a hasty dinner they wended their way along the narrow cobbled streets worn smooth by sledges, for they were so narrow that no modern cart might pass. As they neared the waterfront, the crowds increased—a rough and tough seafaring lot, swarthy piratical types, blond Vikinglike giants, a plethora of every type and tongue. The local merchants were there in force, supervising the unloading of their wares just arrived from the New World or seeing to the stowage of goods to the old.

"Look," said Philip, pointing.

They approached to where a small vessel was being loaded with provisions.

"Where are you bound?" Philip called.

A seaman flung a sack of flour on board and answered: "West Indies."

"Barbados?"

"No, my cully, you be wanting the *Rose of the West* for Barbados. Ask for Captain Crooks."

He gave them rough directions, and after many more inquiries along the route, they at last found Captain Crooks of the trim little ship *Rose of the West*.

"I hear you're bound for Barbados? Have you room for two more passengers?"

"If I take you, you'll be my only passengers. I'm loaded with household goods and gewgaws for the settlers."

He quoted them a figure for the passage that seemed reasonable enough, so they agreed without haggling.

"Pay as you come aboard," he advised. "Then if you change your minds, it'll be no loss to you."

"We won't change our minds," said Philip firmly and counted out the gold and silver coins from among those he hadn't concealed about his body.

"You'm best be careful, young sir, how you flash y'r gold. Bristol is alive with rogues and cutpurses. Well, we sail on the tide at three of the clock. Best be aboard betimes, the tide won't wait . . . and neither will I."

With that he tucked the money for the passages into his waistband and ran lightly up the rope ladder that hung over the side of his ship.

"Let us purchase some warmer clothing for the journey," Robert suggested. "A doublet and breeches of woollen worsted and some heavy wool hose."

"Indeed," Philip agreed. "It'll be cold at sea of a night. I noticed some stalls selling such gear back toward the town, though I'd liefer not go far from the *Rose of the West,* for L'Estrange's men may be here if they suspect at all we might try to leave the country. I feel a foreboding in my bones."

"Then we'll stop at the first stall and buy whatever rough and ready clothing they have to offer," Robert said, glancing around apprehensively, for Philip's unease had sparked a similar feeling in his own breast. They set off at a fast pace, their eyes sharp for possible followers, but could see no one who appeared in the least interested in them. They had only covered a few yards when from a side alley shot a running youth, nearly knocking them over. He staggered at the impact but kept running, throwing over his shoulder:

" *'Ware* . . . the press. Take to your heels."

They stood irresolute, puzzling his meaning, then as his words registered, a mob came pouring from the alley, hysterical cries and hoarse screams ousting all other noise, and before they could escape, they were caught up in and a part of its heaving mass. They struggled vainly against the onrush of bodies and were separated, carried away from each other by the flailing arms of the terrified townspeople. Robert glimpsed Philip in the clutch of two burly ruffians: before he could strive through the press of bodies to help him, he felt a searing blow on the side of his head. As the last shreds of consciousness slipped away, he was flung over an ill-smelling shoulder.

He woke in darkness, a darkness that seemed at first to be an extension of his unconsciousness.

How long?

Minutes?

Hours?

Then he realized that this was no dream; his hands were manacled; his body bruised and cramped among other bodies, bodies that gave off the stench of stale sweat, and there were such groans from men in pain and despair, he felt he must have been transported to one of the lower planes foretold by Dante. His head ached, he could feel blood caked in his hair, stiffened and dried on his face. He was bitterly cold; he could just make out that his doublet had been stripped from him and that his feet were bare.

His money?

He couldn't feel the leather band and pouch about his waist, but it was possible that it could still be there, for he was so battered and bruised that normal feeling had vanished.

39

"Philip?" he called hopefully, his voice thin and reedy amid the cacophony of sorrow.

"Over here."

Philip's voice was almost unrecognizable in its weakness. By dint of much calling to him, Robert managed to inch himself through the darkness, accompanied by curses and railings. He found Philip at last, wedged against the bulkhead, which provided some little support.

"Where are we?" Robert asked fearfully, the shadow of Newgate black in his mind. "Did L'Estrange's men get us?"

"Nay, lad. Perhaps we would have had more of a chance *if* he had us. We're aboard some stinking ship. We've been press-ganged, Rob, lad. Bound for one of the colonies, I'll be bound . . . not in a more or less comfortable cabin aboard the good ship *Rose of the West,* but in this malodorous hold."

Philip's voice was bitter, even in its extreme weakness.

"Are you hurt much?" Robert queried, knowing how Philip feared physical pain.

"My eyebrow's split open again and my left collar bone feels mighty odd."

"If they'd only take these plaguey things from our hands, I could help a little."

"Help? What with? We'll see no water for washing these next few weeks, nor little to drink, I warrant."

They could feel the toss of the boat on the open sea now, but this only added to their misery, for some among them began to retch and vomit, so increasing the stench that pervaded every square inch.

The first night passed with agonizing slowness, and soon after dawn a hatch above them was raised; by the little light that filtered down Robert could view the extent of their misery.

He shut his eyes in revulsion.

A villainous-looking lot they were among: faces grown hard in a life of poverty or from spending years in prisons; faces ravaged by tears and encrusted with filth; old faces, young faces, all with haggard eyes and an air of doom.

Robert opened his eyes and looked at Philip, whose face was pale and drawn beneath the caked blood encrusting his wound. Then from the hatch a leather bottle of water was lowered. A mad scramble ensued for it, but it was brackish and warm. The food which followed was fought over by men who behaved like animals, though it was nothing but moldy ships' biscuits and strips of tough, evil-smelling beef.

Robert could make no attempt to join the scramble, but by nightfall hunger and a raging thirst made him wish that he had done so. When the hatch was raised again, he managed to get a palmful, half of which he dribbled into Philip's mouth. The food he still ignored; the mere sight sickened him and so temporarily assuaged his hunger. Philip had lapsed into an uneasy sleep and moaned and muttered; Robert feared that he had a fever and that the untended wound would suppurate. That day dragged imperceptibly into night and night into day: the hours unmarked, the sun never seen except as a pale glow when the hatch was raised each morning and evening.

After what must have been a week or so, they were let up on the deck in small parties of about six at a time. The joy of breathing fresh, salt-laden air was more than Robert could bear. Tears ran down his face unchecked and unheeded. A leather bucket was hauled up from the side, and they were allowed to douse each other in turn with cold seawater, difficult enough to manage with their manacled hands. This cleansed much of the filth from their bodies, but they had no change of

41

clothing, so the muck and sweat, blood and grime that clung to and stained their rags would not be dislodged.

Although it was now well into early summer, it was chilly enough on the rolling gray Atlantic to keep them shivering after the cold shock of the dousing, and Robert feared that Philip might contract yet another fever, for the first had not entirely abated. It was due solely to his youth and normal well-being that he had not succumbed to a severe infection from his neglected wound. But he appeared to come to no harm and gradually became accustomed to the daily dousing.

Despite their initial disgust at the fare, Philip and Robert forced themselves to eat enough to avoid starvation. Both had lost weight: their features had become gaunt and pallid from the long sojourn in the dark of the hold. Philip's former good looks had gone; the wide livid scar puckering his brow over his right eye gave him a rakish, cynical appearance; his long fair hair was a tangled matted mass. Robert's former air of innocence and wonder at all that chanced was replaced by a bitter wariness, his gray eyes held a cynicism they'd never known before.

"I learned today when we were up on deck," Robert said one night, "that we are bound for the island of Jamaica."

"Jamaica?" Philip said thoughtfully. "I mind when it was taken, back in fifty-five. Cromwell's famous Western Design that he thought would wrest all the West Indies from the Spanish . . . but it proved a great fiasco, only Jamaica was taken."

"It was in that campaign," Robert said bitterly, "that I lost both father and brothers. It seems my bones will join theirs yet."

Philip said nothing but thought with compassion how his young friend had changed over the last weeks.

"What will they do with us there?"

42

"Sell us into bondage, I suppose," Philip stated flatly.

"Sell us? *Sell?* To work and sweat in the fields? Phil . . . they . . . couldn't. . . ."

"Why not? Just because we are who we are? The press-gang takes no note of quality, 'tis quantity they want. I've heard 'tis a big trade now: a new way to make money, trafficking in men's bodies . . . women's too. They are encouraged to breed indiscriminately, to get more slaves without the exertion of buying . . . oh, yes, it's a constant traffic now, ships to Africa with goods and wares load up with slaves and back across to the New World."

"Yes, but . . . *blacks* are . . ." Robert began.

"Do you think it more permissible to make a black man a slave than a white man?" Philip broke in.

"I don't know, I've never had to think of it before. But surely to compare savages . . . ."

"*Are* they savages, as you call them? Isn't it just possible that they have their own civilization, their own way of life, customs, religions? Just because their ways are different from ours, their skin a different color, must we term them inferior? Must we invade their country, snatch them from family and friends, and condemn them to a life of servitude in an alien country? Don't you see the inhumanity in it all, the injustice? Don't you, Rob?" Philip spoke with passion, his drawl replaced by a swift intensity.

Robert turned in the gloom of the hold and peered at his friend curiously:

"You speak as if you would have them as equals," he said wonderingly.

"Why not? They are men, created by the same process as us. If there is a God, then so too by him."

"*If?*"

To the boy brought up under the sternly religious eye of Ann Darby, this was heresy of the highest order.

43

"If," repeated Philip firmly. "The idea of an omnipotent Being I find increasingly hard to believe in . . . especially as the scriptures would have us believe. Too much wickedness is performed in the name of religion for me to believe that it is other than man-inspired."

Philip lapsed into silence after his passionate outburst, and Robert pondered over his words until he fell into the uneasy slumber that he had grown used to: a slumber ever conscious of the discomforts of the body, the snores and groans of their unfortunate companions, the creaks of the ship's timbers, and the pitch and roll as she sailed through the seas.

The weather was becoming hotter now as the rolling ship entered deeper tropical waters. One day, two of the youths who had been press-ganged died: who could say from what cause? The next day one of the political transportees died. In spite of pleading by the whole company in the hold for the bodies to be removed, this was not done for nearly two days; not until the putrescent odor permeated to the upper deck.

"If they treat us so ill," Robert said, fearful that the terrible stench would cause an epidemic through the hold, "they won't get much of a price for us."

As the sixth week drew slowly to a close, they were allowed to be on deck for longer intervals, long enough to wash after a fashion their now tattered and faded breeches. Their shirts were washed on them and dried clinging to their bodies; the manacles precluded their removal. The time spent in the open gave more color to their skins, and some of the youth crept back to their gaunt faces.

One evening as the sun was sinking in a rose and golden splendor, casting broad bands of brilliance across the deep blue sea, a voice rang out from the lookout: "Land. La-and. *Laa-aand.* Ahead-o."

There were joyous cries from the cabin emigrants and

hold prisoners alike. Feet pounded overhead with added zest, ropes smacked the decks with a new vigor, and the little ship with her assortment of human cargo surged ahead as if drawn to land by strong invisible guidelines.

Robert and Philip hardly slept through that long stifling night. They were in a fever of impatience to get on deck the next day and see the island, but it was not until the early evening that they were allowed up.

Robert drew in his breath at the sight.

" 'Tis the fairest scene I have ever yet beheld," he said softly.

The mountains reared high into the heavens, their slopes covered in blue-green lush vegetation of trees and shrubs, their highest peaks wreathed with pink and violet wisps of cloud, serried rank upon serried rank, deep purple clefts, contrasting purple shadows against high ridges of emerald green. The late afternoon sun cast shadows and highlights that made the colors constantly change, so that the shapes of the mountains seemed to shift and alter.

Clustering palm trees came down to the water's edge, their fronds waving in the warm breeze like giant feather dusters.

They were making for what appeared to be a town at the tip of a long, thin, curving causeway that was strung out from the mainland and snaked across to practically enclose an enormous natural harbor. Apart from the town at the uttermost tip, the rest of the causeway seemed to be sand and scrub, giant cactus raising prickly fingers to the sky, while all along its edge were spreading mangrove swamps, unapproachable and mysterious in their hidden depths.

The long journey had ended at last.

Soon, they all thought, they would be taken ashore at Port Royal and their future decided, but before that could happen, everyone was herded back to the hold. It was anticlimactic after their first glimpse of land, of people free to walk the streets.

That last night in the hold passed even more slowly than the first night aboard. The heat was like that from a furnace now that the ship was stationary, and there was a concerted groan of relief when at length the hatch was raised and they were all ordered on deck, where at last their manacles were removed. The feeling of freedom was like wine, but the sores and suppurations on their wrists stung with sudden exposure to strong sunlight and salt-laden air.

Philip and Robert gazed in astonishment at the scene before them.

"It's a little London," Philip murmured in awe. "A little *hot* London."

The houses were jammed close together, some being four stories high, some so close to the water's edge that they had been built on pilings driven into the sand, their upper stories hanging over the sea.

They could hear all the sounds of a busy prosperous town, voices raised in anger or bargaining; the raucous quarreling of drunkards, even at that early hour; the oaths and curses of seamen in a dozen different languages; the screams and shrill laughter of women; the sudden high-pitched cry of a child; and a cacophony of barking dogs, neighing of horses, and rumble of traffic.

It was so unlike that which they had anticipated that they were lost in wonder and had not noticed that a group of prosperous-looking men had come aboard. Their attention was distracted from the bustle of Port Royal by a rustle of anticipation that ran through the ship.

It was with a sickness at heart and a knot of fear tightening in their stomach that they realized the dreaded moment had arrived. . . .

An auction block had been set up in the center of the

deck, and one of the political transportees had been roughly urged on to it. He stood there, shaking with fever and fear, a pitiful object in his tattered and filthy clothes, his beard and hair a tangled mass.

The bidding began, and man after man was subjected to the humiliating process of being told to strip naked, to be pummeled and examined all over, jaws wrenched open to inspect teeth. . . .

Robert felt a surge of revulsion at the sight and glanced quickly at Philip, pale by his side. The utter degradation of holding men up for sale, like cattle in the market place. . . . For the first time he realized that they might be parted, that they might be bought by different buyers. . . .

"Phil," he whispered. "We may be called at any moment. If . . . we go to different buyers . . . we may not see each other again . . . for years."

Philip nodded, eyes suddenly bright with tears.

"I know. This may be good-bye. Hang on, Rob, don't let them get you down. I'll . . . I'll not forget you, Rob. These last few weeks in this hell ship . . . if it hadn't been for your presence. . . ."

They clasped hands warmly, not noticing the pain in their manacle-eroded wrists, trying to give each other courage to face the future.

Then Philip was pushed to the block.

Despite the filth that covered him, there was in his very bearing a promise of what he once was and would be again, so that the bidding was brisk and he was soon sold for twenty pounds to a coarse-faced, thickset man in a sweat-stained doublet and dusty sagging breeches.

Two felons took the stand and went for small sums.

It was now Robert's turn.

He stood, shivering in his nakedness despite the heat, and through a shocked haze heard the bidding for the body of one Robert Vane, male, last of a long line of

47

country gentlemen, heir to the large estate of Vane Court and untold wealth: his only crime the name he bore. . . .

Bidding for the freedom of a human being, so that his every action from now on was at the command of others; his own wishes subject to those of others. To possess nothing, to *be* nothing. . . .

He went at length for twenty-one pounds to a man who had bid continuously, topping each offer; he had prodded and poked Robert with an odd gentleness, almost in the nature of a caress, and Robert had shivered anew, convinced that here was something to be feared and avoided.

He stumbled from the block by the side of his master, this man whose hands held his future. He cast a last look of despair at Philip.

Philip raised his hands slightly and tried to smile, but his lips trembled and he abandoned the attempt. He shut his eyes so that the tears would not fall.

Five

Robert's filthy clothing was left on the deck and he was given a pair of breeches of rough Osnaburg and a loose shirt of the same material. Though the garments were made with no thought for cut or fashion, they were clean and their roughness held a strange comfort.

He dimly noticed that his purchaser had bought two other men, both felons, though guilty of what major or minor crimes he had no knowledge. He learned later that the younger of the two, Jem Marston, had stolen a hen to make broth for his sick child; for this he was sentenced to be hanged, then the sentence had been commuted to transportation for life. He was from Kent and had been a blacksmith and would therefore fill an important post on a growing plantation. The other, John Hastings, older than Jem by a dozen years, had defended his daughter who was to be ducked in the village pond as a supposed witch, but the screaming mob forced him to watch her dying struggles. He had gone berserk and wounded the leader of the mob before he was subdued, then hauled before the local justice and sentenced to be hanged; but men were needed in the young, underpopulated colonies, and he was thrust aboard the trading ship with hundreds of others.

By now it was long past noon, the sun blazing down on the oil-calm waters of the harbor, hazing the distant mountains to a smudged gray-green. Robert and his

49

two fellow bondsmen were herded into a small rowing boat and made to man the oars across the great expanse of the harbor, their destination being Passage Port, a bay that cut deeply into the coastline. He was weak with fatigue from the exertion, after the long weeks of enforced idleness and the scanty diet on which he had existed, as were the other two, and they made but slow progress.

Once ashore, they joined a group of Negro slaves who had arrived by another ship two days earlier. Robert viewed them with compassion and shuddered to think what *their* journey had been like. He felt a kinship with them, but they only gazed at him and the other two white indented servants with dull glazed eyes, too broken by their fate even to feel hatred. There were about fifty of them, joined by ropes around their necks and ankles to form a coffle; even the women and young girls, who made up about half their number, were joined in like manner. Again Robert felt a swift revulsion at men who could treat another human being in such a fashion; he knew now what Philip had meant on board ship when he gave vent to his impassioned outcry against slavery. There was a white overseer in charge of them, astride a prancing black horse, holding by a loose rein two others, a gray and a brown colt. The latter made Robert's eyes smart in memory of Brown Boy.

"You can ride, boy?"

He jumped at the gruff question.

"Yes, I can ride."

"Good. You can travel on the colt. He's a present for the colonel's daughter . . . so treat him gentle. Right, boy?"

"Right, sir," Robert replied, wondering who "the colonel" was.

"We'll make all speed to St. Jago de la Vega, where

we lodge tonight. We'll start as soon as you've had a bite of food."

A piece of salt pork and a flat cake made from some kind of meal was thrust toward him, and Robert ate the food gratefully. He stole his first real look at the man who had bought him—not an overly pleasant sight: short, thickset, broad of shoulder, mean blue eyes set between puffy lids; lips that were thin to the point of nonexistence; a skin weathered brown and leatherlike by the sun, with a welter of broken veins that spoke of an addiction to strong liquor. Now his voice held a gruff kindliness, sounding oddly to Robert, who felt that it was more assumed than real.

The rough meal ended, they were astride the two horses, and Robert caught his last glimpse of Philip, just landing from a similar rowboat, as they went trotting along the road beaten flat by the passage of many feet and rutted by wagons. The coffle of Negroes moved off behind them, their bare feet shuffling through the dust, the white overseer riding alongside, cracking his cowhide whip at those who stumbled and slowed the others—the whip that was to become the symbol of their domination. Robert felt a traitor to the other two indentured white men, as they trudged along with the coffle and he rode easily on the frisky little colt. They soon drew ahead of the coffle, and Robert felt that it was good to be astride a smooth glossy back again, his fingers twined in a silky brown mane; he allowed himself, just for a moment, the luxury of thinking of Brown Boy and all that he had left behind. . . .

He was startled out of his indulgence by his owner slowing his mount to come alongside the colt and the question:

"Your name, boy?"

The voice had a rough burr, from Devon or Somerset, Robert guessed.

"Robert Vane . . . sir," he added.

"Well, Robert Vane, mine's Jez Davies." Ah, I was right, Robert thought, *Somerset*.

"I'm head overseer at Wells, Colonel Wells' property . . . oh, no, I didn't pay your price . . . your master is a man of much property and likely to be a very wealthy man, come a few years more. But you do as *I* say . . . you play your part, I'll play mine. You keep your nose clean and I'll see right by you." There seemed no reply to this, so Robert kept silent. "How'd you come to be aboard the *Martin?*"

This was the first time that Robert had heard the ship's name, and it stuck in his memory as a word or a name to be shunned ever more.

"I . . . we . . . were caught by the press-gang."

"I thought as much, too young to be one of the political prisoners, don't look like a criminal."

He swung sideways in the saddle and viewed Robert in the bright afternoon light. "You'm a turn o' speech that sounds of the gentry?"

"Yes, I . . . I was a student of law."

"Well, you'll need no law here . . . we make our own, as we need 'em . . . just a civil tongue and a willingness . . ." he slid his eyes from Robert's face . . . "a willingness . . . to work." He spurred his horse and drew ahead. "Follow close, Robert Vane, we must reach St. Jago afore night catches us."

It was almost dark when they cantered along a broadening road, so that Robert could scarcely make out the ruins of once lovely buildings that had been torn apart or razed by Venables' invading army seven years before. He vaguely made out the outline of a church on his left, then they passed through what seemed to be a large square, with high buildings on all four sides. Now darkness was quite upon them, and they picked their way by starlight to a small tavern in an alley that branched off from the square. This tavern had once been a Spanish nobleman's house, one of the few to escape complete destruction by the English soldiers, but Robert was too tired and dispirited to appreciate its decayed exotic beauty. After a supper consisting of some highly seasoned stewed green bananas with okra and what tasted like some form of shellfish—a supper that tasted like ambrosia after the diet he had grown accustomed to on board ship, though later it sat uneasily in a stomach shrunk and unused to such fare—he was shown to a small room off a paved courtyard, in a wooden building that housed the slaves. There was no light to examine his surroundings. The room was stuffy and practically airless, its only ventilation some horizontal slats in one wall; but after the filth and stench of the ship's hold, it was a palace of delight. He flung himself on the pallet filled with coconut fiber that served as a bed, and despite his mixed feelings of outrage at the sale of his body, his despair and hope for the future, he fell into a deep untroubled sleep. It was the first time for many weeks that he had been able to sleep lying down.

At dawn Jez Davies and Robert were astride their horses and cantering out of St. Jago. The road, once out of the town, was little more than a trail and wound across a great plain upon which cattle were grazing. To their right rose mountains. Overhead, great vultures lazily circled, black against the vivid blue sky, their broad wings motionless as they drifted on the eddying air currents. A heady air stirred by a breeze from their left dried the sweat on their bodies even as it formed: an air heavy with strange exotic perfume of wild vanilla and jasmine. Robert felt a lift of spirits as some of his apprehensions for the future left him. He thought again fleetingly of Philip and wondered how he was faring, then pushed all such thoughts firmly from his mind.

He became aware that Jez Davies was talking, his rough homely voice barely audible above the clop of the horses' hooves and the sough of the breeze:

"When a man's bought for bonded service, that service lasts five years. After that you're free, you get a bit o' land an' you work it, make a living. You try and run away before that five years is up, you break the bond and you stay in service for life. Don't try it, you'll get lost in the swamps or caught by a runaway Spanish slave. Oh, yes, there's many o' them left up in the mountains, call themselves Maroons and still cause plenty o' trouble. They fled with Ysassi and fought us for years . . . a year or two back you couldn't travel like this, just the two of us, had to be a strong-armed party: that was before we chased Ysassi from his stronghold; you'd be stalked for hours by one o' the blacks, then either ambushed and tortured or a quick knife in the back, and believe me, boy, the last was a better fate. It was tough then, boy, five long years we had of it. I was a bond servant in Barbados and on promise of freedom I joined Penn and Ven-ables. . . ." Jez Davies paused, his mind back in those far-off days, and Robert asked at length:

"So you were here right from the beginning?"

"Aye, boy. Those early days, men died like flies from lack of food, yellow fever, and all manner of ills and strange tropical humors. It was easy enough to take the Spanish capital, they'd all fled to the hills, it was the resistance in the mountains that got us down, and still the fever took its toll. Five long years, a battle against the land, the weather, and the Spanish."

"How did you come to your present position, Master Davies?"

"Colonel Wells was a good soldier, and when he settled on his piece o' land, I reckoned he'd be a good employer. He started with only three hundred acres, now he's got four hundred . . . reckon it'll soon be five hundred. He sent for his wife and family two years after we took the island after it'd quietened down a bit when we'd penned the Spanish up in the hills. . . ." He shot a sideways glance at Robert's intense face, and again the boy felt a spasm of uneasiness at the expression in the man's shifty bloodshot blue eyes. "Aye," he went on. "His wife and two children. He'd built a house of wood, now he plans another of brick and fine hardwood." Jez Davies' voice had a note of envy in it, and Robert wondered when the former implied admiration of Colonel Wells had turned to covetousness for his growing wealth.

"And what does Colonel Wells grow or farm on all these acres?"

"Why, *sugar,* boy. This is the land of the sugar cane. A part is planted with the food we need; plantains, yams, corn . . . we done start a coffee walk, got some young trees from an East Indian merchantman . . . a part for pasturage and cattle . . . but the greater part is sugar. The plantation is a little world of its own, as you'll soon find out."

His last words dispelled the feeling of well-being Robert had felt as he listened to Jez Davies and his account of the early days of the settlers, and a renewed fear for the future took hold, which was again partially dispelled as new sights and sounds greeted him. They were passing through cane fields now. Robert saw a group of black slaves heaping a cart, others working in the fields. They stopped working to watch the two horsemen, then began again at the crack of a whip from a mounted gang leader. They passed more fields, with numerous slaves hoeing and weeding: to Robert's sur-

55

prise he heard the sound of singing, an alien chant with an insistent rhythm that stirred his soul with sadness. Now they were in sight of the buildings: a water mill by a running stream; what he was to learn later was the boiler house, an adjoining curing house raised on strong timber piles; close by were barracks for the slaves, and many other buildings in the process of construction. There was much activity and sound; the loud sawing of wood, the ring of an axe in the nearby wooded area, the hollow clang of iron, subdued murmurs from the slave workers and shouted orders of the overseers. On a slight elevation some way from the other buildings stood a large roughly constructed timber house, low and sprawling.

"The Colonel's house," Jez Davies said shortly. "And up there"—he indicated a flat-topped hill, which had been cleared of trees and underbrush—"will be the new great-house."

Robert gazed at the site in astonishment: the foundations were vast.

"It will take a while to build," he murmured.

"Aye," Jez Davies said shortly, then he led the way to the stables, where Robert slipped from the colt and stroked its velvet nose in farewell. He watched sadly as the creature was led away by a young Negro. Then, at Jez's impatient command, he followed the overseer to his allotted quarters.

He viewed the rude walls of wattle and daub, the palm-thatched roof, the moldy straw pallet, a roughly hewn palmtree trunk that served both for table and chair, a calabash gourd that was the main utensil for drinking and carrying water for washing . . . and his heart grew yet more heavy. There were a number of these huts, a little apart from the slave barracks, and one larger wooden hut—too roughly made to be called a house—which was Jez Davies'. He was issued with

provisions—salt beef, corn meal, and a piece of yam—
and shown where he could cook over a charcoal fire in
a three-legged coal pot.

Jez Davies looked at him meaningly and said: "Like
I said, you do as I say, I'll see you right. I'll tell you
your duties . . . later." Then he was gone, while Robert
was left again with a feeling of unease.

Robert was left to his own devices for the rest of the
day. A vast anticlimax took possession of him after the
interest of the journey. Later he ventured out into the
yard, hungry enough to eat the food provided, yet not
versed in the way of cooking it. He stood looking down
at the raw ingredients in his hands, then at the cooking
pot, in a hopeless puzzled way. There was a muffled
snort of amusement behind him. He turned and saw a
young Negro girl watching him. At his expression she
burst into laughter. It was a gay and joyous sound, the
like of which he hadn't heard since his days at the
Inns of Court, and he felt a lift of spirits. She came
close, and he glimpsed white teeth in a round dark face,
eyes big and almost black, fringed with dense short
curling lashes. She was plump under a blue cotton
gown, hair braided in numerous pigtails, her feet bare
on the sunbaked earth. Robert gave a rueful smile at
her laughter, and she said:

"You soon learn fe cook. Let I show you."

She took the food from him and disappeared toward
the barracks, returning in a few minutes with a heavy
iron pan and a long sharp knife. He watched her slice
through the meat and the yam and toss them in the
pan in which she had heated some oil, then add season-
ing. She added a scoop of water, using a small calabash gourd, and fragrant steam wafted from the pot.

While the food cooked, she examined his wrists and
exclaimed at the sight:

"Eh, eh. Worse than I see since me born."

Her voice was soft with an intonation that was strange to his ear. She darted away again, then returned with a calabash containing some evil-smelling substance. She led him to the water butt and laved cool rainwater over the sores, patting them dry with a rough cloth. She then smeared the gray unguent over his wrist; at once, despite his initial skepticism, he felt an assuagement of the pain and discomfort he had endured for weeks.

"Thank you," he murmured as she darted back to the now bubbling pot. "What's your name?"

"I call Maria," she answered.

"Have . . . have you been here . . . long?"

She gave a trill of laughter. "Lawd, a baan-ya . . . I here wit' the Spanish, afore the English come. Me mumma she cook in the great-house, but me don' member the fighting . . . we all run quick quick to the hill, dem."

"And how did you come here?"

"It hungry hungry we get on the hill. So we go back to the house, an' fin' the Colonel tek it. So 'im say 'im wan' a cook when 'im start 'im house, an' me mumma come here wit' me an' me brother." ·

Robert had difficulty in understanding her quick talk with its odd syntax, but he was grateful to her, and the food she had cooked was surprisingly good, though too hot with peppers for his English palate. He offered to share it with her, but she was suddenly shy and darted away with a quick: "Come sundown, I cook again fe you."

He slept during the afternoon and woke to find the two other indented servants had arrived, together with the weary, footsore coffle of Negro slaves. These had been put in the slave barracks in care of those who had been on the plantation for some time, to settle down and learn a smattering of the English tongue and generally recover from the journey.

The two white men, Hastings and Marston, were put together in one hut; when they all met in the yard that evening for the communal use of the cooking pot, they ignored Robert's greeting, looking sourly beyond him, believing him to be favored in having ridden the colt. They resented, too, his quiet manner and way of speech, muttering and grumbling together in their rough dialect voices. The fact that all three of them were stripped of class privilege or distinction now didn't occur to any of them; the fact that they were chattels, at the mercy of a capricious owner's whim, had not yet impressed their minds.

Maria appeared and cooked Robert's supper and inspected his wrists. She seemed satisfied and applied more of the dark, sticky, odorous unguent.

The quick fall of the tropic night with its accompanying swarms of mosquitoes drove Robert into his hut, though tonight he was not so troubled by the mosquitoes, as the unguent seemed to act as a repellent.

He lay naked on his pallet, unable to sleep with the strangeness of it all, wondering what he would be called upon to do in this spreading plantation, reflecting that he had no training for any work that might be assigned to him, wondering when he would meet his owner, Colonel Wells: wondering . . . .

He was roused by a sound at the door and sat up in alarm as Jez Davies came in, a gust of rum-laden breath preceding him. He swayed slightly on his feet as he surveyed the naked boy, whose body glimmered white in the filtered light from outside.

The man laughed, a sound with no humor in it, his voice rough and slurred:

"So, you knew I'd be along, you were waiting, eh?"

In the shaft of moonlight that shone through the doorway Robert saw the man move toward him, fingers fumbling at the laces of his breeches, releasing the obscene jut of his belly. At the sight Robert sprang from his pallet and tried to reach the door, but Jez Davies caught his arm. He was thrown to the ground, where stubby sweaty fingers explored his body. He struggled wildly, but the last weeks had weakened him. Now the man began to speak in a low wooing tone that came strangely from his lips, lips used to coarse speech, shouting orders in the field, ranting at the slave drivers and slaves . . . the sound filled Robert with shame and a sickening despair. . . .

"Now, boy, don't fight me . . . you'll like it once you've had it . . . I need you, boy, need your young white body . . . it's been so long . . . don't fight me, I'll be good to you, you'll see, come on now, boy . . . ."

The mumbled entreaties went on, the exploring fingers became more urgent. . . . His senses almost gone, Robert lay still. With a grunt of triumph the man flung him over onto his face, but as the boy felt the wet scabrous body pressing against him, felt the mounting desire of the man on his back, the goatish delight, a surge of strength swept through him and with a sudden twist he had turned on his back, then with an upward jab brought his knee sharply with all the power he could muster up into his attacker's groin. There was a bellow of pain, animal in its intensity, as the heavy body rolled from him to the ground.

Robert caught up his breeches and ran to the door . . . then stopped. Where could he run to?

To whom could he turn for help?

He was a slave at the mercy of Jez Davies and God knew how many more like him. The man heaved himself convulsively from the packed mud floor and hobbled toward Robert. His eyes were filled with agony and hate; he raised a hand and hit the boy across the face: ringing stinging slaps that made him dizzy but were infinitely more desirable than a renewed passionate pawing.

"You'll come to me, boy, before I've finished with you. You'll come crawling, begging." The man's voice was hoarse with frustrated desire, and anger. "You could have had it easy here, boy, labor in name only . . . but now, I'll break you, I'll *break* you. . . . You'll work in the fields beginning tomorrow. Y'hear? *Tomorrow. Y'hear?*" His voice rose to a scream.

Robert nodded. "I hear."

"You'll work till you drop, till you come to me and beg to come to my bed . . . and maybe . . ." the spite and malice were tangible in the soft night air . . . "maybe . . . after that . . . *I* won't want *you*."

Six

All this passed again through Robert Vane's mental vision as he stood in the canefield some two months later under the midday blaze.

That first day in the field had been a white-hot day taken from the very depths of hell. He had been woken by the sound of a conch shell being blown just before dawn, and he dressed swiftly after pouring cool rainwater over his head and shoulders. His soul was still seared by the remembrance of the night before, and when Maria appeared by his side, her wide eyes grave and questioning, he felt as if his shame was known throughout the plantation.

"You goin' to the field, dem," she stated, rather than asked. "Tek this, huh?" She thrust a large coarsely woven straw hat at him. "Tek it, man." She shook it fiercely under his nose as he hesitated. "You need it fe sure, to shade you milk white skin."

At her words his cheeks flamed as he recalled Jez Davies' hoarsely uttered endearments. He took the hat with muttered thanks. Maria anointed his wrists again and rubbed yet another unguent across his back and shoulders. "Help fe stop the blister," she explained.

"Walk good," she murmured as a huge Negro joined them.

"You in my gang," he stated briefly.

Robert followed him, with a growing determination

that, come what may, however hard the work, however hot the sun and long the day, he would not give in. He would never submit to the degradation of bowing to Jez Davies and subjecting his body to his perverse desires.

For the first half hour it was bearable work. He wielded the heavy machete, called a cane bill, awkwardly at first, then with more dexterity, but after less than an hour he was staggering, trying desperately to keep up with the long line of Negroes. They paid him no heed after the first sidelong glances, tinged with contempt for a white boy who could allow himself to be sent to the field. They offered no word of comfort when he slumped exhausted to the brown stalks and the slave driver's whip cracked for the first time across his back, nor any help to get him to his feet again.

Why should they?

Had the white seamen on that long nightmare across the rolling, tossing sea in the dread Middle Passage ever eased their misery with a kind word or a cup of water held to gasping parched lips? If they paused in their rhythmic cutting, the whip would whistle toward *them* . . . let the *white* flesh rise in bloody weals for once. . . .

Robert rallied from the whip and kept on raggedly, doggedly. Always at the back of his mind was the thought: Better this than Jez Davies . . . God, let me be strong to hold out, even if death comes as a result. Sweat drenched his body, running from under the straw hat into his eyes, into his ears and mouth, making his hand slip on the handle of the machete that seemed to have doubled its weight.

Then came the wail of the conch shell, and each man downed his machete and hurried to the shade of a large cotton tree and a group of low-spreading wild almond trees. Robert followed them, his feet stumbling in

63

weariness. The big Negro slave driver reined in beside him, his deep-barreled chest gleaming like polished ebony in the strong light.

"It sorry I has to lay whip to you, boy, firs' day. Mas' Jez say I mus' . . . but 'im away to the north piece up yonder soon, you tek it easy, y'hear bwoy . . . I look the other way." He cantered off, then called back over his shoulder: "Water tank a chain up, nex' shell blow not fe two hour."

Robert was grateful for the man's rough kindness; he stumbled toward the slave-tank, its deep stone depths serving cattle and humans alike. He laved water over his head, then staggered to the shade under the trees and stretched out in exhaustion. Two blessed hours: he had no food but was beyond hunger, too bemused to notice that the rest of the work gang had brought food, some in little lidded pans, some wrapped in a banana leaf. He fell into an uneasy doze; his shoulders and back, despite Maria's ministrations, had begun to smart from sunburn and the lash from the whip. . . .

It seemed as if he had hardly shut his eyes when Shell-blow sounded again, sending them scurrying back to the field. It was still fiercely hot, Robert's muscles had begun to stiffen, and he felt light-headed from his weakened state and his lack of food all day. But he kept on as best he could, amid jumbled emotions of despair and determination.

When at last Shell-blow came, telling them that the hard grueling day was done, Robert stood where he was, the machete hanging from a slack hand. The driver paused by his side. He regarded the boy's strained face with something very near to compassion and murmured in his deep voice:

"You not goin' to stan' it, bwoy. Give up, nuh? You could has it easy. . . ."

64

Robert's blue eyes, bloodshot now with the day's glare and labors, looked into the black ones above him.

Was he being a fool to act like this, like some prissy girl frightened of her first kiss?

Then the memory of Jez Davies' pawing, clumsy, sweaty hands, the thrust of his heavy obscene body, and the rum-laden endearments strengthened his wavering determination; he straightened his aching body and said firmly:

"I'll stay in the field."

The driver contemplated him for a long moment, then nodded and murmured: "You're all right, bwoy." He cantered off in a flurry of small trash thrown up by his horse's hooves.

In the compound Robert found Maria waiting for him; she exclaimed under her breath when she saw his condition, then coaxed and bullied him to the water butt, where she doused him from head to foot with water, again anointed his back, chest, and face with the potent soothing unguent, then helped him to his hut, where he collapsed onto his pallet. This, he noticed with limp gratitude, had been changed for a clean, fresh-stuffed one. There was even a thin rough cotton covering across it.

He looked up at Maria. "You did this?" He indicated the pallet.

She nodded, then suddenly hung her head.

"Don't go back to the field. You goin' fe die, fe true. Tell the boss-man you . . ." she trailed off at the expression on his face. "A'right, Mas' Robert, I help you to get t'rough. Let I have you breech, dem, I wash 'em for mornin'."

He wriggled out of the filthy breeches under cover of the thin cotton sheet.

"Thank you, Maria, you're very kind," he said weakly.

She brought him a thick soup, with scraps of meat and vegetables in it, none of which he could identify but which he ate gratefully. Then she brought a cool citrus fruit, peeled and speared on a sharp stick, followed by a long thirst-quenching drink which she told him was water from a coconut. He gave her a tired smile at the end of what was to him the most magnificent repast he had indulged in for many a long week. As he drifted into a deep sleep he assumed his decision to stay in the field would be conveyed to Jez Davies by the driver and that he would be left unmolested.

So the pattern of the days was set.

Each day when Jez Davies rode by, and this he did too often, his mouth cruel, his taunts loud and bitter, the driver, Moses, hounded Robert to work faster, but he had such dexterity with the long curling whip that it skimmed like a feather across his shoulders, until one day Jez Davies became suspicious of the lack of red weals and threatened the driver:

"Whip the boy, good, y'hear, Moses, man? Lest *I* wield the whip on him *an'* you."

After this the whip stung a little more, but never when Jez was off about other business on the plantation.

Maria tended him at night, cooking his food, easing the torments of sunburn and whip weals. She gave him news of John Hastings and Jem Marston; the latter was working as a cooper and blacksmith, making iron rings for the hogsheads and barrels and attending to the shoeing of the horses. John Hastings had been put in the carpenter's shop.

She began to tease him with her body, letting her hands pause, linger, as she smoothed unguent into his now nearly healed wrists or across his shoulders after

66

a lashing. She would allow him a glimpse of her full rounded breasts as she bent over the cooking pot, the neck of her thin cotton gown falling away from her throat. Her taut buttocks had a new provocative swing as she walked away from him, her voice a new breathless husky quality.

The agitation and disgust aroused in him by Jez Davies' advances began to diminish as he became all too conscious of her ripe young body, his for the taking; he looked forward at the end of each day to seeing her, hearing her strange little voice with its overtones of her original Spanish tongue, her sudden childish giggles or peals of uninhibited joyous laughter, or swift transition to provocative woman. One evening she didn't meet him at the hut or arrive later to prepare his meal; he fretted until nightfall, slept badly, and worried all the next day.

He trudged his weary way home that night, dispirited at the thought of another lonely evening, another ill-cooked supper. . . . He pushed open the hut door and there she was, sitting on his pallet.

"Maria," he exclaimed, and at the joy in his voice she was up and into his arms. All thoughts apart from the immediate fulfilling of the swift, engulfing rush of desire left him. . . .

After all it was easy; his shame in his body's functions left him, replaced by a fierce delight in his own and in Maria's slim yet softly rounded body.

She cooked a special supper for them both later that night, and they celebrated with a little of the fiery rum, filched by Maria from the distillery, in their coconut water.

They made love again, fierce demanding young bodies, then slept . . . that special sleep that comes after complete fulfillment.

She was gone when Robert woke next morning, and

he lay for a few minutes exulting in his new state of discovered manhood until the urgent wail of Shell-blow made him leap from his pallet.

The news swept through the compound and the fields with the usual speed of the grapevine, and Robert received a knowing wink from Moses, the driver. The news reached Jez Davies, too. He arrived just before the noon Shell-blow, his horse lathered and sweating, his face red and bloated with anger. He uncoiled the thick cowhide whip he always carried and snaked it across Robert's back, even though the boy was working industriously, manipulating the big, hooked machete with an ease he would never have thought possible a few weeks ago. He stopped in midstroke as the whip curled itself cruelly around his chest, an involuntary cry escaping him.

Moses cantered up.

"De bwoy work well, Mas' Jez, no cause fe whip this morning," he said in mild reproach, a glint in his eye showing that he understood the reason for the savage onslaught. The whip curled back, then was raised for an even more brutal attack.

"Mas' Jez . . ."

"Don't tell me, Moses, what I must do. The boy needs taking down, with his uppity ways and his law-student talk." It was then that he bent down to Robert and said: "So you cry, boy? Look at the sun and weep, weep for what you were and what you *are*."

In the days that followed there were repeated lashings until Maria protested, weeping as she tended his raw bleeding back: "I goin' tell the mistress, fe sure. The man out fe kill you."

A few days later, when he could hardly stand with pain and fatigue, he heard the thud of hooves and Jez Davies' hated voice. He waited for the expected high whine of the whip, eyes closed against the promise of renewed pain, flesh quivering with fearful anticipation.

Then a new voice commanded: "Hold, Jez, enough. Boy, come here."

Robert opened his eyes and raised his head to look up at the man who had the power to stop Jez Davies. This must be Colonel Walter Wells himself, he thought. He saw a straight-backed figure, a hawk face under a wide-brimmed straw hat; keen dark eyes were fixed on him in stern inquiry. A snowy white shirt, ruffed at neck and wrist, brown breeches, with knee-high glossy riding boots. Slender hands lightly held loose reins. Slowly Robert walked toward the man and stood by the horse's head.

"Your name, boy?" The voice cultured, such a voice as Robert had not heard since parting from Philip.

"Vane, sir. Robert Vane . . . at your service."

"Vane?"

"Yes, sir."

The man's eyes traveled over the pitiful figure before him, lingered on the deep red sunburn on chest and arms, the haggard face with lines of pain and anguish etched on its youth, the shoulder-length tangled hair.

"Turn round, Robert Vane," he commanded.

Robert turned slowly, feeling the long scrutiny from those deep-set eyes: then at last: "Face me."

When Robert turned back, the man was looking at Jez Davies, a mounting flush of anger burning his gaunt cheeks.

"I have told you before, Davies, I will not tolerate senseless lashings. This boy's back has been mercilessly beaten, lacerated almost to ribbons . . . *for what cause?*"

The rasped question caught Davies off balance. He floundered:

"Colonel . . . the boy's sullen . . . surly . . . a bad worker. . . ."

"How long have you been at Wells?" the colonel cut in, turning back to Robert.

Robert said tiredly: "A little over two months . . . I think no more."

"And how long have you been in the field?"

There was a quick movement from Davies, then he dropped his hand back to his horse's neck.

"I . . . went into the field . . . the morning after I arrived, sir."

"S'death, Davies." The colonel's rage mounted to fever pitch. "A boy like this . . . no time to recover from the journey. The Negro slaves have two months to season and settle. Are you mad, man?" He turned back to Robert. "You speak well; have you learning?"

"Yes, sir. I was a law student at Gray's Inn, at the Inns of Court in London, when . . . when I was impressed by the press-gang."

"Law, eh? You have Latin, French?"

"Yes, sir. Also mathematics, a little rhetoric. I can pen a fair hand."

"Why was I not told of this?" The colonel's voice was terrible in its anger now, and Jez Davies' bullying attitude was reduced to an abject cringe. "You *knew* of the boy's learning, you were told expressly to look out for someone such as Robert Vane here, and you *put him in the field.*"

"I knew your orders, colonel sir, but I thought the boy too young for such work as you had in mind. . . ."

"You thought . . . surely I'm the judge in such matters . . . you *thought. . . ."* His eyes went from Davies' coarse face to Robert's face, which showed a promise of what good looks he must possess despite the layers of dust runneled by recent tears. He said coldly: "Yes, I can well see *what* you thought. Remember, Davies, I made you overseer . . . I can *un*make you, today, tomorrow, any time. Remember that."

Jez said nothing but shot a look of bitter hatred at Robert. Then Colonel Wells was speaking again:

"Vane, you say? Where did you live in England?"

"At Vane Court, in Cambridgeshire, sir. Near to the university."

"Your parents?"

"My mother died in giving me birth. My father and two older brothers were all killed in the expedition to further Cromwell's Western Design in the Spanish Indies."

"Major John Vane and Lieutenants Roger and Michael Vane," the colonel said softly. "My fellow officers on the *Marston Moor*. Killed in that foolhardy disastrous raid on Santo Domingo. So you are the son of my old friend and comrade in arms, here on my property as an indentured servant. Strange are the ways of destiny and coincidence. Robert, follow me to the house, where I will have your . . . wounds . . . dressed. Davies, *Master* Robert Vane will not be returning to the field, and *you* will see me first thing tomorrow. . . . There are yet more explanations to be made."

Seven

And so began a period for Robert that was dreamlike in its serenity. He followed the colonel up to the house that sprawled on a low elevation. Now that he was close to it, he could see that it was only intended as a temporary residence.

He was taken to a stone outbuilding by the colonel's own body servant, a young Negro boy by the name of Samson. Here there was a shallow tub. He washed, his back was treated, and linen dressings applied. His filthy breeches were discarded and he was given a pair of light blue cotton ones, a loose-fitting white shirt of fine lawn, and a pair of soft black leather boots.

"The massa say to have you measure fe new clothe' come mornin'," Samson informed him cheerfully, then set to work with scissors and comb to convert his hair into some semblance of order before he tied it back with a length of ribbon. Robert felt clean and cared for for the first time in four months: a new sense of freedom possessed him, a slight hope for the future invaded his thoughts. He was then led to a small side veranda where a wickerwork table was set for one. To eat off a white cloth, off fine delft ware, a coffee pot of silver before him. . . . He ate and drank in a kind of mental maze while Samson hovered, watching him with a growing proprietorial pride, his wide gap-toothed smile ever flashing in his dark face.

"Colonel say fe you to eat hearty, Mas' Robert."

Mas' Robert. . . . From, "Hey, *you,* boy" to "Mas' Robert" in one day. Only Maria had ever called him that. . . .

Already she seemed remote from him, far from this new world in which he found himself, and he pushed the problem to the back of his mind, telling himself that there was nothing he could do about it until he knew his own fate, which was in the colonel's hands.

It was not until the next morning that the colonel called for him again. Groomed and brisk, soldierlike still in his brevity of movement, he looked up from a well-spread breakfast table.

"Good morning, sir," Robert said.

"Good morning, Robert. You look as if you slept?" The hooded eyes flashed humor for a moment. "You look more like Major Vane's son now than the tattered bundle I met yesterday." The humor went, and he was serious again. "Of all the buyers who *might* have bought you . . . surely it was some stroke of fate. I'm sorry for the treatment meted to you, lad. But that's past. Before I tell you that which I would have you do, sit and tell me how you got yourself into your present position."

So Robert sat and recounted in detail all that had happened to him since that last quiet morning at Vane Court in April. Colonel Wells listened, silent and absorbed to the end.

"So there's no point in my offering to send you back to England on the next boat?"

Robert's heart leaped at the question and his hopes rose, then quickly fell.

"No sir. Sir Roger L'Estrange would clap me straight into Newgate . . . or worse."

"That makes two of us, boy. As an officer of Cromwell's erstwhile army, my life is forfeit. We had a time

73

of it, I can tell you, when King Charles was recalled
and the Monarchy reinstated. Knowing his partiality to
Spain, we feared for a time that he'd hand Jamaica back
to her . . . for he'd promised to do so if Spain helped
him get his crown. But he stated that Spain played no
actual part in his return to England, so he kept
Jamaica . . . and a good thing too, for we'd as likely to
have been put to the sword, at best all our possessions
wrested from us, all our work on the land for naught.
But last year he issued an Order in Council that this
island will stay with England and a Royal Proclamation
that all settlers, whatever their political persuasions,
were promised that they should be 'free denizens of
England and have the same privileges as free born
subjects of England.' Despite that, *I* wouldn't go back
and put it to the test . . . and as for you, boy, like it or
not, you have to stay."

Robert nodded.

"The prospect is not so formidable as it was yesterday," he said. "What would you have me do, sir?"

Colonel Wells answered his question indirectly.

"After I had some sort of a roof over my head and
this place a-building, I sent for my wife and children,
we had two then, a girl and a boy. Now we have another girl, born nine months to the day after my wife
landed." He chuckled. "Now that we begin to prosper,
some of the planters are sending their children to England to study and acquire some little of the social
graces. But I want my children about me, though they
must not grow up without knowledge, with no ability
beyond eating and lounging in the sun. I want you to
take over their tuition, to teach them Latin, French . . .
all the knowledge that you have."

A *tutor* . . . of *children?*

Of *girls?*

"You would be paid thirty-five pounds a year and

would live with us like a member of the family, with food and clothing provided. How does that strike you?"

Robert still sat silent, thoughts tumbling around his mind like a mouse on a wheel. Did he in fact have a choice? The oblique references to sending him back to England could hardly have been more than a token offer. Nothing had been said, beyond the phrase "live like a member of the family," about the remission of his indentured state. Despite Colonel Wells' outward charm and kindly manner, he sensed a man of steel beneath the courteous facade.

"Well?" The question was sharp, confirming this impression.

"I'm sorry, sir. Your . . . request . . . has taken me so much by surprise . . . I wonder if I am capable of teaching . . ." Robert stammered. "I am but sixteen yet, sir."

"And Charlotte is but ten, Richard nine, and Ann five. To them you will seem *old*. They are . . . fairly biddable . . . and would be told from the start to obey you in all things."

Robert felt bewildered anew by this fresh turn his life was taking, but managed to say quietly:

"I will try my best, sir."

"Good lad." The Colonel stood up. "My good wife is not seen until second breakfast, but come and meet your pupils."

And now began for Robert Vane a period of peace and security, which in future years he looked back upon with a nostalgia and realization that he had been perfectly happy, a state which endured in varying degrees for five and a half years, a time when the plantation was his whole world.

That first morning he had followed his employer—already he had stopped thinking "owner"—along the wide back veranda to a narrower side verranda where there was a battered wooden rocking horse, a swing attached to the high sloping rafters above, a low table, and various chairs to match. A small girl sat at the table solemnly eating an orange; at their entrance she gave a little squeal of delight, dropped the remains of the orange on the table, and hurled herself toward her father.

"Papa . . . why are you so late today?"

Colonel Wells swung her to his shoulders, where she buried her face, her exuberance turning to shyness as she became aware of Robert.

Her father set her on her feet again and said seriously:

"Ann, this is Master Robert Vane, he has come all the way from England to teach you your letters . . . among other things."

Huge gray eyes examined Robert, eyes set in a heart-shaped face framed by light brown fluffy hair, hair that was neither straight nor curled but of such an incredible texture that Robert wanted to stroke it. He said formally:

"I am delighted to meet you, Mistress Ann, I'm sure we shall get along famously." He bowed slightly.

Ann's eyes widened still more at this courtesy, then at a twitch of her shoulder by her father's hand, she dropped a curtsey.

"Fetch your brother and sister," her father commanded.

She ran off, small black-shod feet twinkling from beneath the hem of her long white cotton day gown. There were excited whispers from within, then through an open door a boy came, followed by a taller girl, a blonde edition of Ann.

"This is Richard and this Charlotte. Master Robert Vane, your tutor."

Robert regarded his future charges in some trepidation, hardly hearing their father's admonishment:

76

"You will all obey Master Robert's instructions at all times, in all things. He has come to teach you French and Latin, and other subjects which he will decide. If you are troublesome he will let me know. Is that understood?"

"Yes, papa," came a dutiful chorus.

"Why do we have to learn these things, papa?" Richard asked with a mutinous pout.

"Because otherwise you will grow up a dunce, knowing nothing," the colonel said gently. He regarded his young son with some misgiving, this son who was to inherit this plantation he had labored over, this son who was sickly and pallid, with none of his sisters' enthusiasm and exuberance. He had contracted a fever soon after they had arrived in the island six years ago and had been apathetic and disposed to chest colds, odd unexplained fevers, despite all the loving care and herbal remedies lavished on him. Colonel Wells sighed: God grant that the boy gathers strength as the years go by.

Robert looked at Charlotte: calm gray eyes gazed back into his blue ones, appraising, assessing. Then she smiled: "You are very welcome at Wells, Master Robert. I trust we shall give you no trouble." Her voice was high and sweet, but with a singsong quality that he had noted in the slave's voices; he made a mental decision that speech training was one of the urgent priorities in the schoolroom, then smiled at his thoughts: behaving like a tutor already.

After their initial shyness and excitement at the novelty of a tutor wore off, the children became a little rebellious when their complete freedom was curtailed and when they learned that strict attendance to the schoolroom and set times of study must be adhered to. Then they accepted the situation and settled down very well. Those first weeks very little work was done while

Robert waited for desks and chairs to be made for the room that was destined to be the schoolroom.

One morning he went down to the seamstresses' workroom to be measured again, for even in the few weeks he had been at the Great-house he had grown in height and girth. His heart missed a beat and his conscience clamored as he saw bent over a piece of sewing, fingers flying, the slight form of Maria. She raised her eyes to his, a look of deep reproach in their dark depths. Robert knew a passing shame at his neglect in failing to even send a message to her, but he considered that their one time alliance had come to its inevitable end with his move up to the Great-house. That he could think in this fashion was a measure of the change that had taken place in him in recent months; even so, conscience pricked and nagged.

He bent his head and whispered, conscious that the other girls had stopped working and were watching him covertly, their eyes bright:

"Maria, I'm sorry. I was ordered up to the house, not to come back. I . . . I'll see you . . . sometime . . . soon. We'll manage somehow."

It sounded pitifully weak and half-hearted, even to his ears, and he was not surprised when she said tartly:

"I see you when I see you, Mas' Robert." She kept her eyes lowered and now her voice was bitter. "Now you grand with the white girl, dem, Maria don' matter."

"You *do* matter . . . I . . . I can never be grateful enough for what you did for me. . . ."

"*Grateful?* Cho, Mas' Robert, is *grateful* I wan'?"

The first months passed with gathering momentum: in November Ann joined the early-morning riding lessons and some sessions in the schoolroom. The crop was in, and the pre-Christmas festivities swept through the plantation. Although there was a marked lack of religious observance in the young colony, Christmas was a day of rejoicing, mainly because there was a three-day respite from field work and added rations, so that it took on something of a pagan festival and had nothing in common with the Christmases that Robert had known as a child.

The field slaves were given, besides the extra food, new clothes, and casks of fiery rum were broached. Drums pounded all night, insistent rhythms from their native Africa, strange and pulsating with messages that spoke to the senses and induced a wild recklessness. There were attempts to dress fantastic mimes in outlandish costumes, reminding Robert of the Morris dancers in England, yet having a bizarre quality that was wholly foreign to anything he had seen before. The house slaves kept aloof from these activities, believing themselves to be on a higher social scale than the field slaves, while indulging in their own watered-down celebrations, aping their masters.

The crop had been a good one, many hogsheads of sugar had been dispatched to England, together with a good consignment of pimento berries.

As the new house neared completion early in the new year, that year of 1663, a state of excitement pervaded the household: the plantation was prospering beyond all expectation and expanding rapidly; another two hundred acres came under cultivation; more slaves were brought when the slave traders docked at Port Royal; more and more settlers arrived from England, from the other islands . . . some voluntarily, some indented.

Robert's outlook changed as time passed: he held a favored position in the family now, memories dimmed of his days in the field, ideas re-formed. Slavery was not such a bad thing. Slaves worked hard, yes, but at Wells they were fed and clothed, with no worries beyond that of doing their work well. He had no idea of the misery on some of the other properties, or of the soul-destroying despair at being separated from others of their tribe, from family and friends, plunged into a strange new land, with an alien language, hard work under the broiling sun, the ever-present whip.

Robert's eyes and ears were closed to all this, he only saw the luxury, growing each day as more fine furnishings and fabrics arrived; he lived in a cocoon spun by his absorption in his work, the growing love of his pupils, and the trust in him by Colonel and Mistress Wells. All that went on beyond the confines of the plantation, and more especially beyond the confines of the gardens surrounding the house itself, was not acknowledged. Life was bounded by the microcosm of Wells. Beyond these boundaries nothing seemed important.

He came upon Maria again quite by chance one early morning as he ran lightly up the steep path in the hillside that led from the stables to the back veranda. She was spreading an armful of new-washed clothes out to dry on the short-cropped turf. He stood still, watching her, recognizing her immediately despite the double transformation from sewing maid to house slave, from girlhood to young womanhood. She wore a full-skirted white and blue cotton gown, covered by a stiffly starched white apron whose wide strings hugged her trim waist, the low-cut neckline scarcely covered by the white fichu about her shoulders, showing all the soft plumpness of breasts that he remembered from so long ago. Her dark face framed in a full white mob cap, its whiteness repeated in the flash of white teeth. He felt a swift surge of desire, not experienced for many months . . . she looked up, eyes widening, catching her breath at discovering his presence.

He said softly: "Maria . . . Maria . . . you here in the house and no word to me?"

She stood up and he noticed now that the promise of

80

her child's body of a year ago had ripened to fulfillment. He took a step toward her, but she ducked her head and said in a dutiful, low, remote voice, accompanied by a little bob:

" 'Morning, Mas' Robert. Miss Charlotte wait on me," and with a flash of pink-soled black feet she was pattering back along the veranda to Charlotte's suite.

So the pattern was set: she would afford him the merest glimpse of her, her big eyes sometimes tender, sometimes teasing, until he became obsessed with the thought of her and the urge to possess her once more.

One morning, just before dawn, he went out into the cool air, unable to sleep, erotic pictures chasing his mind's eye, and took the trail to where the new mill was being built, then struck up the hill beside the gurgling mill stream. He sat down on the bank and watched its diamond sparkles in the light of the new-risen sun, the turbulent sight soothing his own turbulent emotions. There was a rustle in the long grass behind him. He turned his head, knowing in advance whom he would see. She was without her cap or apron; the thin cotton gown clung to her body, revealing every lovely line. He reached up a hand and pulled her down to him. Then all the pent-up passion of months burst from them. She was naked under the cotton gown, and he drew it off and caressed her satiny skin with tender hands that made her quiver and moan with joy; she responded to his demanding hands and lips more completely than she had in the past, while he reached a summation of desire never known before. Then afterward, laughing, they ran into the middle of the river and splashed under the waterfall, rejoicing in its cool sting on their lust-fevered bodies.

When Robert returned to the house, he learned that Charlotte and Ann had already left for the morning ride. He hastily followed them on the big gray he always rode.

"Sorry," he said as he caught up with them. "I overslept."

Charlotte turned cool gray eyes on him: "You look as if . . ." she began, then bit her lip and cantered ahead of him.

Robert felt a moment's qualm; she must have missed Maria's help in dressing. Would she connect the two incidents? Surely not, she was not yet twelve, although of high intelligence and perception. Living in the Greathouse away from the sight and sound of easy coupling among the slaves, had she even so picked up enough knowledge of the ways of men to arrive at the right conclusion? He gave a mental shrug. In this new world, this tight little microcosm of the plantation, it was becoming the norm for the planters, overseers, bookkeepers, to pick a mistress from among the slaves. He suspected that Colonel Wells was not above such practices; a pretty young girl who waited at table had been banished to the field after Mistress Bridget's loss of temper over the breakage of a valuable glass bowl. She was back in the house the following day, a slight smirk on her face, giving a covert display of arrogance to her mistress who sat, tight-lipped, ignoring her husband.

It was not safe to repeat the morning's escapade too often, but Robert would steal from his bed after the household was asleep at night and make his way to the waterfall. One night, when rain was falling with all its October vehemence, Maria went to his room, slipping away just before dawn to her own quarters in the newly built slave barracks.

And so the months passed, crop followed crop, and there was still rising prosperity. War broke out between England and the Dutch in 1665, but this only added to the increase, despite the fact that one consignment of sugar was lost when the ship was set on by a Dutch man of war and sacked. More buildings went up—a new boiler house and threshing mill; more acres were added and brought under cultivation; more slaves swelled the barracks and toiled under the broiling sun. And more time passed. Suddenly Robert realized that he had been at Wells for five long years. Charlotte was fifteen, her girlish prettiness ripening into beauty, her eyes wide, clear gray and calm; her blonde hair hung below her waist, a shimmer of silken moonlight. Behind the surface prettiness was a growing strength of will, an imperiousness that matched her father's: just as her mother faded, sapped by the heat, the monotony, the certain knowledge of the colonel's long succession of concubines, so Charlotte blossomed and developed.

Colonel Wells made no attempt at concealment of his amours now, and his current mistress would have only the lightest token work to do. A few lighter-skinned babies appeared among the growing number of picca-ninnies in the slave compound, while the colonel was changing from the taut military man Robert had first met to a typical West Indian planter: overfed at table; overindulgent in the consumption of the potent home-stilled rum; overindulgent to his bodily desires. His features had coarsened and blurred as his body thick-ened, but still he kept a tight rein on the development of the property, and still it prospered. While his father thickened, Richard Wells wilted, his puny body too often a prey to the fevers that were still a scourge. Mistress Bridget worried over the boy helplessly, leav-ing him to the care of his old slave nana, but the colonel's heart was anguished over the boy's frailty, and after each bout of sickness, his eye would rest on Robert's broad, healthy frame with a speculative look.

Ann Wells, ten years old, was willful and lovable, exasperating in her swift changes of mood. She plagued

Robert in the schoolroom, but her quick mind that sped to meet his patient explanations, her enchanting smile that burned her large gray eyes to silver, touched his heart and turned away his impatience or annoyance at her impishness.

One night in the summer of 1667, Maria stirred in his arms and sat up.

"Is it true what I hear roun' the yard?" she demanded.

"How am I to answer if I don't know what you hear?" he asked lazily, stroking her bare thigh.

She pushed his hand away and slid from the bed, holding her gown to her breast.

"I hear you goin' to wed wit' Miss Charlotte."

"You heard *what?*" Robert sat up, all amorous thoughts shocked from his mind.

"It all roun' the yard. Come Miss Charlotte sixteen, you to be wed."

Robert laughed.

"For once the grapevine's wrong. Not a word has been said of the matter or will be. She's just a *child*."

"She the same age as you . . . when first we couple," Maria said tartly, and then she was gone. Toward evening he was called by Samson to the colonel's study, where he sat at a long table piled high with ledgers.

"Sit down, lad. We have to talk . . . these last years, they've been happy ones for you, eh?"

"Yes, sir. In fact at times it seems but yesterday that you found me bloodied and torn in the cane piece."

"Aye, so it does. And you've done a good job: kept the children from being lazy good-for-nothings, the like I see on other folk's property. How'd you like to stay on at Wells . . . for always?" he asked abruptly.

"Stay on for always? But, sir, in a few years Ann will not need my tuition, indeed now I feel I can teach Charlotte no more, and Richard . . . ."

"Aye, lad, Richard. Robert, I looked for Richard to be my heir and take over the property, but the boy's sickly and likely to remain so. Whereas you . . . I'd like you to stay and learn the running of Wells and . . . marry Charlotte . . . then if Richard . . . ." He faltered, then went on firmly: "The little lad ails so, I fear he'll not make manhood. What d'ye say, lad?"

Robert sat in stunned silence. He had heard no more of the colonel's words since he had said "marry Charlotte," and despite the warnings he might have taken from Maria, he refused to believe his ears.

"Well, boy?" It might have been the same barked question of five years ago, after the offer of the tutorship.

"Why, sir . . . I . . . don't . . . I mean . . . what about Charlotte?"

"Maids don't have much choice in these parts of a well-set-up young bridegroom. More often someone fresh out, never seen before, of doubtful parentage, or some rum-ridden old planter. No, I reckon she'll be well pleased at the prospect. Well, lad?"

"I . . . can do nothing but accept, sir. I'm overwhelmed and fearful that I'll not be able to run the property. . . ."

"Tush, lad, you said the same thing about teaching . . . look how you've managed. I'm not asking you to start right away, I'm good for many a long year, God willing. Meanwhile you'll ride along with me, learn all the ropes. I'll speak to Charlotte tonight."

"Sir," Robert rose to his feet. "If . . . Charlotte is unwilling for the match, I beg you not to force her. I would not have her unhappy at the bargain."

Colonel Wells nodded. "She'll be willing, Robert, she'll be willing."

Later that day Robert came upon Ann weeping bitterly in the deserted schoolroom.

"What is it, love?" he asked tenderly.

She turned on him like a little fury, face ablaze, eyes awash.

"I hear you're going to marry *Charlotte,*" she gulped.

He nodded, wondering how she could have heard so soon.

"That's almost certain."

"Why *Charlotte?* Why not *me?* When I've loved you so . . ."

He gazed down at her tear-streaked face with deepened tenderness.

"You're too young to know what love is, Ann."

"I'm *not.* I've loved you, you must have known, ever since I can remember."

She was shaken anew with sobs, and he drew her childish light body into his arms and stroked the soft brown hair. The touch tingled through his fingers and he recalled with startling clarity that first morning when he'd first seen her and wanted to stroke her hair.

"You are but ten years old, going on eleven," he said gently. "When you are as old as Charlotte, you will have forgotten me and love another."

"I won't . . . ever." She shook her head against his chest, then looked up at him with eyes that were suddenly shrewd. "Do *you* love Charlotte?" she asked softly.

His own eyes widened. "Of . . . course I do," he said at last with as much firmness as he could muster.

She held his gaze for a long time—the eyes of a woman, not those of the child he knew her to be—then she said so softly that he hardly caught the words: "If you *do* love Charlotte now, *one* day you'll love me."

The next morning, only Charlotte was ready for the morning ride, for Ann kept to her room and Richard hardly ever rode these days. The girl rode in silence until they reached the far side of the cane walk, then said in a small voice:

"Papa has told me that you wish to marry me, Robert. I . . . I am very happy that is so."

Robert reined in the gray and turned to face her, containing the surprise he felt at her broaching the subject. "Charlotte," he said solemnly. "Are you sure? Not just because your father . . ." he stopped, aware that it would be less than gallant to disclaim the colonel's fabrication of an "offer."

"I am quite sure, Robert," Charlotte said softly. "Sure, I believe, since first I saw you, five years ago."

She bent toward him and he kissed her gently on the lips: as he did so, Ann's tear-drenched face swam before his eyes, and again he heard her clear voice: "Do *you* love Charlotte?" and again he felt doubt. Was it right to marry without love? They were both so young, too young perhaps to love. He consoled himself with the thought that so many people married for convenience, that such marriages, so he had heard, were sometimes the best . . . he was very fond of Charlotte . . . the fact that the brief kiss had meant nothing to him he refused to acknowledge . . . love might grow between them. . . . His musings were broken by Charlotte saying:

"But *I* will not be so complaisant as my *mother* has been."

She cantered off before he could reply, leaving him in no doubt as to her meaning. How long, he wondered, had she known about Maria . . . and how many others knew or suspected? He found himself hoping that no report of his alliance had reached Ann's ears.

The betrothal was announced with much celebration, with guests arriving from other plantations from as far afield as Stokes Hall in the east and staying for many days. The Great-house was all bustle and excitement, and Robert had no time to examine or question his feelings. Charlotte was radiant, leaving no doubt as to her feelings on the matter, but Ann was quiet and subdued, her laughter stilled, her gray eyes shadowed. The wedding was to be in the following January, 1668, and as soon as the guests had departed preparations for the event began with the beginnings of a trousseau.

Robert began to accompany the colonel around the property and found that he enjoyed the work despite the memories the cane field recalled.

"I have not seen my old enemy Jez Davies," he remarked one morning as they stabled their horses.

"I sent him away long ago," Colonel Wells said shortly.

Robert wanted to ask why, but at the expression on the colonel's face, he refrained.

Early in August the colonel told Robert that he wanted him to make a journey to Port Royal to supervise the purchase of a new shipment of slaves and merchandise. He prepared happily for the journey, realizing how little he knew of the world outside the confines of Wells' boundaries. The night before he left, he went up to the waterfall, hoping that Maria would be there, but she wasn't, and eventually he went slowly back to the house. Since the announcement of his pending marriage she had avoided him, and he wondered uneasily if Charlotte had spoken to her. Would an innocent young girl of sixteen speak so frankly to her future husband's present mistress? Remembering her lack of coyness in broaching the subject of marriage, he thought that Charlotte might very well do so.

The next morning he bade them all a cheerful farewell as they clustered on the veranda to wave him Godspeed. Ann clung to his hands. "Don't stay away long, Robert," she implored.

He pinched her cheek. "I'll be back long before you

know I'm gone." He avoided her eye as he kissed Charlotte dutifully on the cheek, then with a final wave he was astride the gray and cantering down the long driveway. As he entered the highway, that same road that he had traversed over five years ago with Jez Davies and the following coffle of slaves, he thought how his life had altered. He felt free and lighthearted at the prospect of his visit to Port Royal, a city that was fast becoming legendary. He was anxious to see for himself how true were the rumors of privateers, buccaneers and untold wealth. He told himself as he trotted along the deeply rutted road that wound through wooded grassland, that a week or so was just the holiday he needed before settling down to his new duties at Wells and the responsibility of marriage.

A week or two . . .

It was to be many a long year before he saw either the plantation or any of the Wells family again.

Part Two

~~~~~~~~~~~~~~~~~~~~~~~~~~~~~~~~~~~~~

1667-1673

One

At the end of the driveway Robert was joined by Dick Gough and Jake Matlock, the former red-faced with a shock of red hair above. He came from the country of Salop on the Welsh border and had replaced Jez Davies as overseer. His singing Welsh lilt could be heard at all times, belaboring the field hands mostly with words, his coiled whip hardly ever brought in use.

Jake Matlock, a quiet boy from Derbyshire, still stunned by the shock of being taken by the press-gang, the horrors of the long voyage, and the prospect of five long years of bondage, stood awkwardly by his mount as Robert paused. The two men greeted him with deference, which he acknowledged distantly, for already the promise of becoming the heir to Wells had produced in him a sense of dignity bordering on arrogance. He cantered on ahead of the two indentured men, reveling in the beauty of the wild countryside and the fresh breeze that carried the mingled scents of wild vanilla, frangipani and jasmine, their sweetness in sharp contrast to the acridity of smoke from a nearby wood fire.

Wells property was in the district which the Spanish had called Anaya, at the foot of some rocky limestone mountains covered with dense scrub and forest. The road was little more than a track, narrow and of difficult going, and it would take them the best part of a

93

day to cover the fifteen or twenty miles that stretched before them before they reached St. Jago de la Vega, or Spanish Town, as one or two people were beginning to call it. They had Colburn Gully to cross and numerous small streams that tumbled down from the mountains, but once they reached the wide St. Catherine Plain with its herds of roving cattle, the going would be much easier.

Robert let his horse have his head. The gray picked his way delicately yet sure-footed over the track. He let his thoughts roam while behind him Dick Gough softly sang a tune of haunting loveliness from his far-off home and Jake began to lose his haggard stunned look, which sat so oddly upon his youthful features, the farther away they drew from Wells. Robert, too, felt a surge of lightness of spirit and a sense of release: he had been cooped up at Wells for five long years, and now the freedom of the outside world was like heady wine; he felt free to make decisions and order his own life.

It was now past noon, with the sun beating down mercilessly, the vast expanse broken only by a flock of lazily wheeling vultures. The three horsemen pulled off the track toward a stream and tied their horses to a low overhanging branch, where they could drink their fill and crop the short sweet turf that lined the bank.

Dick Gough burrowed in a wicker carrier slung across his horse's rump and produced corn pone, salt pork, a roast chicken leg apiece, and a welcome gourd of sangaree. While they ate, Robert chatted to the other two about their homes, how they had managed to find themselves in their present setting, and their hopes and plans when their bonded period ended. In doing so he lost some of his haughty "young master" bearing and became more like the Robert Vane of a few months ago. He didn't unbend sufficiently to confide that he too had been an indentured servant and that only through

94

the grace of God and a lucky coincidence was now in his present enviable position. He believed that the knowledge of his previous status, as against any rumors or gossip that they would most probably have heard, would lessen his position of authority.

They arrived at St. Jago de la Vega just at sunset, with the threat of rain heavy in the air. Great storm clouds, gray and ragged, hung over the distant hills, their drabness colored below by the setting sun, gradually sharpening in outline and taking on more color until the whole sky was a riot of amber, gold, and deep orange against a pale green sky; then the sun dropped from sight behind the western hills, and the clouds returned to their dark lowering gray.

Robert was amazed at the change in the capital since he had passed through over five years before. New buildings had sprung into being, old ones had been refurbished. The beautiful Spanish Hall of Audience still stood proudly in the Square, while nearby the governor's new residence was almost complete, for the governor, Sir Thomas Modyford, had declared that to live continuously in Port Royal was to court disaster from rioting buccaneers and licentious pirates.

Groups of scarlet-jacketed militia clattered by, spurs jangling, swords flapping, or lounged on foot at every corner ogling any slave girl who had ventured out about her own or her mistress's business. There were a number of English wives taking the early evening air on the arms of their officer husbands and young maids, chaperoned by older women, shyly walking with admirers. There were unchaperoned apple-cheeked Irish girls, their wild rose complexions somewhat impaired by the tropic sun, but their laughter and lilting brogue was heard at every corner as they chaffed or flirted with hopeful troopers. There were donkeys laden with produce from outlying farms, their wicker panniers a high-piled clash of color of the strange, exotic fruits and vegetables. There were vendors with chicken for sale, feet tied but clucking in alarm at their approaching demise and consignment to the stockpot. Vendors of litters of squealing piglets cried their wares with:

"Get y'r roast sucking pig. Young 'n tender, crisp 'n juicy."

Vendors of flaky little patties of pastry-enclosed meats kept their wares hot over portable charcoal braziers, while others carried sweetmeats of every kind on a tray held against the body by a stout leather thong about the neck.

Clouds of flies and darting dragonflies swarmed over the refuse that lined the way, and a stench of human excrement hung in the hot air from the slops that had been flung, in careless disregard of passers-by, from the houses whose wooden slatted doorways and shuttered jalousied windows opened directly onto the thoroughfare.

There were a number of taverns and grog shops to choose from, and the three young men booked lodgings for the night at one of the more respectable places in a little lane off the main square, hard by a compact whitestone church, in whose inner court could be seen the slow pacing of shaven-headed, brown-habited monks. There pervaded a great air of bustle and excitement over the town, for the governor and his staff were expected from his other residence, King's House on the Point, at Port Royal.

Early the next morning they set off to cover the few miles to Passage Fort, where Jake would stay and see to the stabling of the horses and Dick would accompany Robert by ferry to Port Royal. The threatened rain of the previous evening had not materialized, and the countryside through which they passed showed signs of drought. Their horses' hooves kicked up a following cloud of fine dust that seeped into their eyes, ears, and nostrils and clung grittily to parched throats, but the surface was good, the way short and when they arrived at their destination, they were lucky enough to board a ferry without having to wait longer than an hour.

Robert recalled all too vividly his first journey across the wide expanse of the harbor, with his raw and stinging wrists above hands that could barely grip the oars. As ever when the memory of those days returned, he covered his wrists anew with the ruffled laces which he always wore, for the sight of the raised weals that encircled them, although lessened by time and reduced in color as the years brought their healing, always stirred memories that he wished to forget.

Now he stood aft while other arms plied the heavy oars and strained his eyes for his second sight of what had now come to be called the wickedest city in the world. The ferry nudged its way into the busy, bustling port, nosing through the dozens of craft riding at anchor in deep water or tied up alongside the many wharves and jetties that thrust out from the narrow spit of land. Robert and Dick Gough were the first ashore. They gazed with all the countryman's wonder at the sights of city life: at the continuous line of wharves that stretched between the two forts of Carlisle and James, bristling with cannon manned by red-coated militiamen; at the packed warehouses close by, their contents spilling from the doorways. Every other building seemed to house a tavern or grog shop, a brothel or a gaming house, or a combination of all four, and early as it was, each one was doing a vigorous roaring trade, the sounds of drunken and bawdy revelry vying with the cries of the street vendors and the vociferous citizens of the town.

Dick Gough's red honest face expressed the bewilderment of his simple country soul faced with an unknown, unimagined sophistication.

"Lord, Mr. Robert, it's like that I have been hearing, but the hearing don't give the half. There's more wealth here than I dreamed was in the world."

His Welsh voice sounded oddly soft and rounded among the harsh cacophony of a dozen different tongues.

"And all this ill gotten, I'll wager," Robert said in wonder. He was still young enough to be thrilled at the prospect of being in the very heart of the buccaneers' stronghold and looked about him eagerly in the hopes of seeing at least one of the famous freebooters. Any citizen of Port Royal that Robert's eyes lingered on that day could have been a pirate or a buccaneer, for all who were abroad were in the colorful garb of seamen, many with gold rings in their ears or on their roughened weather-beaten hands, and with woollen seacaps atop greasy, curling hair. The more respectable settled citizens kept behind locked doors that day, for the rumor had flown through the town that the notorious Dutchman, the pirate Roche Brasilano, would dock later that day: the unmistakable outline of his famous ship, the *Juanita,* had been sighted on the horizon. The fact that the Dutch and English had been at war for the past two years hadn't deterred his brazen use of Port Royal as his terrain headquarters; not that that in itself was cause for comment, for the merchants of Port Royal took no account of wars if they could help it: they traded with ships of all nations, the illicitness of such transactions ignored if the profits warranted such ignorance. The authorities encouraged this by not prosecuting offenders for disregarding the hated Navigation Acts, for their pockets, too, were lined in the process. No, it was the fact that Brasilano's visits held terror for the townspeople, for used as they were to violence and bloodshed, they were not used to the wild unpredictable moods of Brasilano. Whereas most of the visiting buccaneers and pirates caroused, whored, drank the taverns dry, and emptied their purses in gaming, in a spirit of gaiety and joy at the release from confinement of their ships, Brasilano went ashore with a grudge against all humanity: he was capable of slashing viciously at innocent bystanders, of running his sword through the precious silks of the street vendors or grinding his high-heeled boots into a pile of gleaming pearls.

Unaware of all this, Robert and Dick approached the slave-trading area to see if the expected ship had arrived. It had docked the previous evening, and the auction block was already set up. For all his new-grown carapace of harshness and indifference, Robert found his task little to his liking and made his purchases of eight males, four females, and two children with as little display as possible, relying on his eyes rather than his fingers to make judgment and making a poor showing as a businessman in paying the first price asked, with no attempt at bargaining.

Despite his distaste for his job and the dispatch with which he concluded it, he still found time to be amazed at the variety of gold and silver coins that changed hands: pieces of eight, ducats, moidores, piasters and doubloons, from Spain, Italy, and Portugal; louis d'or from France; the recently introduced golden guinea from England which had been struck and named expressly for the slave trade, after the slavers who traded on the Guinea Coast. Coins that were handled carelessly as if they were of no value, tossed into heaps and left seemingly unguarded.

As soon as his purchases were completed, he left the slave ship, where the seeping stench from the hold and the sweaty and filthy bodies of the slaves, together with the sweat-encrusted clothes and rum-laden breath of the crew, sickened and disgusted him, recalling memories best forgotten. He gazed across at the open space that was to house a large vendue hall for the sale of slaves, and hoped that by the next time he came to town on such a matter, it would be completed and in use. He viewed his huddled group of frightened humanity with growing compassion and wanted to reassure them, give them some word of comfort, but instead said gruffly to Dick Gough:

"Give them fresh clothing, then get them in a loose coffle . . . make it as loose as practical. Across at Passage Fort, Jake will be waiting. Give them rest and plenty of food to get them into shape for the march to Wells. I'll join you at Passage Fort in two days. . . . I have sundry commissions for the ladies at Wells to complete."

Dick Gough nodded, his feelings somewhat modified toward Robert after his show of near-compassion.

"Right, Master Robert."

"We'll take our time in getting back to Wells. The slaver's being on time has cut our stay away from home considerably, so I think we are justified in taking these poor devils at a reasonable pace."

Dick nodded again and raised a hand in farewell as Robert turned from him and went slowly along the crowded wharf.

Robert felt disturbed in mind and unclean in body after actively engaging in traffic in human flesh, and he pushed his way blindly through the seething mass of people who were gathered to watch the sale. Then his attention was caught and held by the sight of a strange figure battling through the throngs, tattered black gown flying from a bony gaunt frame, long tangled gray hair matting into a flowing beard, eyes wild and fanatical as he clutched in gnarled hands a roughly made cross of undressed wood, the while declaiming in the high accusing voice of prophecy:

"Repent, ye sinners. Repent, all ye that trade in

human flesh. For human flesh is God-given and cannot be traded in this world. This town of sin and sloth, of debauchery, lechery and godlessness, the streets will be rent asunder and the earth shall swallow all, and those that are saved will cry unto God: Babylon is fallen, is fallen, that great city. For the devil has come into your hearts to lure you to even greater sin, and the lord God grieves because you heed not his exhortations to repent, and is having great wrath, because he knoweth that ye have but a short time to save your souls from eternal hellfire and damnation. Therefore, heed the Word of God and repent, repent before the earth shall swallow the wicked and the innocent alike."

And with this and similar exhortations and much misquoting of the scriptures, which added in fact to their aptness, he plowed his way through the insensate citizens, whose only reactions to his dire prophecy of judgment and the wrath of God were scorn and amusement.

Robert had stopped under the lee of a house to observe the man, when a quiet voice at his elbow said:

"In truth he expresses many of my own sentiments, phrased more colorfully, but there is . . . ."

Robert turned toward the speaker, arrested by the familiar drawl, and his blue eyes widened in complete disbelief as he viewed the tall figure by his side. Elegantly dressed in what must be the latest fashion in Europe, a short doublet with huge ballooning shirt sleeves escaping from the shoulder, petticoat breeches plentifully bedecked with ribbons and lace, falling cravat under the chin, and the whole topped by a periwig of alarming elaboration, this in turn half concealed by a flat-crowned wide-brimmed hat, with a huge ostrich feather encircling it.

The face so near his own was thin and stern-looking, unknown yet hauntingly familiar: a man's face that he

101

had never seen before. But the long jagged scar that puckered the right eyebrow was that which he had last seen on the face of a boy, a boy who had shut his eyes so that the tears would not fall.

"Philip," Robert breathed. "Philip Lonsdale, as I live."

The look of lazy languor went, complete disbelief taking its place.

"As you live? But you don't . . . *Robert?* It can't be. . . ." His eyes widened as he recognized in the deep blue eyes and the bronzed face of the stalwart young man before him the thin and tattered youth of five years ago. "But . . . Rob . . . Rob, lad. I was told that you were dead."

"Dead? Who on earth . . ." Robert began, but Philip clasped him around the shoulder in a flurry of perfumed laces.

"Enough for now. Let us to my lodgings out of this confounded heat, and we will acquaint each other over a good dinner all that has chanced since we parted almost on this very spot."

Robert was too dazed at this unexpected apparition of Philip, and somewhat taken aback at the presumption of his own death, to do more than meekly accompany his new-found friend.

They made their way from the wharf area through one of the narrow streets that radiated from Fishers Row and soon found themselves by way of Lime Street in Queen Street, where Philip's lodging was housed. The houses here, as everywhere in the town, were densely packed, their doorways flush with the narrow unpaved streets. Philip paused before one, identical to a dozen others, and pushed open the shuttered wooden door. A central passage ran through to a courtyard in the rear, so that some slight breeze could circulate and ease the heat of the arid atmosphere. Philip led the way to a door at the end of this passage and motioned Robert to enter. It was a fair-sized room, tastefully enough furnished with the usual four-poster bed, a long wooden trestle table, and the unusual luxury of two velvet-covered chairs in place of the more common stools. The hangings about the bed were of fine lawn edged with Valenciennes lace, while the table was graced by fine pewter goblets and platters. Philip spun his hat onto the bed post and lifted off his elaborate wig with care, revealing his own blond hair, cut short now to just below his ears. It was darkened with sweat caused by the close-fitting wig, and he said as he flung off his doublet and loosened his cravat:

"Plaguey hot clothes in this climate. Yours, though of an execrable cut and a fashion that is a very bastard of style, are yet more suitable to the tropics."

"Then why not follow my example?"

Philip shut his eyes in apparent pain: "You ask me to be garbed like that? My dear Rob, what has this place done to you?" He sank down gracefully onto one of the chairs and waved Robert languidly to the other. Then, throwing off his affected manner, he said briskly: "Now, begin, tell me what has chanced with you . . . you look well enough, I vow, despite no sop to reigning fashion . . . and prosperous enough."

"Let's have your tale first," Robert said.

"As you will."

Philip took up a leather wine bottle and poured two good measures, then settled back in his chair.

"The man who bought me, though unprepossessing, was a kindly soul. He was agent for one Jacob Stokes who has a goodly property beyond the district known as Yallahs, eastward in the island. This man was the son of one of the settlers who came here from Nevis some ten years back . . . *their* story is remarkable enough in its own right, though not for the telling at

103

this time. Anyway, though bonded, I was treated with courtesy and a rough kindness, though I had to labor in the fields . . . but so then did Jacob Stokes alongside us with his brothers. That part of the island is completely isolated, there is no through road and one has to make the journey by sea . . . no doubt roads *will* be cut in time to come, but Lord, the going will be rough; high rugged mountains on one side, rushing rivers, forests and swampy mangroves on the other." Philip paused to take a draft of wine, and Robert waited, impatient to hear more. "Well, I'd been at Stokes upward of eighteen months or so when a ship put in at Morante . . . or Port Morant, as it is coming to be known . . . with James Knowles, an agent of my father, aboard. My father had learned of my whereabouts from Hugh Russell after communicating with your old tutor and had petitioned the King himself for clemency on both your and my behalf. Knowles was authorised to 'buy' us back with no thought to cost, but Jacob Stokes, bless his kindly heart, said he wanted no more traffic in human merchandise and sent me off with his good will and blessing. Back here in Port Royal I spent weeks inquiring of every one I met as to your fate and whereabouts. I almost despaired of discovering anything, when I ran into a seaman in a tavern who claimed that he had once worked at Wells and that there you had succumbed to yellow fever . . . ."

"A *seaman?*" Robert interrupted. "I know of no seaman. You say he worked at Wells? His name?"

"Davies . . . yes, Jez Davies. A villainous type. Since turned pirate, I hear, and sails with the notorious Roche Brasilano."

"Jez Davies? So he thought to revenge himself by preventing my rescue . . . you will hear *why* when I tell *my* tale."

"I can hardly wait. Well, with no cause to doubt the

man's story, I set sail for England, though I came devilish near to making the journey to Wells to hear more of your 'death' but thought it would be but a fool's errand. Once back in England and reunited with my family, I discovered that though you would have been allowed to return, your lands and wealth are still forfeit. That need not bother us now, the rest of my story can wait until I have heard yours. First, more wine and I will order food."

Two

Philip listened in silence as Robert recounted his story, his lips tightening in distaste and his eyes darkening in pain as he heard of the lashings and brutal attack by Jez Davies. Then, as the story progressed and Robert's position improved, his expression lightened.

"So—you're going to marry the beautiful girl and inherit the property. Like a French romance. All sweet sentiment, happy endings, and virtue will triumph," he said lightly, then his expression hardened. "The property? You have slaves there . . . slaves from Africa?"

"Oh, yes, one couldn't run a plantation without, these days. We have over three hundred. That was the point of my journey to Port Royal, to . . ," Robert broke off as Philip cut in coldly:

"The point of your journey to the town? To buy more slaves? Is that it?" He slammed the table with his clenched fist, his face white with anger, the long pucker-ng scar livid. "What irony, that on the day you and I meet in joyous reunion we should find ourselves in opposite camps."

"I don't understand the reason for your anger . . ." Robert began.

"Don't understand?" Philip rasped. "That shows the change wrought in you. From the day I returned to England I have been trying to make people see the wicked inhumanity in this filthy traffic in human flesh.

106

My task is made doubly difficult by the King's charter to the Company of Royal Adventurers in England trading into Africa. Also the King's brother himself shows interest in the venture. Despite this I *have* influenced a few powerful people. The sole purpose of my visit here is to talk to the planters and to get them to see the injustice of the system. Then I find *you,* after all your experiences, upholding the trade, condoning it, actively engaged in it yourself."

"You're becoming too emotional," Robert retorted coldly. "You speak as if *I* had invented the system of slavery. . . . S'life man, it's hundreds, thousands of years old. These same people who have been shipped here would no doubt have been enslaved in other countries . . . these people were *born* to be enslaved."

"No . . . no man is *born* to be enslaved. . . . To accept an evil merely because it has endured over the years is as base as the originator of that evil. Longevity does not imbue a virtue, the evil persists and corrupts. You use the fallacious argument that men always use when confronted by such a situation. 'It was always so, therefore it must be right.' " Philip flung himself back in the chair and viewed Robert's flushed set face, his own anger spent, his eyes strained with exhaustion. "I'm sorry, Rob, to attack you like this, but the shock of hearing your views after the joy of finding you alive. . . ." He spread his hands and shrugged wearily.

Robert sighed.

"Don't think that I disagree with you . . . I don't, up to a point. My conviction is, though, that no one man can fight the world, especially against such an established and profitable system. 'Tis better, surely, to agitate for better conditions for the slaves, and perhaps achieve some measure of success in that field, than expend your energies on a hopeless cause. Come back with me to Wells and see for yourself. You will be very welcome."

Philip nodded. "Thanks, Rob," he said formally, but there was no warmth in his voice. "We must see about lodgings for you for tonight."

Robert was accommodated in a room in the same lodging house and retired early, his thoughts and emotions chaotic after the events of the day: the shivering frightened slaves at the auction block; the voice of doom of the proclaiming prophet; the unexpected meeting with Philip, then Philip's fierce denunciation of his acceptance of the way of life in the island. These thoughts chased around in his mind like a mouse on a wheel as he tossed on his bed unable to sleep, the sounds of carousing a cacophonous background. The oppressive heat added to his discomfort, as the breeze from the hills failed to penetrate the shuttered windows. At the back of his mind was the uneasy conviction that Philip was right in his denunciation, and he wondered wearily how Philip had come to change his views on the existence of God and man's possession of a soul, in direct contrast to his views uttered so long ago on the long voyage across the Atlantic. But then, he reflected bitterly, just as my views have changed, then so might his. He wondered if they would ever resume their easy camaraderie and if he would discover the reason for Philip's conversion. So wondering, he fell asleep at last.

The next day was spent in shopping for the women-folk at Wells. Apart from the specific commissions, Robert bought an exquisite ring, a fine, deeply colored emerald surrounded by pearls, for Charlotte as a betrothal present; delicate pearl eardrops for Ann, who had just had her ears pierced; and after much deliberation, a length of Chinese silk brocade for Bridget Wells.

The townspeople were still keeping behind closed

doors, as Roche Brasilano and his men were carousing in a tavern on Thomas Street. Sounds of drunken revelry, the screams of women, broken glassware, and a continuous stream of obscenities were borne across the still, hot air.

Robert and Philip maintained an uneasy truce, a tacit understanding not to refer to slaves or slavery, and by nightfall they were practically back to their former lighthearted gaiety. They decided to sup out, as this was their last night in Port Royal, for they planned to take the dawn ferry to Passage Fort and hoped to reach Wells by sunset. They chose an eating house in Tower Street near St. Paul's Church, a place comparatively quiet and unassuming after the rowdy places nearer the wharves, yet still rowdy enough to make Robert wish himself back in the peace and serenity of Wells Great-house.

They chatted easily now, back on their old footing, when the door was flung roughly open and a group of seamen, obviously pirates by their garish dress and loud-mouthed oaths, lurched in, jostling the other diners, demanding seats at the table and immediate service. The tavern keeper sprang to attend these unwelcome customers, his face showing servile fear as he recognized them as Brasilano's men. Robert and Philip sat in silence, unwilling to call attention to themselves, when one of the pirates gestured toward them, waving a full tankard of ale, spilling half its contents down his already soiled doublet.

"Hey you cullies there, you fine young snottie-nosed gentlemen. Too proud to drink a toast, eh?"

Philip raised his goblet. "Your very good health, sir," he murmured politely.

The man, his face bloated and purple-veined under a grizzled beard, roared with raucous laughter and mimicked Philip's quiet drawl before turning toward

Robert. "And you, young cockscomb . . . I see *you* keep y'r compliments to y'self?"

Robert raised his goblet and, ignoring the warning pressure of Philip's foot against his, said with ill-advised irony: "No, sir. My compliments are yours to command. I wish you the future that you deserve." He drank deeply.

"Do you, by God," the man roared. "Ye think I'm too much in my cups and dull-witted not to understand y'r meaning."

He lurched to their table and leaned two huge ham-fisted hands on either side, slopping more ale, his eyes bloodshot between puffy lids, his breath foul from rotting teeth and a stomach ill-treated by cheap and copious liquor. Robert drew back in disgust, his nostrils narrowing fastidiously, his mind triggering swift alarm. In the bloodshot eyes so close to his recognition dawned, mingled with an unholy joy.

"By the blessed Mother of God . . . into my hands . . . my very hands . . . *Robert Vane.*"

Philip had recognized the man seconds before as the one who had told him of Robert's death and had sent up a devout prayer that Robert would go unrecognized. Robert's face whitened as he gazed at the hate-filled eyes so close to his. As he made to rise from his seat, Jez straightened, throwing the whole table over with a clatter of pewter ware and a scattering of uneaten food. Robert's hand flew to the small-sword at his hip, but before he could unsheath the weapon, one of Jez's fists caught him a buffet across his temple, a shattering blow that dulled his vision with pain. He dimly heard Philip shout to the taverner: "Quick, man, call the militia." The man either didn't hear or chose not to hear, fearing to antagonize the pirates still further. He heard through a haze Jez's voice: "Just you and me now me cully, no Colonel Wells, rot his soul, to help

110

you now." It was now only a matter of seconds before both Robert and Philip were battered into unconsciousnes, and as black enveloping waves engulfed him, Robert had a vivid memory of a similar happening nearly six years before. Then thought and feeling were blotted out.

Dick Gough waited at Passage Fort with the docile coffle of Negro slaves until long past the appointed time at which Robert had said he would join them. At first he wasn't too worried at the delay. "I reckon how the young master's having a bit of fun afore settling down," he remarked to Jake Matlock with a lewd chuckle. But as the third day drew to a close, he said: "We'd best be getting back to Wells before sun-up in the mornin', lad. There's no knowin' what's keepin' Robert Vane. We'd best get this little lot back home as soon's we can."

There was consternation at Wells when the coffle was sighted and Robert not seen among the riders, for although it had been stated that he might be away a week or two and the fortuitous early arrival of the slaver not yet known, they could not conceive that he would willingly allow a coffle of valuable slaves to travel all the way in the doubtful care of two bonded servants.

Colonel Wells concealed his own worry after listening to Dick Gough's report under testy commands to the womenfolk.

"Enough of this vaporing. The lad's but enjoying the gaiety of town life. He'll be along in good time."

"But, papa," Ann pleaded, her great eyes wide. "If he doesn't arrive . . . by . . . by noon tomorrow, will you send Dick back to find him? *Please*, papa."

Her father pinched her cheek. He could never refuse this child anything, as indeed nobody at Wells could

111

easily resist the soft, pleading look that Ann had early learned to use well to obtain her own ends.

"All right, my love. Despite the chaos amongst the field hands and a shut-down of the boiler shed, we'll send out a search party . . . but I doubt there'll be need, he'll be back before noon."

But the next noon came and went, and despite his promise to Ann, Wells delayed sending Dick Gough back into town until the following day. The household waited impatiently for his return, and on the evening of the third day, when only one horseman was sighted, leading a second riderless horse, consternation broke out again and rose to near hysteria.

"Sorry, sir," Dick Gough reported. "I enquired all over Port Royal, but no one knows anything of him or his whereabouts. It's just as if he was swallowed into thin air. I took the liberty, sir, of havin' the town crier call his name throughout the streets, both mornin' an' evenin', but none came forward with any knowledge."

None came forward, but some did have knowledge: the woman who ran the lodging house kept her mouth shut, otherwise the jewelry and Chinese silk that Robert had bought and left in his room with his other purchases would be forfeit to the authorities. And anyway, she had always fancied a fine emerald ring on her plump hand, and the silk would make an elegant gown. The tavern keeper where Philip and Robert had supped also kept a tight mouth; he wanted no truck with the militia or trouble with Brasilano's men on a subsequent visit. While sundry wharvingers could have testified as to the whereabouts of the two missing young men but kept silent, for their testimony could well be too dangerous to their own persons.

"You did well, Gough," Wells said with a worried frown. "D'you think aught harm has come to the lad?"

112

"Well, sir." Dick seemed reluctant to voice his thoughts. "There was a lot of talk of the pirate Roche Brasilano being about to dock. I hear he's a holy terror, striking down innocent people with no reason, raping young girls in the very streets, the whole town's in fear of him . . . not like some of the other pirates, who I hear just enjoy themselves ashore . . . or the buccaneers who are looked upon as heroes . . . ."

"Yes, yes," the colonel cut in testily, stemming what promised to be a voluble discourse on the debaucheries of Port Royal. "You fear that Robert might have got into a brawl with this man?"

"Well . . . it's possible, though I don't have no facts to . . . ."

"Then where is he? If he'd been killed or wounded, surely the authorities would be aware of the fact and informed you when you made enquiries?"

"Maybe not, sir. The authorities—the militia—are practically helpless against Brasilano and his men. The . . . body . . . could have been dropped into the harbor and no questions asked."

"Or," Walter Wells said thoughtfully, "he could have been taken aboard their pirate ship . . . alive or dead. I think you and I will pay yet another visit to Port Royal and question this ogre. . . ."

"Warn't be no use, sir, Brasilano sailed at dawn yesterday."

"Good God, *what* am I to tell my daughters?"

Charlotte's reception to the news of Robert's disappearance was the calmest of any of the women: she listened, white-faced but composed, to her father's clumsy words:

"A shock to you, girl, but time will heal all. I'll have to be making enquiries about another husband for you. . . ."

The pain in her large gray eyes lifted, to be replaced by sudden anger.

"I'll have no husband but Robert, papa," she said firmly.

"Charlotte, lass, don't build too many dreams . . . I doubt we'll see the lad again. Pity . . . I had hoped . . ." he bit off the unfinished sentence as Charlotte's eyes swam in sudden tears.

"Oh, papa, and we were all going to be so happy here at Wells." She drew a deep breath and controlled her threatened tears. "Papa, teach *me* how to manage Wells. I know you had plans for Robert . . . if Richard—I mean, I can learn, I can ride well. . . ."

"You're but a lass, you can't enforce authority and control hundreds of men, black or white. . . ."

"I *can,* papa, I *know* I can. The men respect me already. I'm young yet, and if I ride with you and learn all that you can teach me, over the years they will come to accept a woman in authority, if *you* show that you respect my judgment. Please, papa, you need me to help you."

Her father shook his head in amazement: a woman, a slip of a girl to learn to manage his fast-growing acreage, his vast crops of sugar, and the intricacies of the rum distillery. Girls were good only in the house to manage children, to breed and do a man's bidding. But he recognized determination and something more in the earnestly entreating eyes of his daughter: an inner strength. He laughed suddenly, the first laugh heard at Wells since the news had come from Port Royal.

"S'life, I believe you will learn and learn well. Tomorrow . . . is tomorrow too soon to start?"

"Oh, no, papa. And thank you. . . . You'll see, you'll forget I'm a girl in no time."

He pinched her cheek. "I doubt the man lives as could do *that,*" he said.

114

Ann had been shaken out of her childish joy in life by the news and had retired once more to the deserted schoolroom, and she wept until there were no more tears to weep. Then a state of apathy and despondency enveloped her, she grew thin and pale, her enormous eyes dominating her pinched little face. She was still a child though, for all her precocity, and as the days lengthened into weeks and the weeks into months, the pain of loss inevitably receded, her youthful resilience asserted itself, she began to eat heartily, her cheeks filled out, and her gay bubbling laugh was heard again throughout the Great-house. But with Charlotte away around the property most of the day with their father, her mother confined now exclusively to her boudoir and private veranda, Richard suffering from one of his recurring bouts of fever, time hung on her hands. She began to associate more and more with the children in the slave compound or take wild, unchaperoned rides with one or other of the young grooms. There was no one to supervise or check her activities, and no one realized that the seeds of recklessness were being sown—seeds that would be reaped in a mixed crop of weeds and wild flowers, watered and nurtured by bitter tears.

Maria accepted Robert's departure and nonreturn with all the impassivity of her slave status. It was ever so, she thought with a resigned shrug, nothing was certain, what was ease and comfort today was hard work and sufferance the next. She experienced a faint regret when she remembered Robert's gentleness, his firm hands about her body, the fierce unions they had known together, his deep blue eyes alive with teasing affection. Then she would toss away the memories and find wild comfort in Noah's strong black arms, oblivious of the child that grew steadily in her womb, the first faint kicks telling her that she would soon have to ad-

115

mit her condition to Charlotte. But meanwhile, the nights were warm and heavy-laden with the cloying odor of ripening sugar cane, the moon swung full in the high dark blue dome . . . and Noah was waiting by the waterfall, as Robert had waited so often.

Three

The *Juanita* plowed through the blue waters of the Caribbean, her destination New Providence in the Bahama Islands, her purpose to intercept supply ships outward bound from England and the east, with goods for the settlers on the North American mainland. Possibly with some profitable wrecking en route. Later, the *Juanita,* a galleon captured from the Spanish, hoped to team up with the *Pedro,* a lighter, swifter treasure frigate, and together they would attack the homeward-bound Spanish flota, laden with silver, gold, spices, and precious gems.

The rigging swarmed with seamen furling and unfurling the many sails as the wind, capricious and fitful, dropped to a mere zephyr or whipped to a gusty squall. There, high in the mainmast, Philip Lonsdale and Robert Vane labored under the fierce midday sun. Stripped to the waist, skin sunbronzed, beards and hair bleached by the sun and snarled by the wind, seamen's wrinkles about their eyes, hard of mouth and hard of eye, they bore no resemblance to the elegant young dandy from London or the sturdy well-dressed young planter from Jamaica. The intervening months since they had left Port Royal had seasoned them and coarsened them to their life among the pirate crew. At first, finding themselves once more captive in a stinking hold, an almost exact replica of their fate

117

over five years before, they had been driven to over-whelming self-pity. But the conditions were by no means the same, they had been abducted partly to assuage Jez Davies' ingrained hatred of Robert and an opportunity to inflict revenge for the imagined wrong that Robert had done him in encompassing his dismissal from Wells, and partly as replacements to the crew, whose numbers had been depleted in a fracas with an English warship on her way to harass the Dutch. They were kept in the hold only as long as it took the *Juanita* to clear Jamaican waters and there was no possibility of escape, then they were hauled on deck before the first mate, a burly Irishman who had been indented in Barbados, had enlisted with Penn and Venables, and had taken to piracy at the first opportunity. Robert noted that Jez Davies kept in the background, that his ebullience seemed muted among his fellow pirates, and that he appeared in no position of authority. Robert's spirits lifted a little at this observation, for he had no illusions as to his helplessness against Jez in his present surroundings. He was jerked out of his musings by a booming liquor-coarsened brogue:

"Now, see here me boys, me name's O'Connor, *Mr.* O'Connor to the likes o' you. Do as I say an' it'll be by you'll be getting . . . any of y'r lip or back word, an' you'll be before the Cap'n, as sure as the blessed Virgin was the good Lord's Mother . . . an' they won't like that, eh, me cullies?"

This last to the crew, who laughed in sycophantic agreement, but with laughter tinged with an uneasy undertone. "Y'r aboard the *Juanita,* a name to strike terror in any Spaniard's heart . . . the devil take their papist souls . . . a name feared by the bloody English and the sniveling French alike, and even, by all the blessed saints, the Dutch themselves, how so's the Cap'n's a Dutchman himself. Y'r'll best be making

118

y'rselves accept that y'r one of *us* now, an' it's join our band y'r'll be doin' and serve us loyally or refuse and be goin' to the bottom of the sea for the sharks to enjoy an' feast on y'r miserable carcases. One or 'tother."

Neither Philip nor Robert so much as glanced at each other; it was as if each could see into the other's mind. What choice had they? Better to take the oath of loyalty or whatever they'd be called upon to do and live, with a chance of escape later, than end their lives now by a pious adherence to a creed that condemned piracy. Neither felt that any oath taken under such circumstances was binding; surely none of the pirates were as naive and as gullible to believe that it was? After all, they were pirates, beholden to none but their leader, not Brethren of the Coast governed by strict laws and half recognized by their respective governments as an unofficial navy. But neither Philip nor Robert realized that to accept so lightheartedly O'Connor's offer, with the intention of escaping at the earliest opportunity, was easier than putting that intent to the test. For months they were to roam the seas, never putting in at an island that was inhabited or anywhere on the mainland that was friendly. But this they discovered too late, and even had they had the knowledge, their answer would very likely have been the same.

"I accept," Robert said firmly.

"I also," Philip said with equal firmness.

The first few days they had scarce opportunity for any private conversation in the close confines of ship life, and it was only when vigilance was relaxed and their presence taken for granted that they had the chance of a few words together. Robert noted with relief that although Jez Davies had been the instrument of their capture, once they were aboard, his vengeance appeared to be satisfied, and he paid them

no more attention beyond occasional jibes at their re-
duction in status in performing the most menial duties.
He had in tow a young black-eyed cabin boy, whose
smooth cheeks and delicate complexion proclaimed
him to be no more than twelve or thirteen years old.
This lad was Jez's constant companion and, as Philip
dryly remarked: "Didn't appear to object to assuaging
Jez's perverted appetite."

They grew accustomed to the bellowing brogue with
which O'Connor issued orders, incongruously larded
with the most devout exhortations to the Deity, the Holy
Trinity, the Virgin Mary, and all the saints by name
and sex ever listed in the Pope's calendar: the adding
inconsonance of his violent condemnation of all Spaniards as "bloody papists" while at the same time he
professed a strong adherence to the Holy Roman faith.
Their views of their dread captain, Roche Brasilano,
were fortunately few and far between, as he spent most
of his time in his quarters with a couple of whores
picked up in Port Royal.

Then at last they were assigned to long spells of duty
high up in the mainmast, to keep a continuous lookout
for possible craft to plunder or to warn of an approaching enemy. At first Robert's senses reeled during the
long climb up the shrouds, but Philip had a good
head for heights and coaxed and bullied him until at
last he could swarm up the rigging without a thought
for what lay below and indeed came to enjoy these
long spells of duty away from the ill-assorted crew,
rejoicing in the fresh salt air.

They were cruising in Bahaman waters, those treacherous waters of sudden depths and equally sudden
shallows, with hundreds of little cays and rocks. They
had sighted a small merchantman, bound probably from
Somer's Island to New Providence, and gave chase. She
bravely crowded on all sail, but the gap between the

two ships lessened. Brasilano knew these waters and tacked away from dangerous hidden reefs, but the little merchantman, thinking she'd outrun the pirate, kept bravely on, unaware of the danger below. Suddenly she began to spin around out of the helmsman's control, her sails to back and fill, then there came a rending crack of ripping timbers, clearly heard by those in the pursuing *Juanita*. She began to list badly, then settled drunkenly, upheld only by the coral bed which had been her destruction. Brasilano swung about and inched up to her, broadside on and as close as he could get, then ordered a longboat to be lowered and to approach the stricken ship. There was no resistance from the frightened crew and handful of passengers, and the pirates swarmed aboard, stripped the doomed ship of all available goods, then rowed quickly back to the *Juanita* with two terrified women passengers, callously leaving the crew and the rest of the passengers to go down with their ship.

Philip and Robert watched from the *Juanita*'s deck, their hearts sick with pity for the victims.

"They can't leave them to die," Robert breathed in horror.

Philip's hand on his arm pressed a warning.

"Don't show what you feel. Whatever *we* do, they'll die . . . and possibly us with them if we make any move to help. Our only hope is to gain complete confidence and make a bid for freedom *only* when it is certain to succeed."

They watched in loathing as the two women—revealed on closer inspection as young girls in their early teens—were hauled aboard and pawed and mauled by the rest of the crew. They were so very young and half dead with terror that it took all Robert's and Philip's self-control not to go to their rescue. But Philip was right; what hope had they? They had no weapons

121

and would be struck down to no avail. The girls' fate would be the same whatever they did. So they had to stand calmly by while the girls were passed from one to another, their clothing ripped until they were both naked, their young bodies pawed obscenely by the lust-aroused seamen.

Then the voice of O'Connor roared:

"Belay that, the cap'n wants 'em first. Y'r turn'll come later."

Robert never forgot in all the years ahead the tortured screams that came from the captain's cabin. Later that night, fired by lust which had increased during the hours of waiting and aggravated by wine taken from the plundered vessel, the porcine grunts and lewd laughter of the crew were heard, along with the renewed screams from the girls, which became increasingly weaker as the night wore on, until at last only low animal whimperings were all that spoke of their hours of torment. Then eventually a blessed silence fell.

"Before I leave this cursed boat," Robert whispered, "I'll send as many as I can to hell. It could not be termed murder to kill such scum."

Despite their nonparticipation in the shameful orgy, not one of the crew remarked on the fact. Their wits had been absorbed only in the quick procuring of the girls to enjoy. One of the satiated seamen said to Robert with an evil leer: "Good sport we had last night, eh, lad? Not but they were a mite worked out by the time we got them . . . the cap'n's a rare one for staying power . . . cor . . . but still . . . ." He licked his stubble-encircled lips in retrospection.

"Yes," Robert agreed ambiguously. "Where . . . where are they now?"

The other laughed coarsely, throwing an arm around Robert's shoulder, bringing an enveloping gust of sweat-drenched clothing mingled with rum- and tobacco-laden breath. "Heh? lad, eh? Want a bit more of the same, eh? Shop-soiled, as it was. Ha, you're out of luck. . . . Cap'n had 'em again after we'd revived 'em with a bucket o' cold water, followed by a tot of rum . . . sort of liven 'em up. . . ." He winked obscenely, his gross body moving suggestively. "But 'twarn't no good. One—the bigger one too—lasted just a few minutes. 'Tother little un 'bout an hour . . . then. . . ." He made a negative movement that left no doubt as to his meaning, followed by a tossing motion seaward. Robert turned away trying to conceal the horror that welled within him. He leaned against the gunwale and stared down into the blue waters, their colors changing from palest aqua to brilliant sapphire as the treacherous depths deepened with their ship's passage.

"All right," he said fiercely to the bleached sky and the glittering sea. "I'll *be* a pirate, I'll get their confidence and plunder and kill . . . in clean blood, a good clean stroke, if need be . . . and *then,* when the time is ripe, I'll blow this cursed ship to Kingdom come and all that's in her . . . if I have to perish in the doing."

The looked-for rendezvous with the sister ship *Pedro* was not kept, and at last it was reluctantly concluded that she had gone down, so the *Juanita* put in at Spanish Wells in the Bahamas, where there was a deep, sheltered bay, a veritable hurricane hole, concealing them from any other shipping that might pass. The waters were barely deep enough to allow the *Juanita* to draw the five feet she needed, and at low tide she rested gently on the sandy bottom while the lowlier members of the crew careened her barnacle-encrusted hull and others filled the water bottles with fresh sweet water from the wells that gave the island its name.

In low whispers Robert confided his vow to Philip.

"Rob, lad, it's crazy, but it's all we can do. To go on as we are is to stagnate to no avail, to be pirates in name only, to be hung for naught if we're caught. Yes," Philip said as Robert jerked his head up in surprise. "Had you not thought of that? If we're taken by an English warship, we'd be tried as pirates and hung, who'd believe the truth? If we're taken by the Dutch, French, or Spanish, we'll be put to the sword . . . in the case of the latter a little touch of the Inquisition first, to save our heretic souls ostensibly, to give immense delight to the Inquisitors in fact. I'm with you, but we've got to gain the crew's confidence gradually and convincingly; there must be no squeamishness when it comes to the point . . . even when those we are forced to kill are innocent. God grant us though that no more women fall into their hands before our mission is accomplished."

And so the months passed. The *Juanita* cruised through the Bahamas, and now Robert and Philip took part in the boardings and the landings, the sacking of rich merchantmen and Spanish treasure ships, in the raiding of towns along the length of the Spanish Main. They won the confidence of the burly Irish mate O'Connor and the respect of their fellow pirates for their valor in being always in the forefront of every boarding party and the last to leave the plundered vessel. They had a complete disregard for their quarries' cannon or musket shot, so that they were now accepted as valuable members of the crew, earning the approval of the villainous Brasilano himself. They were now fully armed: a short heavy dagger, curving machete, a pistol, and a musket apiece. Better than this, they were now made free of the whole ship, barring the captain's cabin, and knew every inch of her, the vagaries of every sail, the intricacies of her rigging, her points of strength and weakness, the approaches and escape routes from every deck . . . and the exact location of the powder cabin.

They let the months pass into one year . . . two years . . .

Then one night Robert motioned Philip to a quiet spot by the brig.

"We put south soon for Port Royal," he murmured scarce above a whisper. "I think the time is drawing near for action."

Four

Charlotte Wells cast an appraising eye over Maria's increasing waistline and at the fuller taut breasts that swelled above her high, low-cut bodice.

"It had better be a boy, Maria," she said dryly. "We can do with more hands . . . we've women enough."

"Yes, Miss Charlotte," Maria said meekly enough, though her heart rebelled at the cold allotment of future work for her unborn child.

"And who is the father?" Charlotte went on. "That handsome groom . . . Noah? Or . . . don't you know?"

There was an undercurrent of scorn in the lightly tossed question which made Maria's dark skin mantle to a deeper hue.

"It . . . it *mus'* be Noah, Miss Charlotte," she said. Despite herself, her voice trembled slightly as that uneasy fear crept back from the deep recesses of her mind however hard she tried to banish it. What if the child favor Mas' Robert? Miss Charlotte fit fe kill me. . . . She glanced quickly up at Charlotte's cool amused scrutiny.

"Well, what certainty, I congratulate you on your fidelity."

Charlotte cantered down to meet her father in the broad grassy ride in the cane-piece. He watched her approach with pleasure and pride: in the few short months that she had been accompanying him around the property, she had shown a grasp of its management with a speed and mature understanding that had amazed him. He had discovered also that beneath her feminine exterior and outward fragility there lay a mind that was fast developing a ruthlessness to match his own and a stamina that enabled her to stay in the saddle from sunrise to sunset, apart from the two-hour break at noon Shell-blow, when the whole plantation came to a standstill.

She smiled as she reined in beside him.

"Papa, my body slave is with child . . . let us hope it is a boy."

"Good, how soon?"

"Two . . . three months. She can work well a while longer." She dismissed Maria's child with a toss of her head and said seriously: "Papa . . . I am concerned about Mama. Have you seen her lately?"

Colonel Wells shifted uneasily in the broad saddle, his conscience stirring momentarily at the treatment he now accorded his wife.

"Dr. Jeffries assures me that nothing bodily ails her. 'Tis all in the mind," he answered indirectly.

"But, papa," Charlotte persisted, "I fear *Dr.* Jeffries' abilities are more feigned than actual. Old Leah knows more of medical care than he does. And that was not what I asked, papa." She was demurely firm.

"Well . . . I'll look in on her tonight," Walter Wells promised with a reluctance that Charlotte noted with displeasure. She was well aware of her father's continuous infidelities. She had come to accept that he was not alone in such behavior; indeed, her small observation of life on other plantations suggested it was fast becoming the norm. She accepted that but could not understand it or condone the neglect to which her mother had been subjected over the last few years. At sixteen Charlotte had not yet awak-

127

ened emotionally or fully developed sexually, she had no curiosity or desire for life to be otherwise, content to continue in an asexual limbo. The abrupt termination of her marriage plans had produced no emotion or reaction other than mild annoyance after the first shock of Robert's disappearance had worn off; but she did show some reaction to her father's amours inasmuch as they affected her mother's health.

Later that night Walter Wells did honor his reluctantly given promise and made his way for the first time in years along the cool veranda to his wife's suite. . . .

She was propped up against a pile of down-filled pillows, the whiteness of their linen covers only a little higher than her own ashen face. He was deeply shocked by her appearance. She had wasted away to a mere skeleton; the once beautiful eyes, so like those she had bequeathed to both her daughters, were sunken in hooded sockets; her hair, now completely gray and lifeless, lay in two wispy plaits down her shoulders.

Despite the heat that lingered in the early evening air, the jalousied shutters were tightly closed and a warm quilted cover was pulled up to her chin. A candle flickered on a low table, its flame throwing grotesque shadows on the four-poster bed with its lace hangings against the whitewashed walls and turning the sick woman's face into a death mask. Wells shuddered, his dormant conscience suddenly awake and clamoring belated reproaches.

He approached the bed.

"Bridget?"

The pale lids flickered and Bridget slowly opened her eyes; she gazed at him dully for a long moment, then recognition brightened them.

"Walter?" her voice was but a wondering whisper.

"How are you, my dear? I—had no idea that you

128

were so ill. I—I respected your apparent wish to be alone. . . ." The false excuses trailed off lamentably.

Bridget said slowly: "I *am* ill. Sometimes . . . Walter, sometimes I'm so frightened . . . the pain. . . ." She thrust a thin hand toward him, and as he took it in his own, its very fragility swept back some of his old feeling for her. He felt the tears prick his eyes, she'd been a good wife . . . until this climate and the plantation conditions had changed her . . . and he'd helped to make those conditions worse by. . . . He bent down:

"I'll have Leah up, she may have something to ease the pain. Where is it?"

She made a vague gesture toward her abdomen, but the effort of speaking the few words and the slight movement had tired her to the point of exhaustion, and the gesture died even as it was born. Beads of moisture lay thickly on her forehead, while her breath came fast and shallow. Walter put her hand gently under the coverlet and went quietly to the door.

Merdina, Bridget's body slave, waited outside.

"Let me know of any change in Mistress Bridget's condition. And don't leave her at any time. Understand?"

"Yes, Mas' Walter. Maria help I look fe she. The missis well sick, sir."

Merdina's great eyes held reproach for his neglect of his wife, ignoring the fact that she herself on more than one occasion had contributed to that neglect.

Leah's plump black fingers gently probed and prodded Bridget Wells' emaciated, pain-wracked body. Her dark eyes clouded with apprehension at what her fingers told her.

"Miss Bridget, Ma'am," she said softly, her voice still holding traces of her early Spanish tongue. "Me fix you a little tea to mek you lie easy. I sen' it quick

129

quick by Maria. You tek little sip an' drink it all. Not to fret, Miss Bridget, Leah tek care."

Bridget managed a wan smile.

"Thank you, Leah, you've very kind. I feel . . . better . . . a little, now that I know you are looking after me."

"Cho, Miss Bridget, you had fe sen' fe me soon," Leah clucked, then rolled her ample form out of the sickroom, wrinkling her nose in distaste at the fetid atmosphere.

Leah found Wells pacing the veranda outside his study.

"Well, Leah?" he demanded as she stood uncertain, twisting her hands in her white apron.

"Not well at all, Mas' Walter . . . Miss Bridget. . . ." She paused, casting a swift look at his set face, not wanting to put her conclusions into words. She *could* be wrong . . . but long years of experience in caring for the sick on the property made her certain of her diagnosis. But, unspoken, it was her thought, her feeling, her belief; once spoken, it was beyond her power to call back those words, beyond her power to lessen the grief and shock they must surely cause. . . . But Walter was waiting impatiently for her to speak; the words must be uttered: "Miss Bridget . . . well sick, sir. Well well sick. She have the sickness that rot you inside . . . an' . . . I try all me can to mek her . . . las' day comforter . . . easy like . . . but me don' . . . ."

"Last days? You mean . . . ?"

"Yes, sir. She ready to dead. It sorry me has to tell you, Mas' Walter."

"How . . . how long?"

Leah spread her hands: "Me can' sure . . . but two—t'ree day . . . ."

"Good God."

130

He felt the enormity of his long neglect like a tangible load crushing him down.

"Thank you, Leah," he said heavily, dismissingly, and she waddled off, leaving him to his own disturbing, accusing thoughts.

Leah's prognosis was as near correct as possible with her lack of academic medical knowledge, and on the fourth day Bridget Wells died. She died at dawn, just as the sun's first rays lit the mountains she had so loved, when the early morning chorus of bird song rang joyously in the cool freshness of a new day.

So the first grave in the designated family graveyard on the property was dug, its lonely mound soon covered by thick grass, and later in the year a handsome white marble tombstone arrived from Europe, making extra ballast in one of the sugar ships. Colonel Wells had neglected his wife shamefully in life, but he was all attention in death. Her grave was ornate, its carved eulogy a marble lie to generations yet unborn.

About three months after Bridget's death Maria was brought to bed of a boy. It was an easy birth . . . her wide hips and strong young body just made for child bearing. After a brief period the child was passed over to one of the wet nurses in the compound nursery, there to be lost in anonymity among the other squalling babies. His lighter skin and straighter hair went unremarked among the color range, which spoke not only of Walter Wells but of his bonded servants as well. Maria experienced a renewed qualm whenever she saw her child, for as the months passed and his opaque newborn eyes changed color, it was all too obvious who had fathered him: looking into those dark-blue eyes was like looking into Robert's; his nose too, gave an early promise of developing into the straight high bridge that was the other distinctive feature of the Vane family.

Maria had returned to her duties in the Great-house

131

and was brushing and braiding Charlotte's waist-length hair.

"The baby well?" Charlotte asked idly.

"Yes, Miss Charlotte. Well an' fat."

"What have you called him?"

The hand wielding the brush paused in its even strokes.

"Me don' call 'im nothin', Miss Charlotte."

"Well, you'd *better*. Does he favor his father?"

Maria caught her breath. "Y'yes . . . 'im favor 'im little. . . ."

"Well," Charlotte persisted. "If he favors . . . Noah, isn't it?" Maria nodded mutely, fingers busy among the long fine strands. "Well, then. I don't suppose you know your bible, you little heathen, but Noah was the father of Ham, Shem and Japheth . . ."

Maria gulped her relief; so Miss Charlotte had no suspicion, an' pray the white man God she never go near the compound.

"I think I call 'im Seth, Miss Charlotte. It's a nice name."

Charlotte stood up, surveying her reflection in the long mirror, dismissing the thought of Maria's child almost at once.

"You do that . . . and you must bring him to see me . . . sometime . . . ."

"Yes, Ma'am," Maria replied meekly, half knowing, wholly hoping that it was an idle invitation, to be forgotten as soon as Charlotte was mounted and busy about the affairs of the property.

"You know, papa," Charlotte said as they cantered toward the coffee walk to inspect a crop of new young trees. "We really ought to do something about religion for the slaves."

"*Religion?* Good God, child, we've no time for notions like that."

132

"But, papa, they *should* be taught the Christian religion . . . . and all those children in the compound, they ought to be christened properly. . . ."

"Well, if it'll please you, m'dear, I'll see about getting a parson feller . . . but it'll be a waste, I warn you . . . the Negroes have their own gods and their own beliefs."

"But that's just it, papa. Their gods are back in Africa, they are losing their beliefs, no idols to worship, no ceremonies. Now that they have taken root here, they need a new form of worship."

"Mind they don't get uppity and think that with the teaching of the white man's religion they become us and expect to lose their slave status."

"Oh, papa, that is fanciful, it couldn't possibly happen."

On one of her subsequent rides around the plantation, over the still increasing number of acres—there were now some seven hundred under cultivation—Charlotte came upon a clearing where Jake Matlock was holding a service beneath the wide spread of a cotton tree. She reined her horse to a standstill and listened, noting the rapt expression on the faces of the Negroes as they sat on the ground, trying to understand the sense of the unfamiliar biblical words. Then Jake led them in a thundering rendition of a hymn, which had none of the prissy solemnity of its usual rendering but seemed to have imbibed a quality pagan in its rhythmic joyousness, as if the singers adapted other songs from their far-off homeland.

Jake didn't see Charlotte until the slaves had dispersed; he approached her diffidently as she sat easily on her restless mount.

"Miss Charlotte . . . I . . . you see, Ma'am, I thought . . . I mean, I've always wanted to be a preacher. I would have been if. . . ." He trailed off

133

under the calm scrutiny of her gray eyes, then felt unutterable relief as she smiled and said:

"It's quite all right, Matlock. I was saying to my father only the other day that we ought to try and give the slaves some form of religious instruction . . . a Christian outlook. He was going to try and find a preacher, but now there is no need to send away for one. . . . I want you to keep up the services. We will also have to have the children baptized, you know."

"Oh, Ma'am, this is like an answer to a prayer."

Jake was delighted at Charlotte's encouraging attitude, and over the weeks and months that followed, this self-ordained parson conducted more and more services, enthusiastically attended by the field hands and house slaves alike. In his blind enthusiasm he didn't perceive that his fervent exhortations to a Christian way of life and a belief in the Holy Trinity were utterly meaningless to ninety-nine per cent of his congregation; to them it was a welcome diversion from the drab daily round, an opportunity to indulge in loud "Amens," fervent "Save us, oh Lords," and an uninhibited singing of hymns, to which solemn tunes they added a gaiety that would have made the resultant sounds quite unrecognizable to an English congregation.

Walter Wells once more broached the subject of finding a husband for Charlotte, but she reminded him firmly of his promise: "Papa, there is time enough for that when I have learned all I can about running the property. I beg you not to insist."

"As you will, daughter, but I beg you . . . not to wait too long. We need heirs for Wells."

The mass baptism and child-naming ceremony took place one cloudy Sunday on the banks of the mill stream. Those same banks that had so often borne silent witness to the expression of love in one form were now to witness the expression in yet another. Jake Matlock, who had become more parsonical as each month passed, had a group of about forty children, ranging in age from about three months to ten years, together with a parent apiece, mostly mothers.

The banks were crowded with practically the whole of the plantation's slave population scrubbed to a shining blackness, their white or blue gowns or shirts and pantaloons laundered to a rough cleanliness.

Charlotte watched the scene with satisfaction: her idea of converting the Negroes to a Christian outlook was burgeoning nicely into fact. Her gaze was held by the sight of Maria, pregnant once more, holding by the hand a child of about eighteen months. There was something familiar about the set of his head on sturdy shoulders that caught at her heart with a premonitory tug of recognition. She pushed her way through the thronging slaves to muttered greetings of: "Marnin', Miss Charlotte." "How you do, Ma'am?" and injunctions to "Give Miss Charlotte de way, nuh, man?" until she stood in front of Maria and her son.

Maria's eyes flared with fear: Charlotte's face tightened and her eyes went slate hard as she gazed down at the little boy.

Those blue eyes that gazed back at her were unmistakable.

Robert's eyes . . . and the baby's nose, so like his already.

The child was lovely, his skin a velvet coffee cream, his hair dark, soft and curling without an inherited crinkle from his mother.

"So." Charlotte's voice was a quiet whiplash. *"This* is your son, Maria?"

"Yes, Ma'am."

"I see *why* now he has not been brought to me." Maria was silent. The child, frightened by Charlotte's venomous tone, crouched back against his mother's skirts. "I asked you once if he was like his father . . . and suggested an appropriate name . . . but surely *Robert* would be more appropriate."

Charlotte was shaking with anger and humiliation, a humiliation that grew as a quickly stifled snigger or two from the watching slaves reached her ear. She gripped her riding crop with both hands in an effort to control her wild desire to strike again and again at the girl before her and the helpless child who proclaimed her betrayal to the whole plantation. Then she said, still in that low venomous tone: "You will return to the fields tomorrow . . . you . . . you filthy little slut." Then she turned and strode, head held high, face white and set, back through the now silent slaves to the empty Great-house.

Five

"It'll never work, Rob, lad," Philip said. "We'll need the devil's own luck."

"It's our only chance . . . we've got to be prepared to take it . . . or stay with *these* devils for many more years."

"They've got to put into Port Royal sooner or later, and from the grumbles amongst the men it'd best be sooner," Philip said. "No, Rob, this crazy plan of yours—to sneak a longboat and conceal it at Cayman Brac, fire the powder kegs aboard here, then row like hell for Jamaica . . . it's beyond any hope of success. The simplest way is when the *Juanita* docks at Port Royal, we go ashore and just don't come back aboard. It happens often enough that someone skips ship, God knows."

Robert viewed his friend, his blue eyes hard and accusing. "And Brasilano and his cutthroats go scot-free? Is that it?"

"Rob, lad, you told me once long ago that one man can't fight the world. Brasilano will get his just deserts one day."

"I hope that your objections to my plan *are* based on the reasons you give and not on the desire to continue this life. Could it be that you've had a change of heart about pirates and a life of piracy?" Robert asked bitterly.

"Don't be a fool, Rob, I want to live . . . I don't want to end my life swinging from the mizzenmast."

Robert thought silently: I suppose Phil's right . . . it *is* a wild plan, but . . . "Good God," he burst out, "I can't stand this life of plundering and murdering. Look what Brasilano ordered for those poor Spanish devils we captured last month before death released them."

"Those 'poor Spanish devils' would have done the same or worse to us, given the opportunity," Philip said lightly.

"Anyway, Phil, think about my plan, don't discard it out of hand . . . we've got about four days before we put in at Cayman Brac."

But as it turned out, there was no need for Philip to consider the plan of scuttling the *Juanita,* for Brasilano changed his mind and decided to put in at Port Royal after all. The men were getting restive after their long spell away from the gay city and were eager to squander their booty in taverns and brothels . . . both of which were plentiful.

They were but two days out from Port Royal, making good headway, with a fair wind and a following sea, the men's eyes bright with anticipation, when the lookout called the warning of *"Sail.* Sail ahead to port." And over the horizon and closing on them fast came a full-rigged French warship, her identity easily discernible by her ornate superstructure even before the French flag could be recognized as it fluttered from the mainmast. The order was hastily given for the Dutch flag to be struck and to run up the French flag, but the ruse was too blatant, and the French guns spat fire on the obviously Spanish-built *Juanita* as she tried in vain to maneuver out of reach. The first salvo fell short, and the *Juanita,* all sail crowded on in a desperate effort to keep out of reach of the range of attack, tacked on a broad reach, but this only shortened the distance between her and her pursuers.

There was no hope of evading a hand-to-hand fight. Brasilano could be heard rasping orders to man the guns, orders interspersed with obscenities in Portuguese and Dutch. Then his voice was cut off in a high gurgling cry as the third salvo raked the stricken *Juanita*. All was chaos now, a confused scrambling toward the guns, toward the longboats: a frantic scurry to salvage booty from below, to save a life while there was yet time. And over all hung a pall of smoke, the sharp acridity of gunpowder joined by a sweeter cloying smell.

"Philip," Robert yelled above the tumult. "She's on fire ... she'll go up in five minutes. ..."

Grappling hooks now locked the two ships together, and as the French victors prepared to swarm over the side, Robert called a warning to them in his excellent French: "Cast off ... we're on fire below. The powder kegs may soon catch." He spoke rapidly in English to Philip at his side. "Keep fast by me, we may yet get out of this." He thrust his way through the now leaderless pirates, who were hopelessly trying to defend their lives with musket and cutlass, and called again urgently: "Don't come aboard. You'll go up with us."

"Who are you? A Frenchman?"

"One captured by this devil Brasilano ... and anxious to be free. Permission to come aboard?"

He held his hands high to show that he carried no weapon and, closely followed by Philip, vaulted from the rail of the doomed *Juanita* to the rail of the French ship. They were immediately seized and held fast. That was to be expected, and they offered no resistance. Now it was obvious that the *Juanita was* on fire, the French crew hastily ungrappled the hooks that held the two ships rail to rail, pushing off hard with boat hooks to speed the process of a quick departure. They ignored the despair-

139

ing cries of the trapped pirates, knocking back into the *Juanita*'s deck some who tried to follow Robert and Philip's example and board the warship, which was now beginning to draw swiftly away.

Robert and Philip were thrust into a poky cabin. . . .

"At least it's not the hold," Philip said with an attempt at lightness but with an undertone of pain that made Robert look at him sharply.

"You're wounded?"

"A glancing blow from a musket ball, but it's plaguey painful, and I'm bleeding like a stuck pig."

Robert took off his shirt, ripped off a sleeve, and tried to staunch the blood and effect some sort of a dressing. "I suppose they've thrust us in here while they get out of the way of falling bits of *Juanita* when she blows up," he said, matching Philip's light tone, and felt no qualms or sympathy at the imminent annihilation of the men with whom he had lived and plundered over the past two years and more. "I wonder what happened that Brasilano was so taken by surprise and destroyed so easily?"

"Overconfident as we were, so near to Port Royal; probably drunk; he certainly sounded so when he did get around to issuing orders. I gather he caught a musket ball from the animal sounds he made later."

"And O'Connor . . . there wasn't any sign of *him* either."

"Drunk too, I wager."

"Without their leaders the whole bloody crew went to pieces. When one thinks how they have achieved success after success all these years, and then when set upon by one man o' war, they crumpled like a pack of Tarot cards."

Their speculation on the causes of the disintegration of the crew of the *Juanita* was interrupted by a con-

140

fusion of running feet aloft as all sail was crowded on in an effort to put as much sea as possible between the two ships. There followed a dull boom, with two more within seconds, and the speeding vessel pitched and rolled violently in the seething waters. There came no outcry of alarm from above, and gradually the vessel settled down and plowed steadily on.

"Are you going to keep up that fiction that we're French?" Philip asked, his face pale from shock and loss of blood. *"My* French won't pass muster."

"No, I'll admit we're English . . . thank God France and England are at peace at the moment, though for how long only He knows. I'll have to try and persuade them of our innocence and ask them to put us ashore at an English island, preferably Jamaica or at worst Barbados."

"At peace or not, if this man o' war tried to put in at an English-held port, every shore battery would blaze first and ask questions afterwards. They'd believe that an invasion was imminent."

Some two hours later, when all activity occasioned by the swift withdrawal from the luckless *Juanita* had died down, an officer entered the small cabin and viewed them with a faint air of disdain. He was dressed in an elaborate short violet velvet doublet, petticoat breeches of a deeper shade, a falling lace jabot with more lace foaming about his wrists, all topped by an overpowering wig of cascading curls. Robert hid a grin. A more foppish dress and manner on board a warship he found hard to imagine. But since their whole future might depend on their manner and on how he answered the inevitable questions, he preserved a suitably grave and courteous expression.

"You are French?" it was stated rather than asked.

"No, M'sieu," Robert replied in his excellent French.

"But you said . . . ."

"No, M'sieu, I did not say that I *was* French. . . . I just did not say I was not. We were desperate to get away from Roche Brasilano—he had abducted us in Port Royal while we were going about our lawful business—and it was a case of pretend to join his crew or end our lives then and there."

"Port Royal? You are English?"

"Yes."

"And your friend?"

"Does not speak your language as well as I do, but well enough. He was visiting Jamaica on private business and was abducted with me. He is the son of an English nobleman," Robert added, elevating Philip's social status a little, knowing how the French loved a title.

"So? How long were you with Brasilano?"

"A matter of . . . months," Robert lied. "This was our first opportunity to leave them."

He devoutly hoped that the French officer would not refer to the shameful raid on Martinique last spring.

"And . . . the 'lawful duties' you were about?"

"I am . . . was . . . about my future father-in-law's business . . . . Buying slaves for his property."

"What we can do with you, I do not know. We are now rapidly leaving your island of Jamaica far astern as we are on our way back to France, and although our two countries enjoy a somewhat uneasy peace at the moment, hostilities could break out again at any time . . . so to put in at an English port might be taken as a sign of renewed hostility, while to take you back to France— well, gentlemen, let us say that Englishmen do not enjoy the height of popularity just now." He spread his hands in a typically Gallic manner. "You see my difficulty. M'sieu . . . M'sieu?"

"Vane . . . Robert Vane. And this is Philip Lonsdale."

"Pierre Escoffery, second in command to my captain, le comte St. Juste de Marigny . . . who is unfortunately unable at the moment to receive you in his cabin. He is, how shall I put it? . . . taking a well deserved rest and relaxation after the chase and turmoil of battle."

Philip's lips tightened to prevent them twitching with laughter, and Robert was hard put to control his expression: turmoil of battle; a half hour's chase, a quick maneuvering, three salvos fired, and that was that . . . more likely taking anything but relaxation with some doxie. . . .

"Of course, M'sieu Escoffery. We appreciate your difficulties. So . . . what is to become of us?"

"I will have a meal sent to you . . . and, if I may join you? . . . we could discuss the matter further? In the meantime I will have the ship's surgeon attend M'sieu—er—Lonsdale."

He gave them a sweeping bow and left the cabin; a bolt slid into its socket.

Philip twitched an eyebrow. "For honored guests we're treated remarkably like prisoners," he said dryly.

"Can't blame them, I'd do the same in a reverse position. I find his attitude strange, though. He could just as well have tossed us into the brig."

"Our innocent young faces plus your excellent French were our salvation," Philip said lightly.

"More likely following orders not to disturb the balance of that 'uneasy peace' he spoke of."

A few minutes later the bolt slid back and an elderly man entered, dressed in a sober black cassock with white bands of linen at neck and wrists. He was followed by a young boy bearing a tray of fierce-looking surgical instruments.

143

"Gentlemen, Gustave de la Gautier . . . at your service."

Robert and Philip bowed in reply to the formal salutation, feeling slightly foolish after all the long months of life with Brasilano's men and their anything but elegant ways.

Philip's wound was examined and probed by surprisingly gentle and competent fingers, despite the strong aura of old French brandy that enveloped the surgeon.

"You were lucky, M'sieu: the ball has not lodged, merely torn the flesh, missing by a fraction vital tendons and blood vessels. A bare millimeter and it would have been a very different story."

He bowed, they returned the bow and were once more alone.

"How'll we get out of this, Phil? Sometimes I feel I'll *never* get back to Jamaica. . . ." He gave a bitter laugh. "Did you hear my braggadocio remark to the surgeon? '*My* property in Jamaica.' What asinine presumption. Colonel Wells has probably married off Charlotte to a fellow planter and made a will in *his* favor. . . . And I, even if I *do* get back, will be no better than the bondsman I was so many years ago."

"Not so bad as that," Philip said cheerfully. "You have a small fortune in jewels in that pouch about your waist, enough to buy your own holding and start your own plantation. Think of it, man, a new Vane Court transplanted from gentle Cambridgeshire to your wild land of wood and water."

"What will you do?" Robert asked after a pause.

"Time enough for that decision when we find ourselves in a position to make decisions," Philip said with a warning glance as the cabin door opened and Pierre Escoffery entered, followed by two young sailors bearing laden trenchers. They set platters and goblets of pewter on the small round table, together with covered dishes emitting a savory odor and a leathern bottle of good French red wine.

"The quarters are cramped, gentlemen, but the food is tolerable, the wine excellent. . . ."

"And the company stimulating," Philip finished with a flourish of his sound arm.

"A pleasure, M'sieu," Escoffery countered. "And your French is not so execrable as you would have me believe."

They ate and drank while making desultory small talk, which Robert felt was incongruous in their present position but which Philip conducted with ease and a serious demeanor which went a long way in convincing Escoffery that they were all that they professed to be, and although his French was not as fluent as Robert's, it was enough to indulge in the lighthearted trivia of such a conversation.

"So, gentlemen," Escoffery said at last as he swirled a fine brandy in a fragile Venetian glass. "I have been giving some thought to your immediate future. We are bound for France by way of our island of St. Christopher, having completed our mission of reinforcing our garrison in St. Domingue, and we could land you on St. Christopher without too much embarrassment either to ourselves or the English. . . ."

"But surely," Philip cut in, "I have always understood that this island that you speak of is unique inasmuch that it is occupied jointly by both French and English, that they live side by side with an amity the like of which is not enjoyed by the larger land masses of France and England with the English Channel between."

"That was indeed so, M'sieu, an amity that extended

even when our two countries were at war, for the respective governors chose to ignore such matters and concentrated on developing and cultivating the land, even joining forces at times against the predatory Caribs who still make devastating raids from neighboring islands. I do not say that this admirable amity was not at times marred by petty quarrels and even bloodshed, but on the whole the island was an example to the world of peaceful coexistence."

"I note that you have used the past tense throughout, M'sieu," Robert said quietly.

"Alas, yes. During the late hostilities betwen our two countries, fighting broke out and the English capitulated. Over eight thousand English and their slaves fled. After the end of the war, at the Treaty of Breda in sixteen sixty-seven St. Christophers . . . the formerly held English parts . . . were to be handed back to the English. . . ." Escoffery put the tips of his well manicured fingers together and regarded them with an embarrassed frown. The pause lengthened. . . .

"Well?" Philip asked at length.

The fingers spread deprecatingly. "I regret to say, gentlemen, that the terms of the Treaty have not yet been honored."

"You mean . . . but s'life, that's over two *years* ago," Philip exploded.

Escoffery nodded. "I regret it exceedingly, but I am just a soldier. . . . I know negotiations have been going on, and I am confident that shortly the lands will be restored to their . . . rightful . . . occupants. I think you will just have to wait, patiently or otherwise, as are your natures, for a ship to put in and take you on your way."

"And is that a likelihood?"

Escoffery shrugged elegantly and spread his hands.

"At *some* date it is a *certainty*. Merchant ships put into the island with supplies for settlers, and many of them are en route to Jamaica. . . . Of course," he added, "a few months might pass between each such arrival . . . but surely the chances of a definite return to Jamaica under the proposal I have presented to you are more certain than if you return to France with me."

There was no valid argument to this, and they agreed to the proposal, but not without misgivings as to the outcome.

At the beginning of the eighth week the island that was their objective rose out of a pale azure sea, the mountains rising in wooded majesty to a clear blue sky. On the far horizon, the very rim of the world, the unmistakable outline of a Dutch East-India merchantman was etched against the pale blue, then she was gone over the edge. The tips of her mast were visible for a few seconds, then they were alone in the world with the island before them.

They were to leave the *Marie Louise* and go ashore in a longboat, so they bade good-bye to Pierre Escoffery and the surgeon.

"Good-bye, gentlemen." Escoffery waved a languid hand, elegant amid its frothing laces, as they lowered themselves to the waiting longboat. "Keep safe the letter of introduction and explanation I have given you for the governor."

They were put ashore under the gaze of a handful of bystanders whose expressions boded them no good, but one of their number was induced by Robert's fluent French to conduct them to the governor's dwelling. There they learned that the governor was sick with a fever and they were received by the acting governor, Louis Bertrecht, who greeted them with a cautious air, which lessened as he read Escoffery's letter and became almost cordial as he listened to Robert's explanation.

"Alas, M'sieu Vane, chance has not played fair with you, a Dutch ship left only this morning—soon after you were sighted—left for Jamaica with merchandise from the Far East."

A huge disappointment swept them both into the abyss of despair: a few hours too late. If only they had not been becalmed they would now be on their way ... if only. . . . But what use is "if only" in the face of fact . . . .

"How long before another, Your Excellency?" Robert asked.

Bertrecht shrugged.

"Who can tell? Two . . . three months . . . maybe six or eight . . . or even a year. . . ."

"A year?"

"We are a very small island, M'sieu Vane: we plant, we reap, we try to build. Until the tragedy of the recent war—as you know, the consequence is still causing us grave concern—we French and English lived side by side for over thirty years, and we had learned to live off our own resources rather than having to rely entirely on those from our mother countries . . . oh, we had our little skirmishes, a few broken heads, an unexplained murder or disappearance, but harmonic on the whole." He sighed. "I wonder if those days will ever return. Or are we to watch each other with suspicion while we dance like puppets at the whims of our national governments?" He looked kindly at Robert's dismayed face. "You may be lucky, M'sieu, do not despair. Come, let me offer you refreshment and a rest while I send a runner to the north with news of your arrival."

They followed him blindly across a flagged courtyard to a cool guest room, blinking their eyes against the harsh sunlight that blazed down on them and on

148

the luxuriant vegetation which encroached beyond the palisades that surrounded the governor's residence—vegetation rare and exotic, which seemed to keep them prisoners with its clinging tendrils.

Six

And so the years at Wells slipped away since Robert had left ... three, four going on for five....

That April of 1672 in Jamaica was one of unutterable loveliness: pink and yellow poui blossoms clustered thickly on branches that had been stark the day before, soft shoots of bamboo plants waved sinuously in the dew-cooled morning air, and Ann Wells, her light brown hair unconfined, her precociously developed body taut under a thin muslin dress, went cantering down the driveway, out beyond the walled garden surrounding the Great-house, through the broad walk of the south cane field and across by devious overgrown tracks to a sheltered beach: a deserted and wild place with seagrapes growing down to the water's edge, palms angled by the winds to improbable shapes, where the silken sea lapped softly against honeycomb rocks and sea birds nested unafraid.

She tied her horse to a low branch, then was suddenly fearful of her temerity in coming, for there, waiting, was the tall Negro she had covertly been taunting and encouraging for weeks.

He was called Malachi and had been at Wells since its inception, the son of a Spanish-owned slave. He was Walter Wells' body slave, a soft-voiced young man of about twenty, with liquid black eyes, broad-shouldered and deep-chested, the muscles rippling with an exciting

150

undulance under his gleaming skin. Ann had been aware of his eyes following her for months, and recently those smoldering looks had caused a new sensation in her body, frightening in its intensity yet anticipated each time with ever-growing delight. She began to respond to his unspoken admiration with provocative glances and half smiles, flaunting her body in low-cut gowns that showed the swell and curves of her young breasts, the handspan waist above maturing hips. She was a true child of the tropics, uninhibited by nature—a quality which had been fostered by lack of parental control—a nature warm with the promise of passion. She had seen how her father acted with his concubines and saw nothing wrong in encouraging Malachi. But now she stood uncertainly as he came toward her, apprehensive as to the immediate future . . . the transition from unspoken admiration and provocation to an unimaginable conclusion.

Malachi was not without experience: he had fathered innumerable children with the placid complaisance of numerous slave girls about the Great-house . . . his duties were light, the empty rooms were many, the girls more than willing. That was very different from violating his master's daughter; the penalty, if he were discovered, would be at least a few hundred lashings and exposure to the stocks, followed by banishment to the field, at most a summary execution. Yet the sight of her white perfection had fired his desire to fever pitch, so that he was blinded to possible consequences. Her gray eyes widened and she could scarcely breathe as he took her by the shoulders and pulled her toward him. His hands moved over her body until she was shivering in ecstasy, all apprehensions forgotten, then they fell to the soft white sand in a transport of desire . . . .

There was no love, affection, or respect in their union, only an animal lust that demanded satisfaction:

he took her roughly, disregarding her virginity. She cried out once sharply, then the pain was forgotten in the delight of fulfillment.

The sun was high in the eastern sky when she left him.

He held her horse's bridle. "You come back come mornin'?" he demanded, the old status of slave and young mistress forgotten.

She nodded: "Yes . . . I'll come back . . . tomorrow."

He watched her go, a deep welling satisfaction flooding his being: at last he'd had her, the arrogant little white bitch. He felt no tenderness, only a triumphant realization that at last he had avenged in some small way the degradation he suffered as a slave.

And so these secret meetings went on, with Malachi becoming more demanding, more masterful, confident that his body would enthrall Ann for as long as he wanted her: she became more reckless in the time she spent with him, going so far as to meet him one night when the moon flung bands of light across the smooth sea, turning its night grayness to shot silk. They bathed in the still sun-warmed waters naked together, and this sight of her completely unclothed aroused such a spasm of desire in him that he flung her down on the very edge of the sea so that the lazy wavelets lapped them, and there subjected her young body to an assault that left her bruised and exhausted.

"Don't . . . please . . . no . . . no more," she begged as he bore down on her again, but he only laughed, a strange savage sound in that quiet place, his teeth white in the brilliant moonlight, and took her again and again, each time with an added ferocity, until at last, when he had left her alone on the beach, dropping her in a huddled heap, leaving her with a contemptuous glance that reduced her to a mere plaything, she felt a deep disgust well from within her, a return to sanity, the beginning of a new adult wisdom.

She kept to her room all the next day, pale and heavy-eyed, avoiding Maria's knowing eyes . . . for Maria was her body slave now . . . and she stopped riding early to the beach . . .

. . . stopped for three whole days, until the sight of her lover moving soft-footed about the house once more aroused her need for him.

So it went on, a see-saw of desire and disgust, until one day in late May she realized with sick despair that she was pregnant.

A wild spasm of fear shot through her.

What should she do?

Maria . . . Maria was surely her only hope.

But all Maria's knowledge failed to produce an abortion for Ann's child. In vain she swallowed strange concoctions, thick and thin, bitter and bland, while the days passed into weeks and the weeks became months. She was wracked with nausea and vomiting, exacerbated by the many drugs she was taking and by her fear of discovery of her guilt.

"I cyan' do no more, Miss Ann," Maria said at last. "You mus' done tell Miss Charlotte."

Ann gazed at her in despair.

"I *can't* tell Charlotte . . . I can't. . . ."

Maria shrugged. "You has to, Miss Ann," she said simply. "No tell she now, you belly speak fe you soon soon."

Maria was right: at last her thickening waistline and the tragic eyes in her wan face could not go unnoticed. Charlotte entered her sister's room one morning early in August and viewed Ann's tear-stained cheeks with concern.

"What ails you, Ann love? You've been keeping to your room and looking so peaky. What is it?"

153

Ann turned her face into her pillow and wept anew.

"Come, come, it can't be as bad as that."

Charlotte put her arms around Ann's quivering shoulders, but she sprang from the embrace and went to the long shuttered door that led to the veranda, flinging it wide open. Charlotte's eyes narrowed as she saw her young sister's body outlined through her thin lawn nightshift against the bright morning light; they narrowed to hard steel as the sympathy left her face.

"Ann . . . you're with child. . . ." Her voice held shocked horror, but Ann didn't perceive any emotion beyond the recognition of her plight. She turned from the doorway and moved toward Charlotte, relief lighting her misery.

"Tell me what I'm to do, Charlotte, I'm at my wit's ends."

"You little *slut*." Charlotte's voice cut like a whiplash, and Ann felt a flood of desolation engulf her. She had yearned for sympathy, affection, understanding, and instead she was being treated with all the scorn and contempt of which Charlotte was capable. "You *fool* to behave so . . . no better than one of the slaves. Who is the father?"

Ann began to tremble. She folded her lips and remained silent as Charlotte gripped her arm.

"Who is it? One of the bondsmen?" Ann bit her quivering lips and shook her head silently. "It *must* be . . . there have been no visitors for . . . how far gone are you?"

Ann tried to speak, but the trembling increased until she was shuddering from head to foot and sobs welled deep from within.

Charlotte regarded her distress and shook her now by both shoulders.

"If it's not a bond servant, then. . . ." Her eyes went wide with horror. *"Not a slave? Oh, no. . . ."* She

154

had her confirmation in the quick flare of Ann's nostrils, the stiffening shoulders under her gripping hands. Then suddenly the anger and contempt fled from her face, to be replaced by deep compassion. "Why didn't you come to me at once, why didn't you tell papa, the man would have been whipped to death . . . to rape a child like you . . . who was it, Ann? . . . it . . . it *was* rape . . . wasn't it?"

Ann was momentarily saved in having to answer that question by sagging heavily against her sister and then sliding to the floor as a merciful unconsciousness claimed her. Charlotte lifted the inert body onto the bed and rang a small handbell. A few seconds later Maria appeared, her eyes wide.

"When you told me that Miss Ann was sick . . . you knew the cause?"

"Yes, Miss Charlotte."

"Why did you not tell me?"

"I beg Miss Ann fe tell you, but she scared, Ma'am."

"And I suppose you've talked of this? The whole plantation knows?"

"Lord, Miss Charlotte, not word pass me mout' 'bout it. . . ."

"Why not? You generally delight in retailing any gossip that would bring dishonor or ridicule to the family." Charlotte spoke cuttingly.

Maria was silent, her hands working nervously in her apron. Since her banishment to the fields and subsequent reinstatement after a year in the hot sun—a year that had taken much of her beauty, a year that had roughened her hands and hardened her heart—a reinstatement at Ann's express wish and against Charlotte's will, she lived in deadly fear of Charlotte's whiplash tongue and ready temper, knowing that if she made one more mistake and was sent back to manual labor, it would be for good.

"I swear I say nothin', Miss Charlotte." She began to snivel, and Charlotte cut in impatiently:

"All right, girl, there's no time for that. We must think of what is to be done. I presume you've tried all the remedies you know to abort the child?"

Maria nodded. "Every one t'ing. It pay no heed."

"You know the man responsible?"

Maria's eyes flared wide in alarm. "Me no know nothin', Ma'am," she said hastily.

"I think you do. . . . That's why you kept silent, not to protect Miss Ann, but to protect this man." She glanced keenly at Maria, as expression chased expression across her dark face. "I'm right, aren't I? Don't you realize that by raping a white girl . . . the master's *own daughter* at that . . . a slave could . . . ." Charlotte stopped at Maria's involuntary movement of negation at the word "rape."

A fearful suspicion crossed her mind . . . *had* it been rape? . . . or . . . had Ann given herself willingly?

Charlotte thrust the insinuating thought to the back of her mind: a delicate, well-brought-up girl like Ann . . . was she well brought up, though? She had been allowed to go her own way without supervision ever since Robert went away and their mother died. . . . *No,* she refused to countenance the idea, it *must* have been rape, the man must be found and punished. . . . But careful, if she spoke too much of punishment, the man would be warned, the whole slave population would do anything to protect him and. . . . Another thought impinged sharply on her fevered imaginings: there might be an attempt to silence Ann; a dose of poison, it had been done before—a case only a few months ago in St. Jago de la Vega, when the wife of Peter Saunders died under strange circumstances and within a month his favorite concubine was openly installed as housekeeper. She spoke more gently: "I'm sorry to speak harshly, Maria,

156

you have done well to keep close about this and to care as best you could for Miss Ann. Continue to do so . . . the only thing that matters is that her condition is not revealed, I will do anything to ensure that . . . but *how* are we to keep this from the master?" She was speaking her thoughts aloud, not expecting a constructive answer from Maria, who surprisingly gave one.

"The master hardly see Miss Ann, an' her dress, dem, cover how she look wit' pickney. If she keep her room the las' two t'ree mont', can tell master she have little fever . . . ."

"A *little* fever lasting so long? He'd send to St. Jago for the governor's physician. . . . Then all would be known."

"But Miss Charlotte, only other t'ing . . . she go 'way till the pickney done born."

Charlotte shuddered at the connotation of the reiterated word "pickney," then said helplessly: "There is nowhere or no one whom I could trust not to spread the tale throughout the whole island, every planter's family would hold us in scorn. Colonel Wells' precious daughters, dragged down to the level of . . . ."

"Not so, Miss Charlotte, it done happen all the time," Maria said simply.

Charlotte bit her lip at the cruelly factual tone, her shame growing: she'd talked too freely already to this girl who had humiliated *her* in the past. She turned back to the bed where Ann showed signs of returning consciousness.

"All right, my love," she murmured. "Don't worry any more, I'll see what can be done."

She bathed Ann's wet face and smoothed back her soft brown hair, darkened with sweat, tangled by a night spent in anguished tossing. Holy Mother of God, she thought, I've neglected her in my preoccupation with the property and allowed her to come to this pass; I'll have to do what papa wants though does not speak of: I'll have to marry and get a man to take over and leave me to my duties of caring for Ann and Richard.

Later she sought out her father in his study and broached the subject with calm dispassion.

"Papa, I have been considering your suggestion . . . nay, your desire . . . that I marry. 'Tis foolish to expect that Robert will return now. Four years . . . nearly five have gone by . . . he must be lost to us forever. And though I love to ride with you and attend to the property, I have a duty here in the house and . . ." she paused, loath to mention Ann's name in the discussion . . . . "Richard is ailing and grows weaker with each passing day . . . I feel it my duty to . . . beget an heir for Wells . . . lest all your work goes for naught."

Walter Wells looked keenly at his elder daughter.

"Your decision to wed will have to wait, lass, for as I was going to tell you tonight, I have a journey to make later this year . . . so any marriage plans must wait on my return."

Charlotte's heart leaped at the unexpected announcement. A *journey*? Was it possible that . . .

"Where to, Papa? And when?"

"To England, 'tis safe enough for me now, I'll be bound, and there are urgent problems I have to discuss with our factor there. Maybe I'll find you a handsome, willing husband in England, eh?"

Walter chuckled, but Charlotte wasn't listening, her heart filled with the impossible hope that the answer to Ann's problem had been found.

"When, papa? And for how long?"

"You're mighty anxious to see me go. 'Tis August now, I'll leave on the first available boat in November . . . a plaguey time to travel, but I have militia duties to perform before that . . . chances are I'll not be back before February or March . . . maybe later. Means you'll have to see to the start of getting the crop in. . . ."

"That's all right, papa. With Dick Gough's help I'll manage."

Her voice was light and bubbling, her relief at her father's words overwhelming. If he was away on militia duties between now and November, he would see little of Ann, then February or March: Ann's child would surely be born in January, and the unwanted shameful bastard safely in the anonymity of the slave compound when her father returned.

He raised his eyebrows. "I can hardly say I'm flattered at your enthusiasm for my proposed journey . . . in the bitter cold of an English winter, too."

"Oh no, papa, not enthusiasm for your departure, enthusiasm for your *return.* Think of the commissions I shall give you: silks and satins, pomanders and trinkets . . . all the latest fashion trends . . . oh, how exciting, Papa, you may even see the *King.*"

"Humph, I doubt that. Maybe though . . . what do you say that I take Ann with me? She could . . . ."

"Oh *no,* papa. I mean . . . she has a little fever now, a cough . . . nothing to speak of, but I do not feel that she should be subjected to the rigors of a cold climate. . . ." She floundered, aware of the feebleness of her argument: that Ann had a slight fever in August surely didn't preclude a journey in the following November. But her fears had flared again at this threat which would reveal Ann's condition, and she prattled on in a way quite foreign to her usual calm manner.

Her father laughed. "All right, lass, I can see that you feel that if anyone has a trip to England, then it should be you. I can also see that your decision and my news have caused confusion in that normally well-reasoned head of yours."

"My decision?"

"To find a husband. Isn't that what you came to see me about?" The colonel looked his surprise, and Charlotte said hastily:

"Oh, yes, of course. But your news drove all other thoughts from my mind."

Ann lay inert on the big four-poster bed trying to think: by stating that she had in fact been raped, she would avoid all reproach, all reprobation. But surely they would make her say who the man was?

She didn't know . . . she couldn't possibly know the names of all the slaves.

When and where had it taken place? Down in the fields. . . . But then, she wasn't allowed there, and anyway there were always overseers and bookkeepers around, and the slaves worked in gangs. . . .

By the millstream early, when she was riding alone?

That would point to a house slave who knew her habits . . . if she gave any indication that it was a house slave, then the field would be quickly narrowed. . . .

She tossed uneasily, waves of self-disgust overwhelming her as she realized the direction in which her thoughts were moving. . . .

Why shouldn't she save herself completely and denounce Malachi? He deserved it . . . he had treated her shamefully at times . . . like a common whore . . . .

If he denied it, as he would, his word was nothing against hers, a slave had no rights of defense. . . .

There was a light footfall along the veranda, and Charlotte entered, followed by Maria bearing a laden tray.

"Oh child, you've been crying again. Come, let me wash your face and get you into a fresh shift. Place the tray here, Maria, then leave us."

Charlotte bustled about, rearranging the crumpled bed, brushing Ann's hair with gentle strokes, and finally settling her in a low rocker, a bowl of hot chicken broth and a platter of new-baked bread before her.

And while Ann ate, slowly and reluctantly at first, then avidly as her healthy young appetite was awakened, Charlotte told her of their father's proposed journey.

"The child will be born . . . when?"

"I . . . I don't know."

"Of course you must know. You cannot forget the day or the month of such a happening."

Again suspicion flared: one *could* be unsure . . . if it hadn't been rape but willing cooperation, not once but many times . . . .

No, not to think along those lines . . . .

"I . . . was so . . . shocked . . . I forgot everything for days," Ann stammered. "It was . . . in April . . . or early May, yes, early May."

Charlotte's eyes narrowed. Here was guilt if ever she saw it, but she must preserve the fiction now she'd started it . . . and of course, there was *one* way to make sure.

"Who was the man, Ann?" she asked softly.

Ann dropped her spoon back into the bowl. She stared in hypnotized terror at her sister: here was the moment, irrevocable, the moment on which her future and the life of a man relied.

"It was . . . it was Malachi," she whispered, and a feeling of horror swept through her, mingled with a vast relief. There, she had done it: saved herself and condemned her lover for an act uncommitted.

Charlotte felt a renewed confidence that Ann was speaking the truth . . . no child—for she was still a child at sixteen—could condemn a man—even a slave— without just cause. She spoke wonderingly. *"Malachi?* Papa's body slave? So quiet, so soft spoken, so. . . ."
She bit back the unbidden words: so well set up and good looking . . . .

161

Ann was trembling at the enormity of her betrayal. "What ... will ... they do to him?"

Charlotte frowned.

"It is unthinkable that he should go unpunished, but to punish him openly at this stage might call attention to the cause ... and Papa's most unwelcome attention. No, I think we will wait to deal with Master Malachi until Papa has gone to England ... and *I* am in sole control of Wells."

There was a look of fanatical intent in Charlotte's gray eyes that struck consternation through Ann. Charlotte, always so gentle when they were younger, before Robert went away and Mama died, now so cold, so pitiless ... so *cruel*.

"Don't worry, my love, we'll see this through ... and Master Malachi will be repaid for the anguish he has caused you. Now try and sleep, I'll be back later, and Maria is at hand at all times," said Charlotte, her face smooth and innocent again.

Seven

Charlotte was in a fever of impatience as the time for her father's proposed journey drew closer. She kept a worried eye on Ann's increasing waistline and had Maria make up identical dresses for them both, with a pleated fall beginning from high under the breast, and prayed that her father's eyes would be deceived. Her heart jolted one morning when he said gaily: "S'life m'dear, if I'd found that husband for you, I'd swear that an heir was well on the way."

Charlotte laughed, hoping it sounded more natural to her father's ears than it did to her own. "Fie, papa, what talk to an unmarried maid. 'Tis but a fashion."

Walter Wells' mind was soon diverted from the whims of fashion by the many problems attendant on his proposed journey, an enforced absence from the property for military duties on the north coast, where the Spanish had made a number of raids in retaliation to the buccaneer Henry Morgan's depredations in the Gulf of Maracaibo, and by his latest and most exhausting concubine.

By November, when he was ready to sail aboard a ship well laden with sugar from his own mills and Ann was in her seventh month of pregnancy, Charlotte was in a ferment lest, after all, the deception be discovered. To avoid her father's saying good-bye to Ann and embracing her on her feet, she banished her sister to bed with the excuse of a high fever and chills.

" 'Tis nothing, papa, nothing," she assured her father. "She will be well in a day or so."

So Wells went on silent feet to his younger daughter's bedside, where she lay shapeless under a mound of quilts. "Good-bye, my child." He kissed her gently on the brow. "I've seen little enough of you these last months, but we'll make up for that on my return. Take heed to your sister. I'll see what gewgaws I can find for you in London."

"Yes, thank you, papa," Ann whispered.

"She does not appear overheated," the colonel remarked as they left the room.

"The fever comes and goes, papa, and I have just this half hour given her a cooling draft. Do not worry, I'll take good care of her."

Oh, God, Charlotte sent up a silent prayer: let her not die in childbirth so that I have to account to my father for her and my own sins. She followed her father to his study, hoping he would not pursue the subject of Ann's health. His mind was elsewhere as he produced a roll of parchment and said:

"I have had this document drawn up by a notary in St. Jago. It gives you power of attorney whilst I am away . . . and in the event of my nonreturn—do not look like that, child, anything could happen in these uncertain days on the sea or still, perhaps, in England. Believe me, I'll be back hale and hearty if it's possible . . . *but* in the event of my not returning, I have bequeathed the whole estate to you, and to the heirs which you will produce in God's good time."

"But Papa . . . the *whole* to me? What about Ann . . . and Richard? And will the law allow me to inherit property when the rightful male heir is alive?"

"As to the law . . . fie . . . we are too far from

Westminster to worry about such things, and our own laws are still fluid. As for Ann, I leave it to your prudence and good sense to provide handsomely for her, if circumstance decree, though I look to make a good marriage for her, and beyond her marriage portion she'll need none of my wealth. If I do not return, then *you* must see about a husband for her. I have hopes of Rodrigues Isaacs, he is sole heir to the Isaacs Estate on the Liguanea Plains, and as you know, his father is one of the wealthy Portuguese Jews who espoused the English occupation. By all accounts he is a presentable and cultured young man, having studied at the University of Padua and at the Sorbonne in Paris. Despite this prevalent feeling against those of the Jewish faith, I pay no heed to that . . . and nor should you and your sister. In a small community like this, there is no room for the ancient enmities, and there will doubtless be, over the years, a commingling of faiths and . . . aye, even a commingling of races."

Walter Wells was silent for a moment, then said heavily: "As for Richard . . . all my hopes are dashed that he will recover. He has been spitting blood these last few days. . . ."

"Oh, papa . . . I didn't know. I thought it was but a recurrence of his fever. . . ."

"It is a great burden you have to bear, Charlotte, but I shall be back, God will, and then it will be eased and we will prepare for your marriage rites."

Charlotte eased the tension by laughing suddenly. "How strange, papa, to talk of marriage rites when I have yet to find me a husband."

He gazed with pride at her slim, taut figure, the silver blonde hair drawn back into a cluster of ringlets on her neck, her large gray eyes, capable of sparkling with affectionate gaiety, equally capable of hardening to an unbelievable slatiness.

"I doubt, daughter, we'll have no dearth of suitors when once the word goes abroad."

Yet even as he spoke a doubt intruded into his mind: this daughter of his, so adept at management, so quick to learn skills which he had believed were for men alone to master, able to instill respect and command obedience from slave and overseer—were these attributes perhaps disadvantageous when it came to finding a husband? A man didn't want a wife who was more capable than himself. Again, with all her feminine pretty ways, there was a quality about her . . . an *asexual* quality that boded ill for the conception of heirs. . . . He shrugged off these gloomy thoughts until his return from England. There was nothing wrong with Charlotte, he'd warrant, that a good bedding with a lusty young bridegroom wouldn't cure.

After Walter Wells had left, the house seemed strangely large and empty. Though he might be away from the property for days at a time, his presence had always seemed to be in command. Now there was a vacuum which Charlotte vainly tried to fill.

Ann spent most of her time on the veranda outside her bedroom, unwilling fingers wielding a slow needle, her thickening body repulsive to her, the kicks of her unborn child a constant reminder of the unknown terror that lay ahead.

And Richard, poor frail white-faced Richard, read and reread Robert's store of books, gaining knowledge he would never put to use, discovering the delights of study, and refusing to believe that his body's frailty was a token that his life, hardly begun, was almost at an end. Despite the cough and the nights of sweat-drenched misery he was forced to endure, he spent a happy, tranquil life, surrounded by books and by parchments on which he wrote fragmented thoughts and a few half-finished poems in a spidery hand with ink that faded as rapidly as the writer. He watched the flight and nesting of a myriad birds, their brilliant plumage and joyous song vibrant with life; he watched the hills in their ever-changing beauty; he felt a momentary sadness that his sisters spent so little time with him these days, but forgot this in long quiet games of chess played with Jake Matlock.

Charlotte's day began soon after dawn, and she spent the long hours astride her gentle black mare out in the fields, but one morning about a month after her father had left, she returned unexpectedly and went straight to her father's suite of rooms.

"I suspected as much," she said triumphantly, and Malachi swung around from the big mahogany press, its drawers half open, doors wide, contents rumpled. He held a frilled shirt in one hand, which he instinctively thrust behind his back as his eyes flared in fear, then he stammered: "Lard, Miss Charlotte, ma'am, so you mek I fright. I jus' go t'rough the master 'im shirt, dem, 'im say I mus' fe see they need mend."

Charlotte laughed, a bitter sound, her eyes alight with revenge: she had waited for just such an opportunity. The long whip which she carried loosely coiled flashed with sickening accuracy and snaked across the man's face, cutting it open from brow to jaw. He dropped the shirt as the blow dizzied him and the warm blood spurted, then he took a groping step toward her. She backed from the room and blew a shrill blast on the whistle she always carried tied about her waist.

"Hold him," she commanded two of the grooms as house slaves came running. "And fetch Master Gough," she ordered a kitchen boy.

"Now, Master Gough," Charlotte said when Dick stood before her, uneasy and awkward among the fine furniture and rich hangings. "This man, Malachi, I caught him rifling my father's belongings for which he

167

gave a pitifully thin lying pretext. When I . . . repri-
manded him . . . he came toward me . . ." she paused
fractionally . . . "seized me and if I hadn't been able to
summon help, would have, I am sure, assaulted me. In
fact," she lowered her eyes in apparent confusion, "by
his . . . actions . . . I am in no doubt as to his intentions.
Keep him in close confinement for now. He must be
punished . . . adequately." She turned away so as not to
meet Dick Gough's honest, faintly doubting gaze. "Send
for Peter Golding." There was a sudden silence in the
big room, then Charlotte asked sharply, still with her
back toward him, "You heard me?"

"Aye, Mistress, I heard. You're *sure*, Miss Charlotte?"

Was he asking if she was sure of the need for
punishment or the punishment itself? Either way, it
made no difference.

"I'm *sure*," she said firmly and stood rigidly erect
until the sound of Dick Gough's heavily booted footfalls
had ceased. She could feel the blood pounding in her
head, her throat dry at the enormity of the decision she
had taken. The memory of Malachi's strong-muscled
body, a perfect example of young manhood, returned
unbidden, and a wave of desire swept over her. The
unaccountable emotion, one never experienced by her
before that moment, disturbed her to the very roots of
her being as she recognized and recoiled from it.

She realized that she had not moved since Dick
Gough had left; she stood, hands clenched, eyes glazed,
the only movement the throb of a pulse at her temple.
There was a sound at the door, and Peter Golding
shuffled in. As always, the sight of him sickened her.
One side of his face was seamed and scarred, the hollow socket where an eye had once been was uncovered
and repulsive. One shoulder was hunched and the left
arm shorter by inches than the right. The length of his

legs was uneven, giving him a weird gait, half crablike, wholly disgusting. Once he had been a fine upstanding English soldier, until he was captured by the Spaniards and had his legs broken on the wheel, then was tossed to their Negro slaves for sport, left for dead when an English patrol surprised them. Why he had not died no one knew: one eye had been torn out, his face was a shambles of strips of skin and exposed bone, one shoulder was shattered and the arm broken in two places, his legs were mangled. He was kept in semi-confinement at Wells, for he would attack and maim any Negro who offered him the slightest provocation. His one duty was the punishment of any slave who had been found guilty of a major crime. His mind was slow, at times cloudy, but he could be made to understand orders if they were given clearly and simply.

"You wanted to see me, Mistress?" he asked in his strangely hoarse voice.

"Yes," Charlotte's voice was steady now. "You know the house slave, Malachi, my father's body slave?"

"Aye."

"He is to be punished."

An anticipatory gleam lit up his one eye: to punish, to hear others cry for mercy, a mercy he had not been granted, a mercy he would not bestow, was his only pleasure. There was too little punishment meted out at Wells. . . .

"Aye," eagerly. "How so?"

"His right hand cut off. Three hundred lashes . . . and . . . to be castrated. You understand? Gelded."

The gleam brightened. "Aye. In that order, Mistress?"

"What? Oh, in whatever order you feel will inflict the most pain. If he loses consciousness, revive him before you continue. Take your time and make him suffer."

Down in the compound the news swept through like wild fire, and many a head nodded knowingly and many

169

a heart beat faster at the ruthlessness of their young white mistress, and when the animallike screams of pain echoed and reechoed across the cane fields, up to the mountainside provision grounds, and even penetrated to the heights of the Great-house itself, prayers of thankfulness were offered up to their gods left far behind in Africa that they had not crossed Charlotte Wells' path.

The next day as she rode around the property, head high, eyes slate cold, the salutations of "Marnin', Miss Charlotte," "How you do, Ma'am" were uttered with an added sycophancy, lest she had discovered some slight misdemeanor they had thought had gone unnoticed. One particular pair of eyes followed the slim, erect figure and a bitter hate rose. "Me goin' fe kill she fe what she done. Malachi no done *she* wrong . . . cold white bitch. I kill she . . . how long me wait no matter."

As Robert Vane after his long exile in St. Christopher drew nearer the shores of Jamaica one clear day in January 1673, a great feeling of peace and homecoming enveloped him as he visualized the rearing mountains with their thickly wooded slopes. He spent hours at the rail waiting for his first glimpse of the island's outline against the blue sky, and as the first gray smudge appeared on the horizon, so in Wells Great-house Ann gave birth after a long and agonizing labor to a girl child. Charlotte took the child immediately and gazed down at the unmistakable Negroid features, wrinkled and dusky red.

Ann opened tired eyes. "May I see . . . is it a boy?"

" 'Tis best that you neither see nor know," Charlotte said firmly. "Here." She thrust the child toward Maria. "Take it, and deliver it to a wet nurse. I neither want to see nor hear of it again."

Maria took the child, roughly covered and still unwashed from its mother's womb, and her heart filled

170

with despair at this young woman who had developed from a sweet gentle creature to this woman of complete implacability.

Charlotte turned back to the blood-stained disorder of the bed and watched two great tears slide down her sister's cheeks. " 'Tis better so, indeed it is, Ann. You only feel that you want to see the child because you have suffered in the bringing forth . . . but now it is over, you must forget the child as if it had never been. Now you must be bathed and sleep, and later, when you are stronger, we will discuss a plan I have in mind."

So Ann slept, the initial stirring of maternal feelings crushed by the strong voice of her sister. Of course, if Charlotte said so, it was better so. As she drifted off into sleep, she wondered briefly what had happened to Malachi. She had once asked Maria with as much casualness as she could muster: "I haven't seen . . . what is his name? The Master's body slave? Yes, of course, Malachi. I haven't seen him about the house for days . . . nay, weeks."

"No, Miss Ann," Maria's eyes flashed strangely. "Malachi . . . won't be back in the house."

Ann had not dared to pursue the subject either with Maria or with Charlotte.

Although it had been a difficult confinement, Ann recovered with all the resilience of youth despite the attempts to impose strong rituals by Leah, who had delivered the child. Charlotte had ordered that Ann's room should be swept thoroughly each day and the shutters thrown wide to admit fresh air and sunlight, and each day she held an inspection to see that her orders had been carried out. Each day brought a renewed burst of anger and a tirade against Leah and the house slaves, for there was a persistent belief among them that all windows, doors, and crevices should be tightly sealed for nine nights after a birth and that all

171

dust and dirt must be swept under the bed for the same period.

"Lord, Miss Charlotte," Leah protested. "The way you say I mus' go on so, Miss Ann goin' tek sick an' dead . . . an' not lie easy in she grave . . . sure sure, Ma'am."

Ann recovered rapidly, her ordeal past, her future bright; but Charlotte was tired to the point of exhaustion. She had lost weight over the weeks since her father had left, there were dark shadows round her eyes, and her mouth had acquired a new pinched line that altered her whole expression. She had been sleeping badly, in short snatches that were dream-filled: dreams peopled by Malachi, his body whole and beautiful, then fearful sequences of what his body had become. There were dreams when the whole sugar crop was ruined, when she tried with her own hands to get the canes in in time; there were vague meandering dreams, unformed, drifting from misty sequence to startling clarity, that left her when she woke with a strange haunting certainty of indelible loss.

She wished passionately for her father's return, now that the child was safely born. At the same time the sight of Ann, slim and carefree again, drove her to a state of bitter frustration.

"I have arranged for you to spend a few days, perhaps a week or two, with Mistress Preston in St. Jago de la Vega," she informed Ann about two weeks after the birth of the child. "You leave tomorrow." She glanced at her sister warily, wondering if she would take exception to her high-handed arrangements, but Ann was overjoyed at the idea of a week or two in the gaiety of the Prestons' house in the capital. There were young people of her own age, there would be parties, maybe a ball, riding . . . .

Charlotte watched from the broad veranda as her sister left, a feeling of lassitude flooding her being. She stayed on the veranda long after the procession had disappeared, long after the dust kicked up by the horses' hooves had settled, long after the time she usually went on her rounds of the plantation.

Her eye was arrested by a cloud of dust, kicked up by a single horseman, that eddied up the drive. She started up, alarm banishing her lethargy.

Who could be traveling at such a pace?

Ann . . . something had happened to Ann, she should never have let her travel so soon after her confinement . . . .

She gathered up her skirts and ran to the double staircase that curved its graceful way down to the mounting blocks. The horseman drew rein as she reached the bottom of the stairs, and her heart leaped as she saw his face: older, harder, bronzed, a man now, but the deep blue eyes and the high aquiline nose were unmistakable.

"Robert . . . oh, Robert."

She held out her hands and he drew them to his chest. As she stood above him on the mounting block, her gray eyes were level with his blue ones, and he saw only the soft welcoming look, showing to him nothing of the change that time and life had wrought in her.

"Yes, Charlotte, at last, at last I've come back to you. Back to you . . . and back to Wells."

Part Three

~~~~~~~~~~~~~~~~~~~~~~~~~~~~~~~~~

1673-1680

One

The marriage of Charlotte Wells to Robert Vane took place in November 1673 amid a blaze of elegance displayed by the cream of the rapidly growing planter society. It was the social occasion of the decade, attended by the Governor, Sir Thomas Lynch, his household retinue, every man in the House of Assembly, and representatives of all the influential families in the island.

As Robert stood waiting for Charlotte to appear on the arm of a proud and smiling Walter Wells, his mind went back over the events of the past few months following his return to Wells. It had been a time of flurry and confusion, for within a week of his arrival Walter Wells made an unexpected earlier return from England, Ann had been summoned from her stay in St. Jago, and immediate arrangements for the wedding had been put in hand. There had been no discussion as to whether the marriage would still take place. There was a tacit understanding betwen them all that it should, and the earlier the better.

"My dear lad," Wells had boomed. "No need to wait, we've all waited too long."

He was flushed with the success of his journey and the promise of the bestowal of a knighthood—all past political differences forgotten—his election to the House of Assembly, and now this welcome return of Robert, with the prospect of at last settling his daughter. Robert had recounted his adventures again and again, laying stress on his captive state at the hands of Brasilano, lengthening his sojourn in St. Kitts, glossing over the years of piracy, until at last, after frequent repetition, he came almost to believe his distortion of the facts. For this reason he had kept his pouch of gems and coins secret: a vague premonition that despite his present affluent position, he might at some future date need every penny their worth could realize. He noticed that Ann had been strangely restrained in her greeting, at the same time observing him with a disturbing maturity from under her long brown lashes. There was a quality about her which disturbed him; he sensed that for all her mere sixteen years she was more of a woman than Charlotte was at twenty-two. . . . More perhaps, came the unbidden thought, than Charlotte would *ever* be. . . .

Charlotte entered, on her father's arm. She looked enchanting and fragile in a gown of silver and white gauze, with silver lacings at the low-cut bodice and banding the full sleeves: her silvery blonde hair clustered about her face in shining ringlets, her silvery gray eyes glowed through the filmy veil that covered her face.

All the nebulous thoughts of the last few months vanished from Robert's mind as he beheld his bride's loveliness, and he made his responses in a firm tone, not aware that each clear word of acceptance struck pain anew in Ann's heart. . . .

After the splendor of the wedding and the lavish reception that followed in the Preston's house . . . which lasted for three days . . . the return to Wells and the resumption of Great-house life was almost anticlimactic. It should have been the start of an adventure, a new life together, but Robert had to admit bitterly within a month of the marriage that it was doomed to disaster from the very beginning.

They left St. Jago as soon as their health had been

178

drunk by the reveling guests to return to Wells. They traveled in some degree of comfort the first dozen miles in the newly acquired Preston carriage, then transferred to horseback when the trail became too narrow and the surface too rutted for the carriage. The first night was a failure. Charlotte rejected his ardent advances with frigid disfavor.

"Please, Robert, I am tired with all the weeks of preparation, the ceremony and the journey back home."

He tried to take her in his arms, thinking to woo this unexpected mood away, but her body stiffened and her eyes went slate hard.

"Robert, I thought I had made my meaning clear. Please leave me."

"But s'life, girl, our *wedding* night? Do you deem me less than a man that you deny me your bed and your body?"

Her eyes flashed as she nearly blurted out the words she had sworn would remain unsaid: I *know* only too well how much a man you are, your bastard son in the slave compound gives truth to that. She folded her lips for a moment then said coldly: "I care . . . not . . . for the idea of lovemaking. It . . . it is repugnant to me."

Robert's nostrils flared in anger and his blue eyes matched her gray ones for hardness. "To tell a man on his wedding night that you care not for lovemaking? What kind of woman are you? Already before they are but a few hours uttered you have foresworn your marriage vows. How is Wells to get an heir?"

"An heir? That I will give to Wells, as my duty, in due time. . . . But for now, goodnight, Robert."

He stood for a moment undecided whether to finish this nonsense once and for all or humor her and ignore the situation, putting it down to female nerves and a too maidenly shyness . . . though there had been nothing shy or coy in her refusal—worse, a frigidity that seemed

179

to turn the warm tropic night cold—then he abruptly turned and walked away back to his own quarters as the disturbing revelation came to him that he neither minded the rejection nor desired his bride.

He settled in a deep leather chair and reached for a flagon of wine, then laughed grimly at the irony of his position: to ring for a complaisant slave girl would at least assuage the feeling of frustration at his enforced celibacy, but the news of his rejection by his new bride would be common knowledge throughout the plantation in a matter of hours.

He thought of Maria. He had been shocked at the change a few short years had wrought in her: the plump sparkling girl of nineteen he had left had turned in the space of six years into a haggard woman, her once full, taut breasts pendulous and arid, her features lined and aged beyond her twenty-five years, and that which pained him more, her once brilliant black eyes now opaque and apathetic. She had stood before him that first day when she returned from St. Jago with Ann, her eyes cast down, her hands twisting in her apron and had cringed inwardly at the doubtful recognition in his voice:

"Why . . . *Maria?* You've . . . grown up . . . since I left."

She laughed bitterly.

"It grow *up* me grow before you leave Mas' Robert, it *old* me grow now. It work in the sun-hot that tek the smooth skin from me face an' rough up me han's."

"The sun? But . . . you were sent to the fields? Why?"

She flashed him a look that recalled some of the quality of the Maria he had known and loved. She wanted to cry out, Because me bear you baby, you son, you firs' born chile; but she bit back the words

180

and murmured evasively: "Me fetch up wit' Miss Charlotte one time." She didn't dare to tell him of his child, for Charlotte had warned her as she stepped into the house and learned that Robert had at last returned: "You will not brag of your bastard child to Master Robert . . . or you will be sent back to the fields . . . and not even Miss Ann's wheedling would get you from hence again."

Robert stirred in the deep leather chair and poured another goblet of wine.

A frigid, rejecting non-wife . . . and the sprawl of acreage that was Wells. He stood up, suddenly determined: Charlotte must learn once and for all who was the master in their household. Not bothering to muffle his footsteps, despite the lateness of the hour, he strode to Charlotte's—their—room, and flung open the door.

Charlotte caught the faint odor of wine on his breath as he came toward her and took her by the shoulders with fingers that bruised. Her eyes went wide with alarm as he said coldly: "We'll have no more nonsense. You're my wife in name and *now,* by God, you'll be so in fact."

He took her roughly, impatiently, with no thought for her virginity, no tenderness of a groom for his bride. There was no joy in their union, no fulfillment, only a fierce assuagement of his bodily needs, a frigid acceptance by her, and later, when she lay dry-eyed and wakeful, listening to the unaccustomed sound of his deep breathing beside her, she told herself that she would endure such treatment until she was with child. After that she would lock her door if needs be, and if Robert was therefore driven into the arms of another . . . well, let it be, rather than the repeated indignity of this night. She shut her mind against the

181

memory of her own words so long ago . . . "But I will not be so complaisant as my mother," though they echoed and reechoed a taunting reminder of the girl she had once been.

Two

Walter Wells glanced sideways at his son-in-law as they made their usual morning round of the plantation. He had an uneasy feeling that all was not well with the newly wed pair. He noticed that Charlotte fretted about the house, missing the chores of the bigger world of the property, jealous that Robert was taking the place she had so assiduously obtained. She was an indifferent housekeeper, and the wastage in the kitchen was appalling, the table suffering in consequence. He reined in his mount and asked gruffly:

"Does aught ail you lad? Is the marriage . . . a failure?"

Robert looked surprised at the blunt question and hesitated, then said: "You can see for yourself, sir, we're not in the rapture that every young couple hopes for. But . . . Charlotte . . . well she is somewhat immature and . . ." he floundered, unwilling to elaborate out of loyalty.

"You mean she's frigid?" her father asked with added bluntness. "I'm not surprised, I'd sensed it before, but hoped. . . ." He sighed, then said heavily: "Sorry, lad, give her time . . . give her time."

"Meanwhile," Robert went on hastily, relieved that his father-in-law sympathised, yet unwilling to continue the discussion, "perhaps if she could resume her duties, some of them, around the plantation? She frets at being 'just a housewife.' "

"Spoiled," the colonel grumbled. "Should never have let her talk me into managing the property in the first place. Yet she's a good lass at the job," he added grudgingly. "But s'life, Rob, what of the house, 'tis bad enough as it is . . . ."

"I have it worked out, sir. In fact I have already taken the liberty of writing my aunt, Mistress Ann Darby, in England, to ask her to find a suitable housekeeper. I trust you do not object, sir?"

"Object? Nay, lad, nay. The house needs a strong woman's hand at the helm."

And so, in November 1674, when Robert and Charlottte had completed one year of uneasy matrimony, Mistress Deborah Darby, niece to Ann Darby and so cousin on his mother's side to Robert, arrived at Wells to take into her fragile hands the reins of household government. She was so diminutive in stature, some four feet eight inches in height, with small neat hands and feet, soft brown hair demurely tucked under a cap, large melting brown eyes that never held a trace of anger, annoyance, or condemnation for another's actions, however ill-advised; her voice was gentle, breathless and low, her manner hesitant and effacing.

Robert viewed her with dismay: how could his omniscient aunt have failed him so utterly in this matter? This . . . this *child* would be useless. He glanced again at the long letter she had brought from Ann Darby. ". . . Deborah is well versed in all aspects of housekeeping. She has been under my care and tutelage these many years, she came to me soon after you left us, God rue that day, I am loath to see her leave me, but by sending her to you, my dear boy, I feel that you are in some measure brought closer to me. . . ."

"You are very welcome, cousin Deborah. I trust,

184

though, that you have not come all this way only to find that the duties are . . . not to your liking."

She smiled and he noticed that beneath the sweet curve of her lips was a chin that spoke of a firmness which the rest of her appearance belied.

"I can see that there is much to be done, cousin Robert. If your wife will give me the keys to the pantry and the still room, I shall begin my duties this minute." A small frown flitted momentarily across her smooth forehead when Charlotte said carelessly:

"Keys? They've been lost for years . . . if ever there were any in the first place. Come, cousin Deborah, I'll show you round."

Charlotte was affable and gay again, now that the tedious household cares were to be lifted from her reluctant shoulders. She did not share Robert's misgivings at the sight of this miniature young woman. She sensed a strength of character which Robert failed to observe, though relief at the promised lessening of household chores would have made her cordial to any female, however unprepossessing or unsuitable in appearance.

The change in the tempo of the household was immediate and apparent. Deborah was everywhere at once, it seemed, never raising her voice, never scolding, never losing for one moment her air of serenity, but the effect on everyone with whom she came in contact was electric: the house slaves under Leah lost their air of lethargy and leaped to do her bidding. The white dimity curtains were crisply starched again; the mahogany floors resounded each day at dawn to the swish of brooms. Great bowls of hibiscus blossoms graced every room, replaced the moment they withered into spiraled death. Leah was kept constantly busy between the great brick ovens and her work tables, turning out

185

fresh bread, melting pasties, roast capons and suckling pigs; surprisingly she didn't resent this intrusion in her domain but fell under the spell that Deborah cast on all whom she met. Ann shed many of her wild and sulky moods under her guidance. Charlotte entered a new phase of submissiveness, and on one or two occasions even welcomed Robert's lovemaking. Richard seemed to rally and regain a little strength under her gentle administrations. And Walter Wells: in his sixtieth year, after years of dissolute living and squandering his manhood, lost his heart and fell hopelessly in love. . . .

Within six months of taking over the housekeeping, in the glorious May of 1675 when Charlotte discovered with relief that at last she was pregnant, Deborah Darby completed her gentle dominance of Wells Great-house by accepting Walter's proposal of marriage.

Walter and Deborah decided on a quiet early wedding with none of the elaborate celebrations that attended Charlotte's and Robert's. But it was triumph enough for quiet Deborah Darby, for the honor of a baronetcy had been bestowed on Walter on the king's command by the governor that very day. There was a new tilt to that small head, a new firmness to that soft mouth and chin, and a faint glint of triumph in the limpid brown eyes.

Robert realized at that moment that Wells was lost to him forever. . . . He glanced down at Charlotte, pale by his side, and he wondered that she had not yet realized the implication of this marriage and the effect it would have on their future . . . but her gray eyes were serene as they met his troubled blue ones, and he resolved not to mention his doubts and fears until she broached the subject.

August swept in that year with a great storm, the

186

worst Robert remembered in the islands. He was wakened just after midnight by the sound of the wind that had risen from an occasional moan to a continuous howl, tearing shutters from their hinges and whistling through the jalousied windows, hurling shingles from the roof and fencing from the enclosures.

"Oh Robert, the very house seems about to be torn apart," Charlotte whispered, shivering in uncharacteristic fear at the intensity of the storm.

"Stay here," Robert ordered as she reached for a robe to cover her nightshift. "I'll round up the domestics and get these shutters secured."

"No, Robert, I must go to Richard, he's frightened of storms. . . ."

"No, I'll see to Richard. You must stay . . . think of the child you carry."

He raced through the house to Richard's room, where he found that a corner of the shingled roof had lifted and that the rain was pouring in onto the huddled figure of his young brother-in-law. He snatched him up in his arms: "Heigh, old chap, let's get you out of here before the rest of the roof comes off," he said lightly, but Richard only trembled violently and clung to him.

Then Deborah was there, serene in a gown of white lace and lawn, her hair in two thick plaits to her waist.

"I have the east guestroom ready for Richard," she said in her gentle voice. "The wind is less that side."

Robert carried Richard to the room made ready for him, marveling that his young cousin could take even a hurricane in her stride. She followed him into the room. "Ah, Leah, you have heated the bricks? Well wrapped in flannel? Place them so, Master Richard is chilled with the rain. There, my love. You will soon be warm again." She drew the clothes high under the boy's chin, and her tone was light and comforting as she said: "I will stay with you, the storm will soon blow itself out." But her eyes were worried in the flaring light of the solitary candle as she whispered to Robert: "Fetch Sir Walter, Robert, *quickly*. I fear for the boy, his pulse is strangely weak yet erratic, and a fever consumes his very being."

"You mean . . . ?"

"I fear so. Tell Charlotte and Ann . . . they must be here, and . . . hurry, Robert."

So Walter Wells, Charlotte, Robert, and Ann kept vigil beside the slight form of the fast-failing Richard, and even as the storm abated, so Richard Wells, aged twenty-two, heir to the growing sugar kingdom that his father had founded, heir to the lately bestowed baronetcy, died as quietly as he lived, and Walter wept bitter tears by his son's bedside.

"My dear love, how may I help you to bear this grief?" Deborah murmured softly.

"By your presence, your love . . . and by giving me another heir," Walter said hoarsely.

She smiled behind her outward show of grief and murmured still more softly: "And that I may be able to do . . . come next spring."

"You mean . . . ?"

" 'Tis too soon to be sure . . . and we should not discuss this at this moment." There was gentle reproof in her voice but a small light of triumph in her eyes.

And so Richard was laid to his long rest beside his mother, the second grave in the family cemetery, the second lavish white headstone that gleamed amid the encroaching grasses.

Charlotte sat listlessly on her veranda. The heat, even so late in October, she found oppressive, and her pregnancy irked her. Her movements were heavy, she felt fettered, a prisoner of her own body. Ann was off visiting the Prestons in St. Jago once more; Robert was about the affairs of the plantation; and she, now well into the seventh month of pregnancy, had been forbidden to ride. She curled her lip at the thought: she, imperious Charlotte, *forbidden* . . . then she smiled; oh well, 'twas but for a space, until her son, the heir to Wells, was safely born.

She tensed suddenly, becoming cold in spite of the intense heat.

Heir to Wells?

Heir?

What a *fool* she had been not to have realized the significance of her father's marriage: that sly, insinuating little creature, already so smugly pregnant, would produce the heir to Wells, while she must yield precedence.

Anger was taking the place of dismay: all these years her father had been urging her to marry and give him an heir for Wells . . . and then treacherously wrested her inheritance from her grasp. . . .

Charlotte was brought to bed late that night of a stillborn son and knew for the first time the meaning and nature of the pain she had inflicted on Ann.

Robert accepted the loss of his son with fatality, his sympathy for Charlotte's anguish overshadowed by his concern for her reason.

Walter Wells faced his son-in-law with some embarrassment: "My marriage must have been a blow to your hopes, Rob lad. The property and all . . . and now this bad business about Charlotte and the child . . . but no excuse for her to go on so. Ayi-i, it seems as if she's demented half the time. But Wells could still be yours. This child which Deborah carries might be a girl . . . and you'll soon father a son on Charlotte, I have no doubt."

He paused, sighed sharply, then went on briskly: "This marriage of mine none of us could foresee. I want to do well by you, Rob. You've given me long years of devoted service, you were instrumental in bringing Deborah out here and so have given me a happiness in my remaining years that I had not dared to hope for . . . and you are my son-in-law, Wells Great-house and the plantation may or may not come to you and yours, but I feel that you should have a place of your own. Deborah and Charlotte will clash again sooner or later, and maybe your marriage will have a better chance of success in a home away from us all. So . . . I want you to look at a piece of land . . . smallish, about three hundred acres, but you can expand as you prosper. 'Tis over westwards near the district the Spanish call Savanna-la-Mar, good sugar land and by a fine harbor. Wild enough country and desolate, but the island grows, lad, more and more settlers arrive, and, God be thanked, the price of sugar rises. There are fortunes to be made here, Rob, if you are prepared to work."

Robert's heart leaped: was this the answer? Was this to be the realization of those dreams he had dreamed in St. Kitts?

"Look at the land from what point of view, sir?" he asked cautiously. "Do you want me there as your attorney or . . . ."

"Nay, lad. I'll buy the land for you and give half the monies needed for initial equipment. . . . The other half I'll lend you, and you can repay me out of the profits which will accrue over the years."

It was a generous offer, but Robert nearly blurted out with pride that he had enough wealth to be beholden to no man. Then caution curbed his tongue.

"This is more than generous, Sir Walter," he said formally. "I am agog to see the land. I—I had a little money saved . . . and . . ."

"Think nothing of it, boy," Sir Walter said in elaborate relief. "I kept you here with the promise of Wells . . . and my daughter's hand. . . . Now both seem to be a bad bargain on your side. You've been a great help to me, Rob. I feel I owe it to you."

Robert stood silent, embarrassed.

"What of Ann, sir?" he asked at last to steer his father-in-law away from the subject.

"Ann? *What* of Ann?"

"Should you not be thinking of marriage for her? She is past eighteen."

"Aye, aye. And I have been so thinking. First I had young Rodrigues Isaacs in mind . . . but there are still in force these plaguey laws concerning Jews, and not to be changed in my time, I fear. Pity, pity, 'twould have been a fine match, wealth beyond measure and a property second to none in the island. Then I spoke to her of young Preston . . . she has spent much time lately in the Preston town house, but the minx tells me haughtily, 'He's but a youth, papa, I'll none of him. Find me a *man* and I'll be willing to wed.' S'life, Rob, when I was a lad, no lass would tell her father so, she'd accept whatever husband so chosen for her and meekly wed him."

"Sir, with all due respect, the life we lead in these islands of the New World has little to compare with that in the Old. . . . As you so often remark, sir, we make our own laws and take little heed to those decreed in England."

"You're right as ever, Rob. But I wish the lass would take young Preston." Sir Walter frowned at the memory of his younger daughter's perversity, then

191

sighed. "She has changed since I left for England . . . a strange and subtle difference . . . as if she had become adult overnight."

Robert laughed. "Only the difference between a girl child and a female grown to womanhood, sir. You had not seen her for many months, therefore the change was more remarkable," he said lightly. But he also had sensed that Ann had reached a peak of maturity at sixteen which Charlotte had not yet acquired, and he wondered uneasily if this had been a natural process or whether some unknown, unguessed-at catalyst had wrought the change.

"One thing more," Sir Walter broke into his musings. "This business that Charlotte started amongst the slaves . . . teaching Christianity and such . . . well, it's got to be stopped."

"Stopped? But why? They seem happy enough, though not, I wager, through a sense of grace. Why, sir?"

" 'Twas decreed in Council that no teaching of religion is lawful. It is like to imbue a false sense of values, and 'tis feared they'll get uppity and think that by becoming Christians they rise above their slave status."

"But, Sir Walter, the practice has been established at Wells for years . . . soon after I left I believe. It *cannot* be stamped out overnight."

"*Cannot?* I say it must. I am looked at askance in the House already on the subject. We were pioneers in starting plantation services, other plantations followed suit, thinking it would do no harm . . . it is our *duty* therefore to obey the decree of the House and be pioneers in stamping out the practice."

"But, sir," Robert argued. " 'Tis just now a *decree*

of the House, 'twill not become *law* until passed by the Lords of Trade and Plantations. . . ."

"Don't quote the rules to me, boy, a decree is the law until the Lords say yea or nay. I am still in command here and I say it must go . . . whatever the cost."

Three

Ann Wells was restless, rebellious and bored. She had enjoyed her visit to the Prestons', though she was overjoyed to return to Wells and be under the same roof as Robert again. She felt a small malicious pleasure when she noted his difficulties attendant on the early days of marriage, then a sharp jealousy when Charlotte became pregnant and at last seemed settled and happy. Her father's marriage to Deborah Darby touched her not at all. She liked Deborah and had learned to assume a demure aspect before her, which assured noninterference with her somewhat unorthodox ways. When she returned from her latest trip to St. Jago, she learned with shock of Charlotte's miscarriage; she tried to offer condolences, but Charlotte was withdrawn and inimical. "Don't be a hypocrite and give me those 'mother bereaved' consoling words. *I* was carrying the heir to Wells."

"You will have other children," she whispered. Charlotte shut her eyes in disgust.

"Yes, and God grant *I* get an heir before . . . before that usurper," she said viciously.

Ann left her sister's room quietly. Surely Charlotte had let this affect her brain in some way? This obsession in getting an heir . . . an heir for *Wells* . . . couldn't she realize that Deborah would probably forestall her? The talk and thought of heirs and children centered her

194

mind on her unknown child: she didn't even know if it were male or female . . . or even if it were still alive. She picked up her skirts in sudden determination: she would visit the nursery in the slave compound under the guise of inquiring for the children's welfare, would try and discover which child was her own.

It was with a sense of physical shock and complete disbelief that she found herself confronted by a small boy of about seven or eight, his olive skin like dusky velvet, his hair dark and softly curling . . . and the deep blue eyes of Robert himself . . . .

She gazed at the child for a long incredulous moment, then at last asked hoarsely: "What is your name, child?"

He scuffed a naked foot in the dust and hung his head, wordless at being spoken to by this goddesslike white woman from the Olympian heights of the Greathouse.

Ann still gazed down at him in sick dismay: Robert's child, there were the eyes as evidence, the nose unmistakable . . . and the darker skin to proclaim the other half of the union . . . a slave . . . Robert and a slave girl . . . she felt choked. Then, as the child recovered some confidence and looked up at her in questioning surprise, her emotions calmed: after all, why should she . . . how *could* she . . . condemn Robert when she . . . she was about to search for her own bastard half-caste. She touched the soft dark hair gently and turned to go: "It doesn't matter, child," she said softly, then was arrested by the sight of another child, a toddler of about two: from the round dark face beneath a cluster of tight black curls her own gray eyes gazed up at her. Before her mind could register that this child, this unmistakable child, was her daughter, her attention was transformed and riveted on the man who held the child's pudgy fist in his left hand.

Her face went white with shock; the blood pounded so in her head that for a moment she swayed, then found herself steadied by a strong arm. She almost screamed as she glanced down and saw that the arm which supported her was roughly severed at the wrist, the scar tissue pink against the dark skin.

"Malachi? Malachi," she whispered to the misshapen parody of her former lover. "What . . . what have they done to you?" Her voice was so faint that the rhetorical question barely reached him. It was pitifully apparent what had been done to him: he had been stripped of his manhood, his beauty, his usefulness. Her eyes filled with compassionate tears as she said: "I didn't know . . . I swear I didn't know."

He shook his head, and she wondered for a terrible moment whether his tongue had been torn out as well, but he said at last, slowly, painfully, in a voice dispassionate: "No, me know you don't know, Miss Ann. Me not good fe much now, but I ten' the pickney dem, an' this . . ." he pushed the girl child toward her. "This . . . our chil' . . . our chil' . . . you boun' to me t'rough her, Miss Ann, boun' to me as long as life spare."

Ann's eyes widened in sudden revulsion: she wanted none of this child, who proclaimed her shame to all the world, none of this battered parody of a man. Charlotte had been right as always, she should never have come to look for her child. She pushed her hands out blindly, warding off the approach of the child, trying not to see the contempt springing into Malachi's black eyes, then turned and fled back through the heat of the afternoon sun, oblivious of the knowing glances of the resting field gangs, back to the cool steadfast recesses of the Great-house. But the vision of Malachi would not dim as time passed; his twisted body, the strange hoarse voice, and the final glance of contempt he had given her stayed with her waking and sleeping, until in desperation she sought her father in his study and said simply: "Papa, you are right, the time has come when I should marry and set up house. I will marry any one you favor."

There was a hush of expectancy over Wells one day early in April of that year, as the time for Deborah's confinement drew near. This she accomplished with her usual quiet efficiency, and even Leah, normally supreme at a lying-in, was cowed into obeying her whispered orders right up to the final moment, though her calm manner faltered for a second as Leah announced, "It a girl pickney, Miss Deborah, Ma'am," and her mouth tightened as Walter gave a quickly smothered sigh of disappointment. She reached out a tired hand and took his, ignoring the look of ill-concealed triumph in Charlotte's eyes.

"A girl, Walter my love. That means that *next* time 'twill certainly be a boy."

Robert let his horse have its head as it picked its way delicately over the rough trail that wound westward to the land that was to be his own. At first it was fairly easy going, but once they had crossed the Clarendon Plains, the way became tangled and difficult. There were six in the party: stolid Dick Gough, his once red shock of hair graying; two indentured bond servants, anxious to end their enforced days at Wells; and two Negro slaves, as trustworthy and devoted as was possible under the restrictions and tribulations of their way of life.

They were now skirting the foothills of the Mountains of the Manatines. The track was narrow and close to the edge of a precipice that fell sheer to the rocky coast below, then the trail turned inward and sharply

197

upward, and they climbed ever higher, the horses' hooves slipping on the loose scree or slithering in soft mud. Then the track fell abruptly again, and they came to a great valley that stretched between two great mountain ranges, those of the Manatines and the Santa Cruz Mountains.

Robert was possessed by a fevered urgency to reach the end of the journey, the like of which he hadn't known for years. "Surely we can make better going than this," he demanded of Dick Gough, who had made the journey previously with Sir Walter.

"Hold y'self in patience, Master Robert. 'Tis wild untamed country, but good rich soil, I'm thinking. We've many a long weary mile afore we reach our goal, but worth the miles at the end, you'll be saying."

So they plodded on along the coast once more, and Robert was exhilarated by the magnificence of the scenery. To their right reared the mountains from which they had come, to their left the sea, a patchwork of brilliant color, the sands silver white and incredibly fine, while sea grapes, wild almond trees, and coconut palms grew to the very water's edge. Then they came at last to a grove of bamboo and crossed a waist-high rippling river, its mountain crispness cooling their hot, dust-encrusted bodies.

"Here, sir," Dick Gough announced, satisfaction filling his voice, "from this river boundary to the foothills, bounded to the east by a tributary of this same river, to the west by a small swamp, the prettiest bit of land a man could wish for."

Robert drew rein and contemplated what was to be his future domain, and in his mind's eye he saw Vane Great-house atop the highest knoll, vast fields of waving cane, groves of citrus, cocoa walks. . . . He jerked his mind back to the present and Dick Gough's smiling face, a face without envy for the good fortune of another. Robert smiled back, his blue eyes alight with purpose.

" 'Tis magnificent, Dick, but many years' hard work ahead before we can carve a living or even put a permanent roof over our heads."

At the use of the term "we" Gough said with sudden seriousness:

"*We*, Master Robert? Is that just a way of speech or . . . ."

"No way of speech, man. Join me as my overseer. You've given service to Wells and Sir Walter over and over above your bondsman's service, you've trained men under you capable enough to fill your place. What do you say?"

Gough was silent for a long moment. Any dreams he might once have cherished had long since melted in the dim mists of the time spent in the service of another. At last he said softly: "A man could do worse than end his days here, isn't it? If Sir Walter be agreeable, then so am I. And God bless you, Master Robert, for the asking of me."

Four

Ann Preston sat by a grilled balcony and watched with discontent the passing crowds that strolled the streets of St. Jago de la Vega, as the Spanish ladies half a century earlier must have done on such an evening as this.

After only a few months of marriage she was bored and restless, resenting the confines of a town house after the freedom of Wells, resenting her ever-present mother-in-law, whose attitude of welcoming affection had changed to one of carping suspicion. Ann avoided her attempts to instruct her in the art of housekeeping and declined her instructions to minimize the decolletage of her dress. Ann despised her two sisters-in-law, who were typical Creoles, lazy, fat, and without a thought in their silly heads beyond eating, sleeping, and ogling every presentable male. Even all this would have been bearable, she thought despairingly, if only she loved—even liked—her husband. But his boorishness bored her, his fumbling hands and rum-laden kisses revolted her, and she submitted to his ineffectual love-making only when it was impossible to avoid him.

He ambled onto the balcony and gave her a doglike look of puzzled yearning.

"Ann," he said tentatively, and for once she was glad to note that he was quite sober. "Ann, love, it plagues me to see you so quiet and subdued. Before our mar-

200

riage you were always so gay. Is it perhaps . . . I mean, are you . . . ?" There was a spark of hope in his eyes, and she shook her head impatiently and broke out: "It's nothing more than that I'm cooped up as in a cage. At Wells I can breathe, I can ride for hours and not see a soul or swim from a beach that has not been trod by a human foot for a dozen years." He said eagerly: "You miss Wells? Is that it? It's not that you're unhappy with me?"

He looked so abject that she wanted to strike him and say cuttingly that of course he was the cause of her unhappiness, but she bit back the threatened torrent of words and said as gently as she could: "Why, William, how could you think *that?* You are my husband."

He knelt beside her and took her hands and said with as much animation as she had ever seen on his face: "Then how would you like to go to Wells . . . for a few months?"

"A few *months?*"

As a wild joy swept through her, she forgot for the moment her reasons for leaving in such blind haste: that misshapen battered hulk who was once her virile lover; that child with Robert's eyes, a living betrayal by the man she wanted; and that girl with her own gray eyes, proof of her past shame.

"But—you—what about you, William?"

"I shall come too."

Now that Deborah had been delivered of a girl, Charlotte's hopes of producing an heir for Wells rose again. She welcomed Robert with open arms, but even at the height of their lovemaking he realized with distaste that Charlotte's feelings were inspired by a calculating desire to conceive a child, so that it was with relief when he left Wells again to spend many weeks at Vane.

He set off with Dick Gough and a newly indentured

bondsman, John White, a skilled craftsman in wood. The track had been broadened and had acquired a better surface over the months of passage to and fro, and the way was much easier for both horses and men. There was still the anxiety in traversing the swamp and the difficult crossing of the ford that spanned the Rio Caobana, but they made good time and completed the journey in a record four days.

And now the work began in earnest. Robert had at last completed his plan for the Great-house to his satisfaction, and once the foundations were finished, the house began to take shape and rose slowly, the gleaming cutstone walls a promised landmark of note for many miles. Work was started also on clearing the scrub and tilling the lower flat lands for sugar; high up on the hillside Robert started a coffee walk from some precious seedlings brought from Wells, hoping that they would do better at a higher altitude, for the crop at Wells had never been very successful, producing barely enough for the household's consumption.

The construction of the mill was under way close to the river, and the once wild desolation of the area slowly became tamed and domesticated.

Since Ann had returned to Wells with her husband, some of Charlotte's animosity toward her had lessened, though it was with an undertone of envy that she had said dryly one morning: "I see you are with child, sister."

Ann flushed at her tone, knowing that each remembered that other morning long ago, when Charlotte had made a similar observation.

"Yes," she admitted shortly, then with a glance at Charlotte's trim waistline asked maliciously: "And you?"

"Unfortunately, no. And what chance do I have to become so, with Robert constantly at Vane?"

"But Charlotte, surely you want Vane to be completed as soon as possible? So that you may be mistress in your own house?"

"I should rightfully be mistress of Wells. Wells is my home and always will be in my heart . . . wherever my body is forced to live."

"But surely when a woman marries her home is where her husband chooses?"

"Then why do *you* stay here?"

"Because my husband chooses," Ann retorted sharply. "He knew I felt restricted and suffocated in his father's town house. Now William's interest in plantation life has grown. Since he has been at Wells, he talks of acquiring a property in the east, so perhaps in the future *I* will also be mistress in my own house."

Charlotte smiled with all the old sweetness that used to light up her face, a smile too seldom seen now: "Then perhaps you had best begin to take some interest in household management." The smile faded. "I'm sure our lady stepmother will be pleased to impart her knowledge of the art," she added with malicious tartness.

Ann's light remarks about being mistress in her own house had been made to impress Charlotte; she was completely incapable of envisaging any life other than that at Wells, and she was prepared to go to any lengths to persuade William to stay on indefinitely, but to every one's surprise she took Charlotte's suggestion seriously and began to take more than just an interest in the affairs of the house, spending long dedicated hours in the huge kitchen, the buttery, and the still-room.

"Why, I declare," Deborah said one day early in

February 1679, when Ann was but a month from her confinement. "You'll rival me at baking and wine-making if you progress at this rate." The words were lightly said, but Ann sensed an underlying coldness. So my lady stepmother doesn't care for so apt a pupil, she thought, then said aloud: "Why Mistress Deborah, you flatter me instead of taking credit yourself. How could one not learn well from so excellent a teacher. But I believe we should call a halt to my lessons now, for the child lies heavy within me."

Deborah looked at her curiously. "You take the birth of this child very calmly. One would think you had experience of such an event." She didn't miss Ann's quick indrawn breath and swift retort:

"Yet you yourself, my lady, again set an example of calmness at such a time."

"Not to you, you were from Wells at the time."

"The tale was told me in admiration and in detail," Ann said, again too quickly.

Deborah's eyes narrowed. Surely her idle words could not have hit on the truth? Suspicion crossed her mind, to be partially dismissed as she viewed Ann's innocent face, but she was well versed herself in dissimulation and mentally resolved to make a few discreet inquiries around the plantation. It would not hurt to hold the whip hand over this much-loved daughter, on whom her husband still doted, despite his obvious and oft-avowed love for herself.

Ann's preoccupation with household matter had been mostly to while away the tedium of the months of pregnancy, and once the child was born, she told herself, she would return to the delights of riding and . . . yes, then perhaps she could put a certain little plan into action. . . .

Ann's second child was born in circumstances very

different from the first, although the physical surroundings were identical. Instead of being shrouded in secrecy the whole household revolved about her, and William, his faced suffused with pride in his achievement and concern for his wife's well-being, hovered outside the bedroom until Deborah and Charlotte shooed him away in exasperation.

Charlotte would have preferred to attend Ann alone, for she feared that her sister in her agony might let fall some word of her previous difficult confinement, but this time the birth was easy and quickly over—so quickly that Deborah's suspicions were aroused anew. This suspicion gave way to envy when the child was seen to be a boy: a healthy child who cried lustily as soon as he left his mother's womb.

Charlotte also felt a stab of envy: *a boy*. She caught and held Deborah's eye; their thoughts were naked to each other, for Deborah, despite her outward composure, was inwardly chafing that three years had passed since Melissa's birth and she still showed no signs of being again with child: perhaps at last Walter's virility had failed, and all her plans for keeping Wells for the son she longed for would come to naught.

Sir Walter's pride in his grandson did nothing to assuage the envy in his wife's breast or ease the turmoil in Charlotte's fevered mind.

"Good lass," he told Ann. "A true Wells, spitting image of me old father, God rest him."

William was bursting with pride and relief. "My darling." He held Ann's hand in his. "He has the Preston features even at this age, the nose, the forehead . . . even the hairline." He gazed down at the wrinkled wizened face. "What would you like to call our son?"

She smiled back tiredly. "What about Walter William, after my father, you and your father, or . . ." noting a flicker of disappointment, "William Walter?" He bent and kissed her. "William Walter it shall be."

Five

Later that year in October, when the heat of the summer was beginning to wane and the seasonal rains were lashing the island, Ann sought out Robert in the old schoolroom, where he was poring over sketches of furniture that he had ordered from England and France.

"Robert, when you go back to Vane, take me with you," she asked softly.

"Take you with me? My dear girl, the house is far from finished."

"But I want to see it. You said that this time you would be away only a short time and . . . ."

"Impossible. Charlotte would never agree."

"I doubt Charlotte would mind overmuch . . . after all, she is much preoccupied now," she added slyly, for only last week Charlotte had announced joyfully that she expected a child the following May. This announcement had followed quickly on Deborah's own statement that *her* child would be born at about the same time.

Robert gazed down into Ann's pleading face, and his resolution faltered. "You will not be comfortable at Vane . . . and Charlotte should see it first," he added lamely.

"When she makes no pretense of wanting to? Please, Robert, I am bored now that little William is in the nursery all the time and . . . my husband away on business in the east."

"We shall see," Robert said, feebly falling back on the old schoolroom tactic of prevarication.

Surprisingly to Robert, Charlotte offered no objections to the plan. Her world was bounded by the child she carried, and she wished for nothing more than peace and serenity until its birth was safe. Her affection toward Robert had been replaced by indifference since she had been certain that she was with child, and she banned him from her room now, determined that nothing should induce another miscarriage. She was glad when the time came for their departure, although this left her more alone with Deborah. There was between the two women a barely veiled hostility as each grew bigger with child.

Ann packed joyfully for her visit to Vane and left her son in the care of his wet nurse with no deep maternal feelings. Marriage and childbirth had only increased her beauty: her figure was still slim and taut, her breasts had an added fullness, her arms a softer roundness, her eyes an extra sparkle.

Robert had experienced a lightness of spirit the like of which he hadn't known for years as he rode out of Wells with Ann by his side. She was dressed for the long journey in a pair of riding breeches, ignoring the consternation that such attire had caused Deborah.

" 'Tis indelicate, I vow, to display your limbs so blatantly."

Ann laughed. "Fie, my lady, my *legs* are adequately clad, more so than with heavy skirts that may catch on briars and pull me indecorously away from my horse."

And so she rode astride like a man to earn yet more disapproval from the womenfolk and undisguised admiration from the men. With the breeches she wore a severe white ruffled shirt, also mannish, yet she was all woman, Robert thought, in spite of her clothes; indeed, they only served to enhance her femininity.

Dick Gough rode with them, together with a group of five new slaves whom he had bought in Port Royal a month previously.

Ann exclaimed in delight at all they heard and saw: the birdsong, a crash of wild boar in the underbrush; the changing terrain as they moved ever westward; the forest-clad mountains that reared about them, with purple and yellow wild orchids clinging to the trees, spilling their beauty in exotic carelessness; the deep valleys where they gazed down onto the tops of trees, close packed and seemingly impenetrable.

"Oh, Robert, this is wonderful, like riding into a new world."

Robert cantered after her and said sharply: "You must keep by my side or just behind me. This is not a joy ride on St. Catherine's Plain but one fraught with danger and sudden changes of terrain."

She glanced up at his stern face from under her lashes and said demurely: "Yes, Robert."

"Why did you not bring your body slave?" he asked after a short silence.

She tightened her lips. "I can do without Maria for a few days," she said shortly.

"Maria? She is still your body slave?"

There was a note of tenderness in his voice that brought back the pain she had known when she first saw his child in the slave compound, a wistful nostalgic tenderness that made her certain that the mother was Maria. Did he know of his son, she wondered. He was looking at her now, waiting for an answer to his question.

"Yes, Maria is still my body slave, though since . . . she went into the fields she has aged and become somewhat frail. . . . I doubt that she would stand this journey well."

"Sent to the fields? But why?" Even as he asked the question, he remembered that Maria herself had told him years ago that she had been so punished by Charlotte. "Why?" he asked again, obscurely feeling that the reason was important.

Ann flashed him a strange look. "I don't *know* why." But I *do,* her heart cried: because she bore your son, and Charlotte found out, then married you and has still said nothing . . . and I who love you can still say nothing.

The journey took a long, hot six days, but once they crossed the Westmoreland Plain and came at last to Vane, all Ann's tiredness vanished at the beauty of the sight. The Great-house was finished outwardly, a finely proportioned building of two stories, the lower of white cutstone, the upper of golden wood. A graceful double staircase led from the mounting blocks to the upper story, each flight curving to flow and merge into a covered landing that led through wide double doors to the interior. The lower walls of the frontage were only about three feet high, then graceful stone columns took over the support. Through them a wide cool veranda could be glimpsed. The upper story had many windows with louvered shutters, and Ann noted with amazement that the windows were not of the usual plain wooden jalousie type but were of glass, small glass panes set in lead. She turned to Robert:

" 'Tis more magnificent than Wells, much more, and though somewhat similar in style . . . yet so unlike. I suppose . . . what is it, Robert, that makes of this not just a house but a thing of beauty?"

He was pleased by her perception and appreciation. " 'Tis the proportions. I worked many a long night to get them just so."

"I hope you will not be in debt too many years to pay for all this splendor."

He smiled and shook his head. "No debts hang over my head." The house had indeed cost a fortune, and be damned if he would explain to Sir Walter how much or how he had paid for it . . . and yet he still had a goodly portion left in gem and coins to help him over the next few years until Vane would be a self-supporting plantation.

They moved slowly forward toward the house, alone now, for Gough had left them as they gazed in wonderment at the realization of Robert's dream and had taken the group of slaves to the compound, newly finished, away down by the cane fields which were brilliant green and waved proudly with the first Vane crop.

They drew rein at the mounting block, and Ann made no attempt to dismount. She was looking up at a carved crest above the central archway. Robert's eyes followed hers and he said softly: "The Vane crest and motto: *Parem non fert. He brooks no equal.* Presumptuous as was the first Vane to adopt such a motto, yet I still feel pride in seeing it. Although my lands were wrested from me, they could not take my heritage of birth, and here a new generation of Vanes will grow and flourish."

He leaped from his mount and moved toward her. He raised his hands and placed them about her waist and swung her lightly to the ground; in the stillness that encompassed them he heard her quick breathing and felt the flutter of her heart beneath his fingers. His own breath came faster as he said even more softly:

"Welcome to Vane."

She gazed up at him, her own feelings naked for him to see. He released his hold about her waist and took her hand. "Come, let me show you inside." It was dark and cool in the square entrance hall with its inner stair-well leading to the room below, but they saw none of its splendor as they turned without hesitation into each other's arms. Robert made one last effort to retain his sanity. "Ann . . . we can't . . . I am your sister's husband." But her body was pressed against his, her eyes were veiled with desire, and he crushed her even closer, kissing her with a fierce passion. She responded with a passion to match his own, a wild uninhibited abandonment, until they were both exhausted yet exhilarated.

He led her through the dim rooms to a small side room furnished with a single pallet, and they came together in a convulsive, demanding union so perfect as to leave them dazed. She smiled mistily, looking deep into his eyes above hers: "I knew you'd love me—one day. Remember when you left Wells so many years ago? I told you then that I loved you, and I've never stopped loving you."

"What about . . . your husband?"

"I've never loved him."

He kissed her again, tenderly. "You were right all those years ago when you demanded in your childish rage why I didn't marry you. What a fool I was not to have realized then. . . ." He got up from the pallet and reached for his breeches. . . . A wordless longing possessed him that the heirs of his body for this domain of his could be borne by Ann and not by his cold and frigid lawful wife.

She sat up, her long, light brown hair her only covering, and touched the scars on his back and the weals on his wrist. "How *could* they do this to you?" she asked wonderingly, then shut her eyes in sudden pain as she remembered what Charlotte had caused to be done to Malachi . . . through *her* treachery . . . . Robert, busy tying the laces of his shirt, noticed nothing. He kissed her again as he prepared to leave. "Put on your shift, I'll find a slave girl to bring you your traveling basket and to act as your tiring maid. I'll have food sent up too, then you can rest, and later in the cool of the evening we will make that—postponed exploration of the house. Now I have work to do with Gough and my man White."

For proprieties' sake she clothed herself in the journey-stained breeches and shirt and waited in a euphoric languor for the slave girl.

There began that day a week of halcyon enchantment, an interlude in their lives that had no relationship to the past or present, an interlude they knew would end on their return to Wells. It was a strange and romantic setting, the huge near-finished house, empty of furnishings except for the little room with the narrow, hard pallet and a veranda with bamboo rockers and a low table. In the first they slept and made ecstatic love, on the second they ate their meals picnic fashion, with calabash gourds for goblets and rough wooden platters for their food; not that they would have noticed if the goblets had been of the finest Venetian crystal and the platters pure silver.

Dick Gough could not possibly be unaware of the change in their relationship, nor could he, with his Puritan background, approve; yet he showed no sign, treating Robert with his usual rough deference and Ann with an Old World gruff courtesy.

Robert would spend the morning hours with Dick Gough. His mind, which was usually completely absorbed in the affairs of Vane and all its spreading acres, not merely half attentive, now was for the greater part still engrossed with thoughts of Ann. Then Gough would again patiently explain a detail or present a problem, sighing inwardly over the plight these two lovers would find themselves in once they were back at Wells.

Then, unbelievably, it was the end; but the spell was

broken and the future of their ordered world loomed menacingly ahead. Ann clung to him in a storm of tears when it was time to leave.

"How are we going to live, seeing each other, meeting at meals, my imagining you lying in Charlotte's arms, while I have to endure William's caresses?"

He stroked her hair sadly, his heart heavy at the prospect before them.

"Don't torture yourself with such imaginings. Charlotte and I live apart, except when she has this desire for a son, which God grant will be fulfilled before many months are past. We *will* endure it, my sweet love, and the memory of these days will uphold us in the dark days ahead. There will be moments, snatched and precious; you'll see, we will manage somehow.

The journey back took six days, each a day nearer to their separation: it was a journey of frustration for the lovers, since to make love in the confines of the camp was almost impossible, so that it was a relief in some measure to sight the familiar fields of Wells and the high sloping roofs of the Great-house.

As Robert lifted her down from her mount, each remembered with piercing sweetness that same action, that action which had revealed their love, in another time, another place, and they gazed for the last time into each other's eyes, their love naked and despairing, before Charlotte appeared to welcome them home. Ann feared that her love for Robert would show for all to see. She had a radiance about her which had not been there when she left for Vane; but apart from saying: "Your trip into the wilds seems to have done you no harm," Charlotte made no comment on her looks.

"It may be the wilds to get there, but oh, Charlotte, Vane is *beautiful,* the house, the property . . . everything. You're going to be . . . so happy there." Ann found herself expressing her enthusiasm quite naturally,

214

despite her former fears that she would be struck with an awkward silence before her sister.

"I doubt that," Charlotte said indifferently. "I want no part of Vane . . . Wells is my home."

Charlotte was completely absorbed now in the approaching birth of her child, and a strange race for delivery went on between her young stepmother and herself. They avoided each other as far as was possible, but when they did meet, they eyed each other's swelling belly with worried assessment. As May drew near and the earth was deluged with rain and humidity hung in the air like a clinging blanket, speculation grew rife throughout the plantation as to "which Missis goin' drop pickney firs'." The tension in the household grew accordingly.

Since their return from Vane, Robert and Ann had managed a few meetings. They were diffident at first, but as the months passed, they became more confident and blatant in their encounters, even after William returned from the east. Now a new fear possessed Ann.

"I believe William will insist that we move into the house in the east, he is so enthused with the idea and talks of nothing but the groves of coconut palms he has there," she said to Robert as they lay clasped in each other's arms one afternoon in early May. They were in the schoolroom, a place where they were least likely to be discovered. "How shall I live so far away?" she complained. "Robert, I *cannot* go all that way from you. I shall die of boredom alone with William."

"You *must* endure it, my love. You have little William . . . whom you shamefully ignore," Robert murmured, then placed his hand on her gently imperceptibly swelling belly. "And someone else to keep you occupied in a few months."

Ann bit her lip. "I hope this child is yours, and yet

215

when I think it may be, I get sick with fear that the resemblance to you will be too apparent. . . ." Again she was overcome by remembrance of the beautiful child in the slave compound, the unmistakable brilliance of his blue eyes in his dark olive face, and bitter jealousy once more overwhelmed her.

Ann was correct about William's plans.

"We will leave for the east as soon as the May rains are over and the muddy tracks have dried somewhat," he announced with a new authority. "And before your pregnancy becomes too far advanced."

"William, let me stay here until the baby is born. Charlotte and Deborah will care for me . . . there is no one at Preston."

"Nonsense, my lady mother and sisters will give you every assistance."

She closed her eyes in desperation: his "lady mother" with her carping ways, those stupid lumps who were his sisters with their Creole drawl and their incessant stuffing of sickly sweetmeats: she felt already the suffocation she knew would engulf her in the eastern estate, which she had not yet seen.

"William, I beg you let me have the child here. To . . ask me to undertake such a long journey in June, at the height of the summer's heat, when I shall be four whole months gone, then to take the last part of the journey by sea . . . that prospect alone makes me feel ill with fear . . . finally to arrive at an unknown house . . . it's too much to contemplate."

William was unexpectedly firm. "I cannot live there all those months without you, Ann. I missed you so much, I couldn't go through that again."

Then Ann wept, accusing him of selfishness and not thinking of her or their child at all, until at last poor, besotted, cuckolded William agreed that she could stay until the child was born . . . "until he's old enough to travel." . . . Ann agreed, knowing that when that time came, she could surely think up more excuses to prolong her stay.

Lady Wells was proudly delivered of a boy on the last day of May that year and smiled in triumph at Walter. "You have your son at last, husband, an heir to your land and title."

"Yes . . . and thank you, my love. He's a fine lusty child, hark to the power from those lungs," Walter said in relief. The memory of Richard and his poor weak lungs receded still further from his mind.

Charlotte felt that she would swoon with frustration when the news was told her; she was well over her time and still no signs of labor, but she kept an iron control over her emotions, determined to do nothing to damage her child, until at last, two days after her stepmother's triumph, she lay in agonizing labor for nearly forty-eight hours. Robert stayed with her, bathing her pain-furrowed brow and brushing the long silvery blonde hair from her tormented eyes. Ann, too, was in constant attendance, her mind filled with wonder at the incongruity of the situation, that she and her lover should attend so assiduously his wronged wife—her betrayed sister—and still she felt no qualm of guilt.

When at last the child was born, Charlotte wept when told it was a girl. Robert feared for her health as the great sobs shook her: he held her close and whispered: "Charlotte, sweetheart, it's not the end of the world. Next year we'll have a son—you'll see, you'll see."

"I want an heir, an heir for Wells," she sobbed.

Oh God, he thought, can she not *yet* realize that Wells is lost to her. . . . Wells *has* a lusty young heir. But *I* need an heir for Vane, that's why . . . he glanced around to look at Ann, but she was gone. She couldn't

217

bear to see him touch Charlotte, much less whisper words of endearment.

In the months that followed Ann realized that it had been a mistake for her to have stayed on at Wells. Robert was hardly ever there. He spent most of his time at Vane, now in the last stage of completion, and when he did appear for brief visits, they were never alone, for Charlotte, still avid to have a son, kept him by her side in an embarrassing display of spurious affection that deceived no one.

There was a veritable nursery now at the Greathouse: Melissa, an imperious four years old, queening it over Ann's William Walter, a sturdy toddler with all his father's stolid somberness and none of his mother's looks or charm, while the two new arrivals—Walter Wells, Deborah's and Walter's much wanted son, and Bridget Vane, surprisingly Robert's pride and Charlotte's shame—were no more than mewling bundles consigned to the care of their respective wet nurses.

Six

The yearly Christmas revels were in full swing in the slave compound when Ann's second son was born. Her labor was accompanied by the insistent thrumming of drums and the high tuneless whistle of fee-fees, a wild pagan cacophony going on far into the night.

She scanned the baby's wrinkled face anxiously for any sign of resemblance to Robert, but his indeterminate features bore no likeness to anyone, and she sank back, relieved for the moment.

Another boy: Charlotte—once more pregnant—would be bitter and frustrated anew. Later that day Ann pondered about her sister as she lay exhausted and drained in the big four-poster bed. Charlotte: so changed in character, temperament, and looks in such a few short years, obsessed with her love for Wells. She doesn't love Robert, Ann mused, she never has, and yet she urges him to father her children . . . in such indecent haste . . . then ignores him while she carries his child.

Each day passed with a renewed fear that William would demand that she join him at Preston. This fear was realized late in January, when he sent word that he would arrive shortly and that she must prepare for the journey east. She sought Robert in his study. "How can I bear to go?" she cried bitterly.

He closed the door and took her in his arms. "It's

been so long since I held you, my love. Yet if you rebel against William and stay here, we will still have the agony of knowing that each is so near and yet untouchable. We have taken too many chances already."

In spite of his words, he kissed her again, a long kiss, and each felt desire that throbbingly demanded to be satisfied now.

"Go to the little guestroom at the east corner," he whispered. "No one goes there, I'll join you in a few minutes."

She hurried off, joy adding lightness to her step and a song in her heart. Once more, just once more, to know his love, his strong hands about her body, once more before the future closed about them and long miles lay between them. Her fingers trembled as she looped the laces of her muslin dress, and when Robert opened the door a few minutes later, her white body gleamed lustrously in the half-darkness. They came together in an agony of passion, a frenzied clinging together in desire to make these last moments endure forever, to blot out the future and the past, to make *now* eternal. Without warning the door was flung wide, and Charlotte stood there surveying their nakedness in shaking fury. They were frozen to shocked immobility until she began to speak, spitting the words out as if they seared her tongue:

"*Adulterers.* I guessed as much: you think I haven't seen the looks, the half smiles, heard the quickened breathing when each speaks to the other? *Incestuous* adulterers. And *you*—whore—slut—strumpet—your ways haven't changed since you were a schoolgirl, have they?" Her eyes glittered as she viewed her sister's ripe body, still flushed with love, her hair tumbled about her shoulders, and Ann snatched up her shift to shield her nakedness from that burning, malevolent regard.

"What were you trying to do? Produce yet *another* bastard to join the two in the compound?"

Ann gasped, then went deathly pale.

Robert pulled on his breeches and stood up. He was shaken by the discovery but not dismayed. "What do you mean, Charlotte? What bastards?"

"One is your own—fathered on my body slave, Maria. You didn't know? You haven't met . . . your bastard mulatto son?"

He grasped her arm.

"What are you saying? Is this your distorted mind?"

" 'Tis sober truth, a likeness to you to proclaim to all the world," Charlotte said bitterly.

He stood stunned. "I have a son, a *son,* and all these years I was not told." He turned to Charlotte. "You said 'two bastards'?"

She laughed, her voice tinged with madness. "Indeed I did, but not yours, oh no, not yours . . . ."

"Then who. . . ." He turned wondering eyes on Ann who cried:

"Charlotte, I beg you . . . ."

"To spare you, sister? You steal my husband under my own roof and expect me to spare you? This woman —my sister—this whore—this harlot . . . ."

"Enough, Charlotte," Robert began, but she went on wildly:

"You don't know this woman you've been deceiving me with. . . . She lay with a slave when she was but sixteen . . . lay with him again and again and then persuaded me it was but once and that was rape. The child of the union is with yours in the compound." Charlotte stopped in her tirade, her breath coming raggedly, then went on with a compressed venom that was shocking in its mordancy: "Get out of my house, both of you, go to Vane, do what you will, but get from under my discredited, violated roof." She turned and left them as suddenly as she had come, and Robert went slowly to Ann where she huddled white-faced and silent on the rumpled bed.

"Is this true?" he asked in a strained voice.

She nodded mutely.

"How could you—give yourself like that?"

She came to life at the contemptuous wonder in his voice and flared:

"How different is it for me than for you? You had a liaison with Maria."

"The two cases are not comparable."

"Why not? What is normal and right for a man is not permitted in a woman?"

"It has ever been so."

"But, Robert, now that Charlotte knows . . . take me with you to Vane . . . I'll not go back to William. . . ."

"Take you to Vane? After what I've just heard? Get back to your husband . . . if he'll have you after he learns of this . . . as learn of it I'm sure he will."

She gazed at him in stunned horror, at this stranger who condemned her so harshly. "Robert, you don't mean it? You're sending me away when your—crime —is like to mine? All this happened so long ago, when we were both so young, I was little more than a child. . . . I love you, Robert, let me come with you to Vane." He stood silently unforgiving and she said at last in desperate pleading: "Where shall I go? Not here, not to Vane . . . and dear God, not east with William."

He looked at her coldly, all the love and passion of the last months forgotten, the tenderness and under-standing destroyed, and said in cruel calculation: "Why not go to Port Royal? You'll find many of your per-suasion there." He picked up the rest of his discarded clothing and left her.

For a while she sat immovable, dry-eyed. Then, as it grew darker outside and the small sounds of evening crept through the shutters, she dressed with clumsy movements and left the little room that had been a paradise and had turned so precipitately to the deepest pit of hell.

She went numbly from the house to the stables, her hair streaming wildly, her dress disordered, and sprang upon the back of the first horse she came upon. Dick Gough, just returned from the fields, called a warning: "Not Mr. Robert's Brown Boy, Mistress Ann, he's . . ." but the rest was lost on the air as she was gone, riding bare-back in an abandonment of grief, her hands entwined in Brown Boy's silken mane. Instinctively she took the track towards Vane, and Brown Boy thundered on, knowing the road and its idiosyncrasies. The sky darkened quickly as the sun dropped below the horizon, a sickly half moon swam in the green-gray bowl of the sky above, and still the miles between her and all that she held dear lengthened, when suddenly there came a thud of feet from the underbrush, a snapping of twigs and trampling of the long grass, and a huge wild boar stood in their path, his little evil eyes glinting redly in the feeble light of the moon. Brown Boy whimpered in startled fear, rearing up onto his hind legs. Ann felt her hold on him give; then, as he plunged, she was thrown violently over his head. She had time to experience surprise but not fear before all sensation, all thought, was blotted out. The boar, as startled as the horse, watched the girl's crumpled stillness for a moment, then turned back into the brush. Brown Boy quieted gradually, then gently nudged the still form, grotesquely twisted on the rough path. Getting no response, he began to crop the long sweet grasses that grew nearby.

The turmoil in Robert's breast subsided as the evening wore into night, his initial ungoverned disgust toward

Ann turning into disgust for himself. His last words to her brought a blush of shame to his cheeks—to say these words to his beloved Ann without giving her a chance to speak. Whatever she had been guilty of in the past, she was his love now, and he would claim her against all odds. He went quickly to her room, but it was empty: should he wait until she returned? Maybe she had gone to the nursery wing to take comfort in the company of her children. . . . At length he returned to his own room and spent a sleepless night, determined to take Charlotte at her word and leave Wells for Vane soon after dawn.

Before first light he went to Ann's room again, and a flash of fear shook him when he saw that her bed had not been slept in, the candle guttering and smoking as the light drowned in a pool of wax.

Where could she be? She wouldn't have stayed all night in the nursery wing. . . .

He hurried from the house, to be met by an agitated Dick Gough.

"Lord, Master Robert, sir, 'tis glad that I am to be seeing you. I marked Mistress Ann ride off west on your Brown Boy last evening. I called to her to stop, as Brown Boy's been something skittish these past days, but she paid me no heed. . . . Lord, sir, I knew I should've gone after her but . . . ."

"Get *on* with it, man. . . ."

"Sir, it grieves me to say the words, but just now . . . these five minutes gone . . . I see Brown Boy come back *alone.*"

West . . . toward Vane . . . toward the sanctuary of the place where they had known such happiness. Oh Ann, Ann my darling—I drove you to this. God save you're unharmed, and I'll spend my life in making amends for my cruelty.

They cantered out of Wells just as the sun rose

above the low foothills. The heat increased minutely as they went as fast as the track allowed, their long gray shadows going before them.

They were far into the deep bush when Gough reined suddenly. "Oh, God, look, sir." He pointed upward: in the innocent clarity of the blue morning sky a flock of black vultures wheeled, their great wings motionless as they drifted in the air currents, circling ever lower, nearer to their prey below.

As he thundered the last few yards that separated them, Robert groaned aloud as one of the vultures rose leisurely from the body, giving him a malevolent glare from yellow eyes and emitting an angry thwarted hiss. Robert flung himself from his horse and knelt beside her, refusing to believe that she was dead. But the angle at which she lay hammered home the truth. At first he thought that she had been unmarked by the vultures' tearing vicious beaks and rending talons, but then he saw the mutilation of her throat; the sight made his head spin and his stomach retch. Then he felt Dick Gough's arm steadying him and the rough consolation of his voice:

"Steady, sir. Steady, lad. Lord love you, lad, don't take on so. The little lady, she couldn't have felt or known a thing. Merciful quick, a broken neck. Lord, lad . . . don't . . . I beg you. . . ." His own voice broke with shocked grief.

The huge vultures were circling lower again, menacing in their silent approach, unafraid of the living, thwarted of their dead prey. Gough fired his pistol and wounded one of them. The others, canniballike, turned their rending talons on one of their own kind. Then Robert and Dick began the grim and dreadful task of covering her broken body and laying it carefully across one of the horses. And so began Ann Preston's last terrible journey back to Wells.

225

Robert raised his head and gazed at the burnished dome above him, and down through the years came an echo of Jez Davies' jeering voice:

"Weep, boy, weep. Look at the sun and weep for what you were and what you are."

What you were? Yesterday I was a lover, and now what am I? he asked himself bitterly. Nothing less than a murderer. And as the soft covered body jolted limply across the saddle before him, tears blinded him, falling hotly unchecked onto his clenched hands.

Part Four

1692-1703

One

Seth pushed the wide-brimmed woven straw hat off his forehead and wiped his brow with the back of his hand. Rivulets of sweat ran down his face, and his shirt and breeches clung damply to his body. He sat easily astride his brown mare as he rode beside Dick Gough on the morning round of the plantation.

" 'Tis plaguey hot, Master Gough," he said. "Not long after sunup, yet the heat as fierce as hell's own. I vow I smell the sulphur in the air."

Gough cast a sideway's glance at the young man beside him, marveling anew at the easy carriage and unselfconscious poise of the boy rescued these dozen years past from the slave compound. Strange, he thought, I always think of him as a boy, yet he's a man in body and mind. Aloud he said: "Aye, 'tis that, Master Seth. It's not liking the look of the sky. See yonder." He pointed to the east where the sky was obscured by a yellowish haze that seemed to eddy and writhe low on the horizon. Seth squinted his brilliant blue eyes in the direction and shook his head.

"Strange . . . not the sign of an approaching storm . . . but something strange and ill-omened."

They continued their rounds through the broad fields of young cane, noting that the toiling slaves were moving more slowly than usual in the heavy, humid, still atmosphere, their black backs and chests gleaming with sweat, yet neither felt the inclination to spur them on to greater efforts. The overseers' whips were silent, as if the exertion needed to wield them was too great in in the enervating heat. An enveloping lassitude hung over all; no bird sang, no dog barked, no cattle lowed or horse whinnied, and man himself was strangely silent.

The two horsemen passed through the cane fields and beyond to the citrus grove, where they found Robert Vane inspecting the new crop of limes and oranges.

"Good morning, father," Seth called.

" 'Morning, son. 'Morning, Dick. Yet I wonder just how good it is."

"What were we saying a moment ago: a smell of sulphur in the air."

Robert laughed. "Sulphur, eh? Think you the earth will open and we'll all be swallowed into everlasting damnation?"

His words brought back the memory of a morning long ago in Port Royal, when the crazy prophet proclaimed doom and damnation for all the inhabitants ... brought back a memory too of Philip . . . .

Philip had been silent for many years. That silence was broken by the unexpected arrival of a long letter from him, announcing that he now owned a small fleet of merchant ships that plied between England and Honduras, where he did a thriving business. He also declared that he would pay a visit to Vane Great-house this very month of June. Robert's eyes lit with pleasure at the thought of seeing his old friend again; then the pleasure turned to pride as he gazed at this son of his, a pride that never kindled for his younger son, Robert Matthew, born shortly after the death of Ann, these twelve years back. Matt, as he was called, was spoiled and wayward, indulged to excess by his mother, tolerated by his father. . . .

Robert returned his thoughts to the present as Seth said:

"Gough and I will tend the citrus, father. Why not go home and rest, this heat is unendurable."

"Unendurable for an old man of some forty-six summers, but endurable for a young one of twenty-four, eh, lad?"

"Not joyfully endurable, sir, but to be endured . . . for your sake."

Two pairs of blue eyes looked deep, each reflecting the profound bond between them, and Dick Gough sighed inwardly: Master Robert was piling up trouble by showing so blatantly his love and pride for this half-caste bastard son of his.

Robert accepted Seth's offer by a warm pressure of a hand on his shoulder, then wheeled his horse and cantered back to the house.

Dick Gough watched him go, his mind going back to that dreadful morning over twelve years ago . . . .

For a while he had feared for Robert's sanity. After the first outburst of grief he had gone about his duties mechanically, his face tinged with gray under his bronzed skin. But as the days of mourning lengthened into weeks, a fatalistic calm had possessed him, and when the pressure of work at the new plantation at Vane engrossed him, the pain lines about his mouth were not so noticeable, and at times his blue eyes would regain their old brilliance, until some chance remark, some memory which evoked Ann, would shutter him from the world again.

Robert was also overcome by memories that morning as he rode back to the house, his mind at first occupied by the sights and sounds of his thriving estate, then drifting to thoughts of Seth, this son whom he loved above both his lawful children. After the upheaval at Wells caused by Ann's tragic death had sub-

231

sided into a hushed acceptance of her loss, he had gone down to the slave compound and sought among the ever-growing child population for his son; but he had discovered him among the grown men in the first gang. The boy was twelve at the time, tall, well-muscled, bare-footed and dressed in the drab gray Osnaburg breeches of a slave, his hands calloused by wielding a heavy machete in the fields, his olive skin darkened still more by long hours spent under the pitiless sun, his eyes, exact replicas of Robert's own, a startling contrast. Robert had reined his horse and shooed away the myriad piccaninnies from the third weeding gang who had stopped work and clustered about him.

"Seth?" he called. "Come here, lad."

He felt a constriction in his throat as he called for the first time to this boy who was his son . . . his first-born.

Seth put down the heavy bill-hooked machete, wiped his hands on the seat of his breeches, and moved slowly toward Robert, a wary look in his eyes, mentally assessing what crime was worthy of reproof from Master Robert Vane himself.

"Yes, sir, Mas' Robert?" His voice, not yet deepened into its manhood register, had the lilt and rhythm of the compound, yet still had a quality which was pleasing to the ear.

"Follow me, Seth, I want to talk to you. Don't worry, you have done no wrong."

Robert let his horse loose to graze the rich grass and sat on a smooth river stone on the bank.

"Sit here, Seth."

Seth sat with reluctance, watchful.

Then Robert told him of his parentage, for even Maria was unknown to him now in the anonymity of the slave compound.

"Had you heard aught of this?" Robert asked at the end of his short recital.

"Mas' Robert?"

"Had you heard that you were my son? Did no one ever tell you this?"

Seth shook his head.

"Not but one time, when 'im say I has eyes like so, an' laugh."

Robert winced at the embracing neutral "im" and compound syntax.

"You understand now? I'm taking you from Wells to my new plantation in the west. There you will not work, either in the fields or in the house. Instead you will learn to read and write and . . ." "speak properly" he had nearly said, but he bit the words back in time.

"Mas' Robert . . ." Seth began, but Robert held up his hand.

"*Not* Mas' Robert. Not ever again. From now on you will call me 'Father.' "

The blue eyes misted suddenly with tears, and on an impulse Robert stood up and pulled the boy into his arms.

"My son," he murmured. "My son. . . . I'll try and make up to you for these twelve years of servitude."

He didn't need to imagine the boy's chaotic thoughts, he *knew* what he was feeling, he had experienced those same emotions himself when he had been liberated from the fields and the whip by Walter Wells . . . and yet not quite the same, for he was white and had known another life, while this boy, Seth, his son, was a mulatto, half white, half black, a bastard born into slavery, who had known no other life but the hardships of the compound.

Later he had given Seth into the care of Dick Gough with a quick word of explanation: "Care for him, Dick, until we leave for Vane. Have clothes made up at once as befitting my son. Meanwhile there is one other thing I have to do."

He sought out Maria in the linen room, where she had been sent to work after Ann's death. He spoke at length, watching the prematurely lined face and dull eyes with compassion. "And I will bring up the boy in his rightful position, as my son," he concluded.

Maria asked hesitantly: "But . . . what Miss Charlotte say?"

"Miss Charlotte will accept that which I decree," he said shortly. "Miss Charlotte has done enough damage in this matter by her silence. Why did you not tell me when I returned?" She kept silent, her eyes cast down. "Miss Charlotte threatened to send you to the fields?" She nodded. "I thought as much; because of the child, she sent you before, eh?"

"Yes." It was barely a whisper. "Not jus' because I has a pickney. Not till she met up wit' 'im an' see he blue eye."

"I'm sorry," he said inadequately. "If I'd known . . . but that's all past. Maria, I have to ask you something, but I want your word that you'll not mention the matter . . . not to anyone?"

She nodded, wide-eyed and oddly apprehensive. "Not one t'ing you say cross me mout'."

Still Robert hesitated: Ann had gone to her grave with a reputation unsullied in the eyes of her husband and her father, for the truth of the events which led to her death had been suppressed by himself and Dick Gough in tacit agreement, and not spoken of by Charlotte because of the shock and remorse she felt over her words and actions which had led directly to her sister's death. But he *had* to know . . . and Maria must have been one of those in attendance when Ann had been brought to bed.

"You knew—Miss Ann—" It was still painful even

234

to utter her name. "She had a child? The child in the compound?"

Maria's eyes flared wide with fear. "Me know nothin'," she began, "Miss Charlotte. . . ."

"Devil take Miss Charlotte," Robert exploded. "Tell me what you know or—mother of my son or not—I'll have you whipped." Even as he uttered the threat, he knew it was hollow: the fragile woman that Maria had become could never be whipped by *his* order, whatever her crime. She sensed this and smiled a little at the knowledge, then said at last: "Is true. . . . She . . . have a little girl-pickney."

"Then go to the compound and find her, take her to Master Gough's cabin. Have clothes made up for her, anything which she needs for a few weeks. And I have your word that you will keep silent on this matter. Maria?" As she turned to go, he added, "I—I am leaving Wells. Miss Charlotte may or may not join me at Vane. But . . . would you come with me and help me look after—our son—and Miss Ann's child?"

She seemed stunned for a moment, twisting her hands in the familiar gesture in her apron. Then she said with difficulty: "Me don' rightly know, Mas' Robert. Me has pickney here fe care . . . ." She stumbled on, her vocabulary not adequate to express what she instinctively knew to be best for her son and the least embarrassing for Robert. "Bes' that me stay, Mas' Robert, bes' fe do bwoy . . . and bes' fe I," she added sadly and not very convincingly.

And so he had left Wells accompanied by Seth and the seven-year-old daughter of Ann and Malachi. The child's eyes were so like Ann's, their startling silver-gray enhanced by the strange contrast of her dark chubby face, that Robert's heart lurched and twisted with pain at the sight of her. He brusquely told his father-in-law that he was taking two children from the

235

compound, offering no explanation, and Sir Walter only nodded heavily, drawing the obvious conclusion.

"Aye, lad, take them, take them. 'Tis a bad business —I'll miss you, Rob, lad, but 'tis best that you go— times change, and bitter memories take the place of remembered joy. . . ." He muttered and mumbled on incoherently, and even amid his own engulfing sorrow Robert felt pity for this shell of a once-robust man, for he had aged almost beyond recognition after the shock of Ann's death, and even Deborah's loving attention failed to rouse him from the near-stupor into which he had sunk.

The morning that he left Wells Robert went to Charlotte's room. She was pale and listless, still ravaged by grief and racked by guilt.

"As you requested," he said with formal irony, as if they were strangers, "I'm leaving for Vane, I'm taking my son with me—and—Ann's daughter." He paused, expecting vituperation, but she sat, apathetic, her swelling belly dominant in the thinness of her body. "If . . . you would like to join me, either now or after the child's born, you will be very welcome. Perhaps we can renew our life . . . on a basis of friendship . . . if nothing more."

The cold gray eyes flickered for an instant. "My place is here," she said distantly.

Now, a dozen years later, Robert entered the cool of Vane Great-house, his leather riding boots loud on the polished floors. Time had wrought the change that Ann had envisaged so many years ago, and the beautiful interior had gradually assimilated a gracious lived-in atmosphere, its furniture and hangings rich and in keeping with the house and the ever-growing prosperity of the plantation and ensuing wealth of the Vanes.

Charlotte Vane heard her husband's approach along

the wide veranda that overlooked the expanse of manicured lawns, dotted with huge gnarled cotton trees, and
rang a small hand bell to summon the serving of second
breakfast. She too had been plagued by memories as the
oppressive heat of the early morning increased. She
remembered vividly that today, June 7, was the eighth
anniversary since she had finally left Wells.

A week before that day, Walter Wells, never fully
recovered from the death of his youngest daughter,
had succumbed without a fight to a bout of the "shivering sickness," as the slaves termed malaria. As soon as
he had joined his first wife, son, and daughter in the
quiet cemetery, Deborah Wells had faced her step-
daughter and issued her ultimatum.

"You will leave Wells now that I am sole mistress.
I have sent word to your husband."

The words were spoken in her usual quiet way, but
with such an undertone of icy implacability that Charlotte went white to the lips.

"*Leave?* Wells is my home . . . my *son's* home. . . ."

"Wells is *my* home, which I hold for *my* son . . . the
new Sir Walter. I hold it in trust until he is old enough
to claim his heritage. You will do well at last to recog-
nize the facts and accept them, instead of clinging to
this fantasy you have cherished all these years. Go to
your real home and your husband."

This was the event for which Robert had hoped: this
was the blow that broke the carapace that had encased
her and made her blind to reality. And so he had
fetched her, their daughter, Bridget, and their son,
Robert Matthew, who had been born in the July following Robert's departure for Vane, whom he had
never seen until this day. Charlotte went with him
without argument, ashen-faced and silent, in numb
acceptance of this act of treachery by her stepmother.
Bridget was a lively five-year-old, excited and chatter-

ing at this unexpected change in her life, working her way into Robert's heart by her freely given affection and ready acceptance of him, while Matt, a stolid four-year-old, sat sullen and watchful against his mother, a look of distrust and active dislike in his flat gray eyes whenever he viewed his new-found father.

Lady Wells had said softly to Robert as he went to bid her goodbye:

"Cousin, forgive me . . . but I could not live in the same house as Charlotte now that Walter has gone. Sometimes . . . she acts so strangely . . . I feared . . . I feared that she might harm my son."

Robert nodded, his eyes troubled as he looked down at the soft plumpness of his iron-willed little cousin. "It seemed a harsh decree at first, cousin, but I see now it was necessary. Perhaps in the serenity of Vane she will recover . . . her reason . . . her perspective."

The first months were not easy. Charlotte had developed an intense antagonism toward Seth, now sixteen and markedly attached to his father. This antagonism was based on a fear that he was a threat to her own cosseted Matt and was heightened by the obviously deep bond between Robert and his eldest son. Over the years her obsessive love for Wells dwindled and a new obsession took its place: Vane . . . not for Vane itself—although in time she came to appreciate its beauty—but for the Vane that constituted the rightful heritage for Matt. This, she told herself, this could *not* be wrenched from him, this house, these ever-increasing rolling acres, this growing wealth, *all* . . . all would be Matt's. She began to instill in the boy an increasing awareness of his future power. This awareness developed into open arrogance, coupled with ignorance, for he was lazy both in mind and body. The children's tutor, Oliver Campion, a quiet competent youth for whom Robert had sought from many a consignment of indentured servants, at length complained to Robert.

"Sir, I can do nothing with Master Matt, he plays truant all the time. When he can be prevailed upon to attend lessons, he idles the time, is insolent when chided, and sets a bad example to the others. And Mistress Charlotte . . . .'"

"Encourages him? Do the best you can, lad. The boy needs a good thrashing to knock some of the nonsense out of him . . . but his mother indulges him overly. . . ." In such a manner Robert shrugged the matter off, although his conscience niggled that he was taking the coward's way out.

Over the years there had grown between Robert and Charlotte a tolerance that at times bordered on friendship. They had never resumed their sexual relationship, and Charlotte was indifferent to the occasional slave girl whom Robert took to his bed for a night or two: casual relationships that served only to assuage his bodily needs between long periods of celibacy, the periods growing yet longer as the demands of the growing estate absorbed all his energies, all his concentration.

Now Charlotte greeted him languidly, the unnatural heat sapping her usual unflagging vitality.

"You look exhausted, Robert, and the morning not yet over. 'Tis more than that we are getting old . . . there is something in the air today . . . we have had a number of earth tremors in the last few years, and it seems as if all were preceded by weather such as this." She went on, apparently inconsequentially, "Your friend Sir Philip Lonsdale arrives soon, doesn't he? He mentioned that he was accompanied by a friend, yet doesn't give the name?"

"No matter, 'twill be good to see him and good for us to have company. We live too much in isolation, despite the hundreds of souls who live and work at Vane. You have rooms ready?"

"Oh, yes, this week past, against an early arrival."

There sounded a slap of bare feet as Cibba, the head butler, came along the veranda, a heavily laden tray balanced on his curly head. As he raised his hands to lower it to the table, they heard a distant roll of sound, sonorous, unearthly, filling the high dome of the heavens, relentless in its majesty, coming ever nearer from the hills; it converged upon them from every quarter, from above and below. Then the house began to shake and undulate as the broad expanse of lawns rippled in the near noonday sun.

The three of them were petrified to immobility, then Cibba let out an animallike moan of fear as he completed transferring the tray to the table. Even as he had it safely down, the tremors increased and the fine delft ware careered onto the floor, scattering fruit and meats and splashing steaming chocolate over all.

"Lie flat on the floor, Cibba," Robert ordered. "Don't bother with the food. Charlotte, don't move."

The tremor decreased as the sound retreated back into the hills and to the depths from whence it came, but before they could collect their wits, another more forceful tremor began. The sounds crescendoed and before their eyes a huge fissure opened across the once immaculate lawns and snaked its way to the cane fields beyond, exposing a tangle of tree roots and once-buried boulders in its path. Then, even as they watched in fascinated awe, yet a third tremor growled its angry way in the wake of the second and miraculously the fissure closed, leaving a heaped swathe of tossed stone and unrooted fallen trees across the formerly smooth lawn.

The sounds gradually died, a brooding silence hung over the whole plantation, then Robert rose unsteadily

240

and helped Charlotte to her feet while Cibba, gabbling incoherent supplications and incantations to half-remembered gods, tried unsuccessfully with scrabbing fingers to salvage some of the scattered tableware and ruined breakfast.

Two

On that same morning, the morning of June 7, 1692, Sir Philip Lonsdale and his traveling companion came ashore from the ferry that had taken them from Port Royal to Passage Fort. As they made their way toward the stables to hire horses for the continuance of their journey, they paused on the crest of a rise to look back across the expanse of the great harbor to the thronging city on the tip of the curving spit of land.

"Aye, 'tis even more inglorious than I remember," Philip said, his drawl deepened over the passing years. "There has been more infamy in those few acres than in any other in Christendom, I'd wager—though Morgan, turned scourge of the pirates after being the greatest buccaneer of all time, did much in his span of office as lieutenant governor to purge the town. But to my mind the merchants and inhabitants are still licentious to a degree unknown before. Every man jack openly smuggles and engages in any illicit trade, however base, that will put more Spanish dollars or golden guineas in his purse."

His companion nodded. "And yet the buildings there are as fine as any one would find in Cheapside, the people dress in silks and satins to rival any gallant in Whitehall, and there is more gold and silver changing hands than in the 'Change. But, faith, I'll be glad to leave it far behind me." His voice changed from a tone of mild censure to one of alarm. "God in heaven, look, Philip, 'tis like the day of judgment."

They watched in stupefied silence as the quiet hills erupted into rumbling sound and the immovable craggy peaks shimmered and danced against the sultry cloudless sky. Then the city, which they had so recently left, seemed to be lifted by a giant up-thrusting hand and tossed into the air before being dropped like scattered building blocks that sank into the boiling, churning sea. They felt the shock waves approach and were flung to the ground, which shook and trembled beneath them like a huge monster waking from subterranean sleep. From the stables came the high whinney of terrified horses, uncalmed by fearful exhortations from the equally terrified grooms. As the sounds and tremors diminished, they raised themselves cautiously to a sitting position and gazed once more across the harbor, just as a huge tidal wave swept toward the stricken city, the wreckage of small craft on its crest, and engulfed what little was left. As they watched dumbfounded, the wave receded and came surging across the harbor toward them, spending most of its fury across the six-mile expanse. They held their ground, certain that they were high enough above sealevel to avoid its destructive path.

"If we had gone by sea to Savanna-la-Mar as we at first intended, I doubt we had lived to see this," Philip murmured. "God rest their damned souls, not many lives in Port Royal can have been saved this day."

They turned at length from contemplating the pitiful remains of the once gay and wicked city, their senses bemused and minds shocked with horror at the cataclysm and set about the belated arrangements for continuing their journey. Eventually, after many hours of patient cajoling, together with the promise of double

243

the normal charge, they managed to procure horses. The poor beasts were still in a lather of sweat, rolling their eyes and emitting little whinnies of fright, but Philip's careful coaxing and gentle bullying succeeded in calming down three, and they persuaded an ostler to act as their guide.

They passed through scenes of devastation. Huge fissures where none had been hours before opened dangerously at every turn; trees and shrubs lay scattered, their roots already drying in the heat; great clefts and rifts could be seen in the mountains across the plain, while giant smooth river stones had been hurled from their wet beds and tossed like marbles onto dry land; and the course of many a river and stream had been recoursed by the upheaval.

The journey took them all of ten days, for in many places they had to make wide detours through untrod forest, their guide hacking a way with his machete. And so it was not until the evening of June 17 that they sighted Vane Great-house.

They set foot to spur in a renewed burst of energy now that their goal was within their reach. The driveway to the Great-house wound upward, a gentle curving climb for about a mile. The grounds were like rolling parkland, with sweeps of smooth lawns, kept closely trimmed by an army of slaves wielding with precise dexterity the ubiquitous machete. Huge trees dotted the emerald turf; the gnarled and knotted roots of giant spreading cotton trees, the many-rooted ficus, and the graceful umbrella spread of the newly introduced poinciana—the *arbol de fuego,* as the Spanish called it—in full glory of crimson petals.

A runner must have sped ahead to warn of their approach, for as they passed through high, delicately wrought iron gates set in a towering cut-stone wall, adorned with the Vane crest and motto, into the domestic gardens where many shrubs and vines spilled color everywhere . . . much as Ann had envisaged so many years ago . . . they were met by a welcoming party of three riders: Robert, Seth, and Matt. Robert and Philip sprang from their horses simultaneously and clasped hands with unashamed emotion.

"You've hardly changed," Robert said in wonder.

And indeed, except for a few silver hairs among the long blond hair drawn back and tied at the nape of his neck, a slight thickening of the jaw line, and a deeper crease from nose to mouth, Philip looked scarce a year older than when they parted. Though the long scar over his right eye had become less noticeable with the passage of years, it still quirked his brow in a sardonic twist.

"*You* have, a typical prosperous West Indian planter," Philip said lightly, and patted the growing paunch that was the trade mark of the plantocracy. He noted, too, the slightly puffy features and small broken facial veins, signs of the heavy drinker. He sighed inwardly but made no comment. "But come, we must not just gaze at each other like young lovers with naught but bedding in their minds: meet my fellow traveler."

Robert turned to greet the man who had quietly descended from his mount while he and Philip appraised each other. Recognition mixed with incredulity played across his face. He saw a man short and thickset, with a compact solid body and gray hair left unfashionably like Philip's in its natural state, unadorned by a wig. Under it were inscrutable dark brown eyes.

"*Hugh Russell* . . . as I live, I am joyed beyond measure that *you* are the mysterious traveling companion. S'life, Philip, why did you not tell me?"

" 'Twould have robbed me of the sight of that look of unbelief and childlike wonder on your face, which I had feared had gone forever." Philip's drawl deepened laughingly, and Robert was swept back by a flood of memories to those years they had spent together . . . as pirates aboard the *Juanita,* waiting out their time on St. Kitts . . . when that drawling voice had teased and coaxed him through many a depressing hour. It was difficult to believe that this dusty and travel-stained but fashionably dressed London dandy could ever have swarmed aboard a Spanish merchantman, brandishing a cutlass and screeching a blood-thirsty battle call . . . .

He recalled himself to the present. "The joy of seeing you both has driven my manners away. May I present my sons: Seth, my eldest, and Matt."

Philip's eyes narrowed as he took note of Seth's dark skin, dramatic contrast to the brilliant blue eyes, of Matt's pallid face with the cold gray eyes and the flash of something like anger in their depths when Robert gave precedence to Seth, but he shook hands gravely with each, refraining from even a twitch of an eyebrow as his eyes met Hugh's as they remounted.

They cantered the rest of the way to the house, Philip and Hugh making appreciative comments all the way, and were greeted at the top of the graceful double stairway by Charlotte, angularly elegant in pale blue muslin, her hair—once so silvery blonde, now silvery gray—drawn back in a neat chignon, a prim lace cap framing her face. Behind her was Bridget Vane, now twelve years old, with her father's brown hair and a more feminine version of the Vane nose. The third member of the group was a dark slim girl of about eighteen or twenty, her face round and dimpled, her hair caught back in close black curls that only just avoided being crinkly; but it was her eyes which made Philip's pale blue ones widen in admiration, for they were of a gray like new-minted Spanish pieces of eight, shining and luminous, set in the burnished teak of her face.

He became aware of Robert's voice: "My wife, Charlotte."

"You are very welcome, Sir Philip," Charlotte murmured in her clear crisp voice, with more warmth than Robert had heard for a long time. Philip swept a bow as if to a queen and kissed her outstretched hand.

"My daughter Bridget."

"Mistress Bridget, my pleasure."

Bridget folded her lips to hide her smile as she dropped a curtsey, these elegant manners from Whitehall a source of wonder in the isolation of Vane.

"And—my niece—Sarah."

He held the soft dark hand to his lips a moment longer than necessary, and the lambent gray eyes gazed deep into his before she veiled them with a flutter of thick curling lashes and sank in a low curtsey before him.

Again Philip flashed a puzzled glance at Robert. He hadn't missed the slight hesitation before the introductory "my niece" or the simultaneous tightening of Charlotte's lips. Two mysteries in as many moments, he thought lightly. Rob's life would not seem to have been dull in this backwater.

The huge dining table was loaded with every kind of fish and fowl and roasted meats. Philip's appetite left him completely, though Hugh waded through every dish offered and drank copiously of the accompanying sangaree and French and Spanish wines, appreciating that each goblet was immediately topped to the brim after a few sips.

"You're not eating, Philip, is it not to your taste?" Robert asked.

"A most lavish repast," Philip replied evasively. "I can see now how you planters increase your girths if this is an example of the board you keep."

Charlotte said in her crisp, dry, asexual voice: "You

247

must forgive the lack of ceremony, Sir Philip, we usually dine at about five, the hour is now late and we felt you would be more content with a simple repast. . . ." She stopped in some confusion at his quickly suppressed quirk of amusement.

"Forgive my ill manners, Mistress Charlotte, but a repast such as this would be termed lavish in the England of William and our good Mary."

That England seemed in another world to this. He felt himself hemmed in by the soft flickering candles throwing grotesque shadows into the high dark-wood tray ceiling and into the far corners of the big room, turning the heavy mahogany furniture into crouching monsters with evil intent. He was seized and held by a swift depression.

". . . did you fare?"

"I beg your pardon?" He jerked his mind from introspections and turned his eyes to Robert.

"I asked how you fared in the tremors that swept from the east these some days past?"

For the rest of that long repast Philip and Hugh recalled the terrifying sight of a city's disappearance, the great tidal wave which followed, and the vast rifts in the terrain coming westward. In the telling Philip lost some of the sense of unreality that had engulfed him earlier.

His hearers listened in shocked silence, then Robert said thoughtfully: "I had no conception of the extent of the disaster. The whole of Port Royal *gone* . . . just like that?"

"As far as we could judge from across the harbor . . . the old prophet was right after all."

"It seems we were luckier than we at first thought. Part of the north cane piece has a great fissure, the water mill was razed, but the mule-driven mill was unscathed. Minor rifts such as those in the lawn were soon filled and returned to normal. 'Twill take days for accurate reports to get to the capital, and if any part of Port Royal is still above sea level, and any citizen left alive, there will be looting and other types of lawlessness, I wager."

"There was precious little left of the capital itself," Hugh said. "Great heaps of rubble and signs of disaster everywhere."

Philip and Hugh rode around the property each day, learning the many facets of plantation life, that microcosm complete in itself. Hugh was intrigued with the crushing sheds and the distilleries, declaring that this was the greatest change from his former drab lawyer's life as could be imagined. Philip's lips tightened to a thin line of disapproval when shown the jail house with its chains and iron ankle and wrist cuffs, the noisome cubby hutches that were used for solitary confinement. He wrinkled his nose at the fetid odor of human excrement, sweat, and blood . . . chillingly reminiscent of those long months he had spent in the hold. . . .

"Is it not possible," he asked with enforced calmness, "to run a plantation on more—humane—lines? Is it necessary to employ such harsh methods of punishment?"

Charlotte turned cool, slightly amused, and scornful eyes on him.

"Necessary? My dear Philip, it is imperative. We at Vane are noted for indulgence . . . too much so, to my way of thinking. My husband will have it so, and refuses to punish at times when 'tis folly not to."

"I will change that when I am master of Vane," Matt interposed with such an undercurrent of adult venom that Philip felt as if he had been physically assaulted. He turned to look at this twelve-year-old boy who rode beside his mother, noting the too-plump flabby body, the pouchy pallid face under non-descript brown hair, the cold slate-gray eyes, and wondered how Robert could have fathered such a child. He looked back to Charlotte, expecting her to utter some reproach for his uncouth behavior and ill-chosen words, but she was regarding the boy with amused, warm indulgence.

"Let us hope that you will not be master of Vane for many a long year," Philip said as coldly and sharply as manners allowed. "Your father is in his prime and looks to be in excellent health." Even as he spoke, he felt a sharp twinge of doubt, remembering the puffy look about Robert's features, the slightly blood-shot eyes. He heard with scarce-concealed disgust the boy's cheerful reply:

"No one lives overlong in this climate. . . . I've heard many of my father's friends say so."

Philip reined his mount abruptly. "Excuse me, Mistress Charlotte, I will return to the house if you will forgive me. I find the—heat—excessive this morning."

When Hugh spoke of the island as a paradise, Philip was quick to challenge him.

"*Paradise?* Have you not seen the hundreds of black backs bent in the fields? The loathesome jail house and the stocks set under the blazing sun? Nor yet heard the whistle and whine of the driver's whip?"

"We have jail houses and stocks in England . . . even if not under such a blazing sun, sometimes amid freezing snow. . . . We have those and worse. Because you do not see them daily and are not so conscious of their use, you disregard them."

"But these men and women are slaves, man, each one bound to another's whim for life."

Hugh sighed and wiped his fingers delicately on a

250

fine white napkin; this was a familiar theme with Philip. He'd grown accustomed to these impassioned tirades over the years, and once again he produced his usual arguments:

"You have to accept the system, Philip. Long ago you learned that one man cannot fight it. You do nothing but tear your emotions to shreds for a useless cause. How much more so are these people slaves than the English peasants, themselves not so long removed from serfdom? They live in wretched huts and are in danger of being hung for stealing a loaf of bread to feed their starving children. These people are better off than thousands of so-called free English men and women: they work . . . all right . . . but they are housed, they have food issued each day, clothing for their backs. These islands of the West Indies depend on slaves for survival, for sugar is a hard master and demands the payment of long hours' work, and white men cannot pay that price. As long as sugar is the principal crop . . . and it will be long beyond our time . . . then slaves will be necessary to tend it."

Philip folded his lips in angry silence. His faith in Robert was somewhat renewed when he noted the worry and care he took over his workers, but his hatred of the system remained unshaken.

About a week after their return, Robert asked Hugh Russell to his study and shut the door carefully.

"You practiced law before you went in with Philip in the shipping business?"

"Oh, yes, for many years. It's only this six months past I've been with Philip. I changed my profession, wisely I hope. Life in England is not what it was. . . . 'Twas well enough in Charles' day, and tolerable under Jamie. . . . but s'life, after the revolution of eighty-eight and the coming of Dutch William, I was glad to get out for a few months each year . . . though he does well enough, I suppose," he added grudgingly. "Why do you ask?"

Robert frowned. "I have a problem which I hope you will help me solve," he said slowly. "Though to my mind 'tis well nigh insoluble." He paused and gazed around at the paneled walls, at those woods of various tones and textures which Ann had loved, then began to speak in a low, unemotional voice, carefully controlled, as if he feared to express his true feelings. As Hugh listened, his own brow creased into a frown: his doubts and nebulous suspicions of the last few weeks were being justified and confirmed.

Three

There was many a long conference held in the privacy of Robert's study between himself and Hugh Russell during the following days. Then one morning he announced that they had business to conduct in St. Jago.

"Perhaps you would care to accompany us, Philip?"

Hugh laughed at the suggestion. "I wager he would rather stay and conduct a little business of his own, eh, Phil?"

To Robert's surprise, Philip flushed like a schoolboy. "For a lawyer, you're remarkably open-mouthed," he said mildly to Hugh. " 'Tis not urgent, Rob, a matter I would discuss with you on your return."

Robert nodded, only a little curious, his own worries absorbing his attention.

They were away for two weeks, and the day after their return to Vane, Robert summoned Seth to his study. To his concern, the young man's usually open and relaxed expression was replaced by one of closed tautness.

"Does aught ail thee, lad?"

Seth hesitated then said quickly: "Aye, father. My position here at Vane daily becomes more difficult. I am . . . neither one nor the other . . . neither black nor white nor master nor slave."

Robert frowned. "What has chanced whilst I was away?"

Seth was silent, his large, well-shaped hands clasped between wide-apart knees, his bowed head concealing the anguish in his eyes.

"I'll tell you how it's been," Robert went on. "My lady wife, Mistress Charlotte, has heaped as many insults on your head as she dared, and Master Matt has been his usual insufferable taunting self, with his constant reiteration of the changes *he* will make when *he* is master of Vane. Am I not right?"

"Sir . . . I thought you were unaware . . ." Seth began.

"Unaware of the position? Nay, lad . . . only too aware, and it has grieved me beyond measure. I have sought to rectify the situation as far as I am able. With the help of Master Russell and a reputable notary in St. Jago, these past two weeks I have had papers of manumission drawn up for you . . . and for Sarah. Before this, you were both slaves in the eyes of the law, although I have tried all these years to blot that fact from your minds and treat you as my dear son and niece. From now on you are a free man, equal to all throughout the land. Your name is now by deed Vane, and . . . well, there is another matter which we will deal with in due course."

Seth closed his eyes against the onrush of tears, and Robert rose swiftly and put his arm about his son's shoulders. "Cry, lad, cry if you want. 'Tis not unmanly to shed tears when one hears such news."

After a while Seth said in a choked voice: "Father . . . I have no words to thank you, but : . . will this change very much? There is still my color."

"That is something I cannot change, and it is small comfort to you now that I believe that the time will come when there will be more men of your color in important positions in this island than of mine. It is up

254

to you to make men, of any color, any race, proud to know you."

After Seth had gone to fetch Sarah, Robert sat for a long time at his desk, the slanting rays of the swiftly dropping sun picking out the silver in his hair. He could still hear Seth's voice: "There is still my color." And *I,* he thought bitterly, condemned him to be a prisoner of his skin. I was the instrument to make a man cry out so bitterly. And he thanked me for giving him his freedom: I, who made him a slave, a child conceived unknowingly, a child born into slavery and unacknowledged for a dozen years. . . . *And he thanked me.* . . . For once Robert understood Philip and his hatred of slavery. . . .

He shook off this feeling of compassion as the practical side of his nature took over: the plantation owner needed slaves to run a property. The analogy between *his* son and those hundreds of anonymous workers just didn't exist, not any more—that piece of paper lodged in his secret wall compartment proclaimed the difference: he had banished the haunting fear that had attended him these many months past that in the event of his death his beloved son Seth was in danger of being sold . . . and he was under no illusion that that would not happen. Seth, his first-born, was now "one of us," not "one of them"! By the time a timid knock on the door announced Sarah's arrival, his usual placid mask was in position, showing no trace of the turmoil of his recent thoughts.

He looked up in delight as she entered. She wasn't beautiful in the accepted European conception of beauty: her nose was too flat and broad, her hair had too close a curl; her eyes, so lovely in themselves, were alien in her dark face, giving a sense of shock at first sight; but to Robert she was beauty undimmed, she was Ann's daughter, all that remained of Ann except the memories he still cherished, and those were Ann's eyes that looked at him, wide and slightly apprehensive at the unexpected summons.

"You sent for me, Uncle Robert?" Her voice was light and lilting, without the drawl she had had when he took her from the compound. He pushed aside the heaped parchments in front of him.

"Come in, child, and sit down."

She sat on a stool of tooled Spanish leather, studded with gilt nails, the legs of intricately carved ebony. Her pale pink muslin skirt swirled gracefully into folds, her hands were folded primly in her lap.

He thought back to that day when Maria had brought her from the compound, a thin child of seven, her hair in a myriad little plaits. Her feet were bare and she was clad only in a rough Osnaburg smock, overlarge and frayed.

"What is your name, child?" he had asked.

She flashed scared gray eyes at him, then hung her head and twisted one grubby foot behind the other.

"What is she called, Maria?"

" 'im pickney-mumma call 'im Juba, Mas' Robert."

"H'm, well, we'll have to change that."

And so Sarah she became and went to Vane with Robert and Seth. There she was put in the care of Susan Grafham.

Susan was a quiet-voiced girl from Sussex who had come to the island to marry her childhood sweetheart only to find him dead of the yellow fever when she arrived. As nursery companion to Sarah, she had shown the child how to give and receive affection, to laugh and play, and gradually to shed the fear that her new life was only temporary and to reassure her that she was not to be thrust back into the maelstrom of compound life. From Susan, too, Sarah acquired poise and good manners, while from Oliver Campion she learned to read and write and lose the slipshod speech she had used from babyhood.

Now she grew uneasy under Robert's intense scrutiny, until at last he said:

"Forgive me, my child, my mind wanders into the past. Did Seth say aught of that which I have to say to you?"

"No, Uncle Robert."

"I—we at Vane—do not often mention the circumstances surrounding your birth and parentage, though you are acquainted with the facts, aren't you?"

She nodded, then he was amazed at the amount of bitterness she injected into her usually soft voice: "Oh yes, I could not but be aware of the facts. Child though I was, brought up in the anonymity of the compound, where half the children never knew their mothers, let alone their fathers, and were looked after by a 'pickney-mumma' who maybe had a dozen other foster children to care for, I cried myself to sleep many a night for the mother who abandoned me. . . ."

"No, she didn't *abandon* you, you were taken from her. She was hardly more than a child herself when you were born and had no choice in the matter. Over the years she knew nothing of you, not even your sex or if you were still alive."

"But . . . I heard tell once she visited the slave nursery and saw me. . . . Sometimes I seem to remember her, so beautiful all in white, and . . . when I went toward her . . . she thrust me off . . . pushed her own child from her . . . and ran. . . ."

Robert sat silent, his whole being wanting to defend Ann, yet engulfed in a vast compassion for this child who would hold the memory of her mother's repudiation of her and betrayal of her motherhood until time dulled the sharp edges of truth and softened the heartache.

"We have tried to make up for all that. . . ."

"*You* have . . . but . . . ."

"I know, I know, child. Mistress Charlotte finds it hard to show compassion to the innocent or forgiveness to the guilty. But now I have something to say which I hope will make you happy."

Sarah's eyes were shining as she left Robert's study. She almost danced along the veranda, unseeing, and ran full tilt into Philip. He caught her before the sharp impact made her lose her balance.

"Why, Mistress Sarah, your eyes are like the evening star, gloriously doubled. You appear like radiance personified. What has chanced to make you so happy?"

His hands tightened about her waist as the thought unbidden crossed his mind: *a man* . . . only a man's declaration of love, a welcome declaration . . . could bring such radiance to a maid's face. He was appalled at the wave of jealous dismay that swept through him.

Her eyes widened at his expression. "Why, Sir Philip, I thank you for saving me from a fall due to my indecorous haste . . . but 'tis not seemly to hold me so."

"What makes you so happy?" he asked intently.

"I will tell you only if you release me."

"Would to God I need never release you," he burst out, then drew her closer to him and kissed her parted lips. After the first startled movement of rejection, she responded in a way that brought a surge of delight to Philip, banishing his former suspicion.

"Walk with me to the mill stream," he urged.

" 'Twill soon be dusk. . . ."

"No matter . . . come. Please, Sarah, there is so much I want to tell you, and I feel eyes on us in the house," he implored, a schoolboy with his first love.

And she, heady with her new freedom and this unexpected encounter, agreed.

"I am quite serious, Rob. I love the girl and she returns my love, despite the great difference in our ages. I meant to speak to you before I spoke to her, but fate ... or the god of love ... planned otherwise."

"Philip, you leave me speechless, though I must find words to answer you. Have you thought what this means in terms of your future life? Or are you too besotted to have envisaged the future?"

"In what way?"

"The only way that matters, man, in such a liaison. I love Sarah as if she were my own daughter, but how think you she will be received in *England?* Oh, I know that there are many Blackamoors in England, but they are tolerated because they are nothing more than fashionable whims of a certain type, a passing caprice ... but a dark-skinned *wife,* born a slave ... a *bastard,* for Sir Philip Lonsdale, the fourth baronet? She would be an object of curiosity at first which would quickly wane and become indifference or, worse, scorn. I cannot allow Sarah to suffer this. ..."

"Wait, Rob, wait. Besotted I am, I agree, but not bereft of my wits. I foresaw all those difficulties you enumerate ... and possibly more. I would not consider subjecting Sarah to the snubs and insults of London society. I am prepared ... nay, happy, to settle here. Buy a small property ...."

"Settle *here?*" Robert exclaimed. *"You* of all people to act the weathervane? So all your fine ideals regarding slavery have been consumed in the fires of love, eh?"

"Not so," Philip said sharply, nettled by Robert's tone. "I shall buy a small property with land enough to support the household in meat and produce. I shall buy slaves to staff it . . . but they will be freed immediately and paid wages. . . ."

"God, man, you'll be hounded from the island as a bad influence."

"Why?"

"To buy slaves for labor and *free* them . . . how will this affect the other estates? We'll all have our slaves clamoring for freedom. . . ."

"I don't see why it should affect other estates adversely. I shall not plant sugar or any other profitable commodity, I shall not be in competition in any way with the other planters. We are too isolated one property from another for the intelligence to circulate quickly. How does my plan differ from that of a planter freeing a slave for any other reason?"

"The numbers primarily."

"The numbers will be vastly less than those on a sugar plantation."

Robert sat silent, thinking of the papers of manumission he had had drawn up for Seth and Sarah. . . . But that, he argued, was completely different.

"Well, Rob?"

Robert looked at Philip's set face and realized that to argue further was useless. "What about your shipping company?"

"Hugh will deal with the English end. I will find me some land hard by the harbor at Savanna-la-Mar, and my ships can put in there. I can make an occasional trip to Honduras. 'Twill work well. Come Rob, don't play the heavy . . . *uncle* . . . with me. I love Sarah, and I'll make her happy."

Robert capitulated with a sudden smile.

"Of course I give my consent, and I wish you all the happiness in the world, but first you should know her history. . . ." He outlined the story of Ann and Malachi as briefly as possible, ending with his recent manumission and legal adoption of Sarah. "So she is now in truth Mistress Sarah Vane . . . and not a nameless brat from the compound."

Philip was silent for a long moment, then stated rather than asked:

"You loved Ann, didn't you? The pain in your eyes as you speak of her tells me so."

"God help me, I loved her more than life itself . . . and I sent her to her death. . . . Both memories are with me always."

It was decided after much discussion and amid conflicting opinions and personal views as to the correct procedure, that a ball would be held at Vane, ostensibly to introduce Philip and Hugh to the leading families of the island, in reality to announce the engagement of Sarah and Philip.

Charlotte was white-lipped with rage when she was told of Robert's act in freeing Seth and Sarah and legally adopting them.

"What can you be thinking of? To bring the bastards into the house in the first place and treat them as you have done was insult enough to me, but to elevate them to a status comparable with your own lawful children . . . my mortification will be complete. And *now* you propose to launch them into island society . . . we'll be the scorn and laughing stock of . . . ."

"Enough, Charlotte. No insult was intended nor given to you. Rather, you should be humble and grateful that some of the wrongs committed so long ago are to be righted . . . however late."

"What do you mean?"

"Must I put it into words? It has always been beyond my comprehension that you, once so gentle in manners and thoughtful for others, could harshly send your own sister's child into that huddle of humanity in the compound and leave her there for seven years without a thought to her welfare. You knew that my son was there . . . I cannot blame you for that . . . but to keep me in ignorance of his existence all those years. . . . I had vowed not to reproach you with this, but your attitude has forced me to do so. We will not argue. You will give the ball, and let society think what it chooses."

Four

It was eventually decided that the ball would take place late in November, when the autumn rains had ended and the days and nights were somewhat cooler. Invitations to every prominent prosperous family were sent out, some taking three weeks or more to reach remote plantations. Among them were three to Wells for Lady Wells, young Sir Walter, and Melissa. Charlotte was mutinous on this point, but once more Robert overruled her.

"I swore that that woman would never know the shelter of this roof."

"Not only will she know the shelter of the roof, she will receive the courtesy of the mistress of the house."

"Why I declare, cousin, I've not seen such elegance since I left England," Deborah Wells exclaimed as Robert lifted her down from her mount.

"It has gained an added elegance with your presence," Robert replied gallantly as he turned to assist Melissa. He looked down at her with appreciation: she was small like her mother and had her large, soft, deceptively innocent brown eyes, but her brow and chin were all Wells. She was sixteen now and, although no beauty, had a promise of great charm and a forceful personality. He bowed over her hand.

"Welcome to Vane, Mistress Melissa. And this must be Walter?"

"Yes, sir." Walter vaulted lightly from his filly and took Robert's outstretched hand.

Robert warmed to the boy at once. At twelve he was taller than either his mother or sister and promised to be taller than his father had been. He had the hooded, keen eyes of Sir Walter, which held a frank intelligent gaze as he looked up at Robert.

"I am very pleased to be your guest at Vane, sir. I hope you will find time to show me the whole estate. I would like to compare your methods of sugar production with ours at Wells. . . ."

"I think that is enough of the subject for the moment, Walter," Deborah rebuked gently. "Master Vane has other guests to attend to."

"Yes, mama. My apologies, sir, but I have so much to learn if I am to run Wells properly."

Robert's eyes crinkled with amused respect at the boy's earnestness and adult manner.

"I doubt not that when the time comes you will do admirably," he assured him. "My sons will gladly show you around . . . after you have rested and washed the dust of the journey from your person."

Robert privately thought that his son Matt, lazy, insolent and arrogant, would have nothing in common with his . . . his what? . . . what relationship was there between the two boys? His second cousin on Robert's side, stepbrother on Charlotte's side. . . . How these island relationships tend to become complex, he thought wryly, and probably more so as the years go by.

Later that day the Prestons arrived from St. Jago de la Vega. Ann's two former lumpish sisters-in-law had now grown into even lumpier matrons. Their red-faced, hard-drinking planter husbands and a brood of loutish offspring accompanied them.

That evening the dinner table was laden with food and drink, and talk and laughter spilled out across the garden. Charlotte sat smiling at one end, though she cast an occasional anxious glance at her young step-mother as each dish was presented. Her own house-keeping is faultless, she will surely try to find fault with mine, she thought, oh *why* did Robert insist on her presence? But Lady Wells' whole attention was centered on Philip Lonsdale on her right. She listened intently to his easy talk of London and his travels to Honduras, her large brown eyes fixed limpidly on his expressive face.

Oh-ho, Robert thought from his end of the table, my lady cousin-cum-stepmother-in-law has designs on old Philip. She'll not be pleased when she learns that such a valuable prize is bespoke. He glanced down the table at Sarah, but she was talking animatedly to the young Sir Walter. Then his glance roamed to Seth across the table next to one of the former Preston girls. Seth had no need to engage in dinner-table small talk, for his companion was concentrating all her attention on her heaped plate, and he was free to fix his deep blue eyes on the demure figure of Melissa immediately opposite him, the expression in their depths plain for all to read. Robert felt a surge of affection: the boy's fallen in love . . . now how is Deborah going to like *that?* Even as he watched, Melissa raised her eyes and met Seth's gaze. She seemed to stop breathing for a moment, then flashed him an enchanting smile . . . a smile of recognition, of acceptance of his homage. No one else seemed to have noticed the silent scene, and after that first explicit look Melissa drooped her long-lashed lids and turned to Hugh Russell on her left, while Seth made a valiant effort to engage his gluttonous companion's attention on something other than food.

At twenty-four Seth had led a blameless life, sublimating his natural urges in long hours of work. Averse to forming an alliance with a slave girl, he had been barred from forming an alliance with any other—until now. Despite the obstacles that were undoubtedly in his way, his heart clamored in his breast at the promise in Melissa's smile, and his thoughts ran ahead unchecked.

Early in the morning on the day of the ball, Seth, Matt, Walter, and William and John Preston went on a conducted tour of the plantation, glad to get away from the last frenetic preparations for the gala event. Matt had been reluctant to leave his bed, but pride urged him to be present. He had developed a sharp antagonism toward Walter and wanted to impress him with the superiority of Vane over Wells. But Walter kept by Seth's side, asking intelligent and probing questions, to which Matt was quite incapable of supplying the answers, although this didn't prevent him from making foolish irrelevant interpolations, to the ill-concealed amusement of the Preston boys, older than Matt by one and two years respectively and obviously well-versed in the law of cultivation. At length Walter said innocently: "Your knowledge of sugar cultivation is not very great, is it, cousin Matt? Not that that is necessary though, as cousin Seth has so much understanding and experience."

Matt's slaty eyes glinted. "I think my knowledge will be adequate when there is need for it. I shall employ a good overseer, and that will be all that is required."

266

"*You* will, cousin? And what do *you* say to that, cousin Seth?"

Seth bit his lip.

"Walter . . . I do not think you understand the position. . . ."

"What is there to understand? You are the heir to Vane, therefore . . . ."

"*I* am the heir to Vane," Matt broke in, his pasty cheeks flushed with anger, and spurred his horse to Walter's side.

"But . . . ." Walter's usual poise deserted him at the venom in Matt's voice, and he looked uncertainly from Seth's embarrassed face to Matt's, rendered bloated and blotchy by ungoverned temper.

"I will explain later," Seth began, but Matt went on regardless of any feelings but his own:

"Vane is *mine*. Seth . . . *Seth* is but a *slave* . . . whatever anyone says. That he lives in the house and wears fine clothes and eats with us at table cannot change that fact. I would sell him tomorrow, was it possible. Vane is mine . . . and my mother says that by right Wells too should be mine . . . 'twas usurped. . . ."

"*Enough.*" Seth had paled under the vicious verbal attack from his young half-brother, but now he cut in commandingly: "Enough, Matt, these are not the words and manners to use before a guest. *Enough*, I say. *Return to the house.*"

For a moment Walter feared that the younger boy would bring his riding crop across Seth's face; his knuckles were white as he gripped it, but at length his eyes dropped before the brilliant blue anger in Seth's, and without another word he wheeled his horse sharply about, cutting the soft mouth with cruel force as he jerked violently on the reins, and galloped back toward the house.

267

"I am sorry for that display," Seth said quietly, though his eyes still burned with anger. "Matt has been spoiled and cosseted by his mother, and his mind is filled with grandiose ideas. But it is true," he added. "He is the heir to Vane."

Walter regarded him from hooded brown eyes, their expression too adult and understanding for a boy of his age.

"And . . . was the rest true?"

Seth smiled a trifle bitterly. "You have eyes to see me as I am. 'Tis true I was born into slavery, but . . . 'tis not known by all yet . . . my father has freed me. *Legally* I am the equal of any man."

Walter was silent for a long moment, while the young Prestons watched in embarrassed curiosity. Then he said quietly: "It cannot be an easy life for you, cousin Seth. For all that you are a better man than Matt will ever be . . . and I am proud to call you cousin. Now that we have got rid of Matt, we can begin to enjoy this tour. Race you to the end of the cane walk."

The strains of music floated out across the rolling lawns to the slave quarters, strains as alien to their ears as their drums and cow horns were to those in the Greathouse.

Robert sought out Lady Wells as she sipped fruit cup and watched the dancers. "My lady cousin, a word with you."

A faint frown creased her still-smooth brow, and her eyes strayed to Philip's blue-velvet-clad back, but Robert took her arm and led her firmly to a comparatively quiet and deserted side veranda.

"May I speak bluntly, cousin?"

268

"Of course."

He sensed her surprise, but the veranda was too dimly lit by guttering, smoky torches set in wall brackets to observe her expression.

"I have noted that you seem somewhat attracted to Sir Philip . . . don't be offended," as she made a quick movement of negation. " 'Tis natural enough, but he plans to marry. One of the reasons for this ball is to announce . . . their . . . engagement."

The silence was charged with suppressed emotion, then Deborah asked in a small voice: "Their engagement? Someone . . . from Vane?"

"Yes. Sarah."

"*Sarah?* But that's impossible . . . he couldn't marry . . . ."

"Couldn't marry a bastard half-caste? He fell in love and proposed marriage before he knew that I had freed her and had legally adopted her."

"But Robert . . . I vow I am amazed and confused at these tidings. How will she be accepted in England?"

"He plans to settle here."

"And *how*," she asked with as much tartness as he had ever heard in her soft equable voice, "how will society out here accept her?"

"With upraised eyebrows no doubt, and a sweeping of virtuous European skirts to one side. But I venture that that will not bother either of them. And I think most people will follow *your* lead in their attitude." He paused, then went on gently: "I wanted you to know before the announcement was made in public."

"I . . . thank you, Robert. We should be getting back to the ball."

"One moment. There is one other matter that has arisen in the last few days. Would you be very upset if—Seth—asked for Melissa's hand?"

269

"Cousin . . . you joke. The boy is a . . . ."

"Is my eldest son, as free as your own son . . . and has my name legally."

"No, Robert, it would never do."

She fell silent, and Robert spoke quietly for a few moments, his voice persuasive, until she said helplessly: "I cannot wholly approve . . . the idea is so . . . new . . . but if Melissa loves him, there is naught I can do . . . her determination matches my own."

There had been much talk and raised eyebrows among the wives of the planters as they observed the presence of Seth and Sarah, both treated as members of the family. Rumors about them had gradually percolated to the most remote plantations, but many of the wives, most of whom had been born in England, Ireland, or Scotland, could hardly credit the truth. Yet here they were confronted with the astounding facts of the dark, handsome young man with the eyes which were the exact replicas of their host's—"And have you noticed his *nose,* there can be no *doubt*"—together with the lovely young girl—"And where did she get those strange gray eyes?"

"Have you noticed that Mistress *Charlotte's* own are very like?"

"Oh *no* . . . she does not seem the type who would lower . . . ."

"H'm, you never can tell . . . ."

"But haven't you *heard* there was *another* sister, she married William Preston—that's him, talking to Colonel Orr—the two young lads who performed in the country dances are *her* children."

"What happened to her?"

"Well, there were all sorts of rumors, each contradicting the other—before your time, dear—and they do say . . . ."

There was a sustained roll on the tabor, and the guests crowded in to the long withdrawing room that was doing service as the ballroom.

Robert took the center of the floor and held up his hand for silence.

"My honored relatives and guests who have traveled from as far as Morante in the east and as near as the new settlement of Savanna-la-Mar and the resettled community of Oristan: I have long wanted to have an excuse to invite you to share our board at Vane Great-house, despite the fact that many of you are strangers to me and to each other, for I feel the time has come when we should get to know one another as fellow islanders, fellow Jamaicans, and not think of ourselves as English, Scots, Irish, or Welsh. In this growing island community, the distances will shorten, the isolation will grow less. This is only the beginning, and with a hard-working, thrifty community, our island home will continue to expand and prosper."

There was an outbreak of applause. It died, and he continued: "This gathering is also in honor of two of my oldest friends: Sir Philip Lonsdale and the Honorable Hugh Russell, who arrived from England a few months ago to visit me and my family."

Philip, resplendent in blue velvet and frothing white lace, his blond hair covered by a wig of cascading silver curls, bowed elegantly to the company, drawing sighs and murmurs of admiration. Hugh, more restrained in russet velvet and cream lace, his own hair simply dressed, bowed low to the gawping company, an ironic gleam in his dark eyes.

"I have also asked you here to celebrate the announcement of a forthcoming marriage."

271

The guests crowded forward as Robert went to Sarah, took her hand, and led her to the center before he beckoned Philip. There was a sudden stunned silence as Robert's voice rang out:

"I am delighted to announce the forthcoming marriage between my friend Sir Philip Lonsdale and my very dear—my beloved—niece, Sarah Vane." He kissed Sarah and shook hands with Philip, and still the silence hung like a palpable living creature over the shocked guests. It was broken by Lady Wells . . . darling Deborah, Robert thought in gratitude . . . rustling forward and kissing Sarah:

"My dear, I trust you will be *very* happy. My felicitations, Sir Philip." Her smile was warm and guileless, yet Philip caught a flash of self-mockery as she held out her small hand to him. "I shall welcome you both at Wells in due course."

At Deborah's action there was a concerted sigh from the watching guests. Then one after another moved toward the couple until the mingled voices were loud in their congratulations. Then Robert gave the signal for the music to recommence and Philip led his bride-to-be in a dashing coranto, and Seth, encouraged by Lady Wells' attitude, approached her and asked formally:

"May I have your permission in asking your daughter for the honor of this dance, my lady?"

There was a flicker of conflicting expressions in her brown eyes as she gazed into his blue ones. How strange, she thought with relevant irrelevance, that both these—mulattos—should proclaim their parentage by each inheriting the most striking feature of their European parent. . . .

She said: "No, I think not. Not *this* dance . . . perhaps the next. *This* dance you may have with *me.*"

And she placed her small white hand on his arm clad in dark red velvet. Her eyes met Robert's as Seth led her to the floor, and she smiled, giving him the faintest of nods.

Five

Before the guests finally departed to make their long return journeys, the engagement was also announced of Melissa Wells and Seth Vane, giving the planters and especially their wives enough gossip to last them, exclaim over, and wonder at for many a long month.

" 'Tis positively indecent," Charlotte exclaimed.

"How so?" Robert asked.

"Why—to think that *your* son is to marry *my* half-sister—I'm sure 'tis within the proscribed degree."

"Nonsense, they have no blood tie—a tenuous cousinship through me and Deborah—I believe that in such a tight community as ours these close relationships will be made yet closer through marriages like this for many a long day . . . at least until we have many more settlers."

Later Robert summoned Seth to his study.

"Close the door fast, lad, and also the shutters. . . . Leave but a crack to see and breathe by."

Seth was somewhat mystified, as it was the hottest part of the day and every shutter throughout the house stood wide to catch the breeze. He was further mystified as Robert's long fingers explored one of the intricately worked wall panels, and a section swung smoothly open, disclosing a cavity of about two feet deep and as much wide and high. He glimpsed a pile

274

of papers and a brown leather pouch. Robert took out the latter and smiled at Seth's expression.

"No one in this household but you and I know of this compartment. The craftsman who fashioned it, my lamented late John White, was the only other person to know of it until this moment. Before you leave this room I will show you how to open it . . . but first. . . ." He tipped the contents of the pouch onto his desk, and Seth gasped in surprised awe as a number of flashing gems tumbled out and lay in a scintillating heap of brilliant color on the wooden surface. "Well?" Robert asked as the pause lengthened.

"Sir, I know not what to say. Such magnificence . . . like unto some pirate's hoard. . . ." Seth drew in his breath sharply and looked the unspoken question that so obviously hung on his lips.

Robert nodded.

"I'll tell you the whole sorry tale one day, Seth lad. 'Tis a fact that many a respectable landowner obtained the means to become so by this method. Think none the worse of me for the knowledge, before you have the whole story from my lips—or Sir Philip's."

"*Sir Philip's?* Mean you . . . ?"

"Indeed yes. We sailed as comrades under the black flag—for far too long. But come, I didn't call you in here merely to look or listen to me reminisce over that which is best forgot. Choose a gem which you think will please Melissa in a betrothal ring, and we'll have it set fittingly . . . if any goldsmith's is left standing in Port Royal."

Seth pored over the gems, touching them occasionally with long, brown, gentle fingertips. Eventually he picked up a stone of a deep brilliant green that glowed and glittered in the dim light that seeped through the partially closed shutters and came from the flickering flame of the one candle Robert had lit while Seth made up his mind.

"Think you she'll be pleased with this, Father?"

Robert laughed grimly.

"She should be, 'twas worn by a Mayan princess and is the apex of my collection."

"Oh no, then I couldn't. . . ." Seth made to put back the stone, but Robert stopped him.

"Nay, lad, I said choose, and I abide by your choice. 'Tis an emerald of the finest quality and worth a fortune. . . . But let no man or woman be aware of its true value. 'Twill grace the hand of your bride better than hiding its beauty in a dark and secret cupboard."

He scooped the other jewels back into the pouch, then reached for the emerald.

"Best that we leave it here until we can get it set. And Seth—if aught should chance to me at any time, keep only to yourself the secret of the panel, and use the jewels to your advantage. I want your word on that."

"But, father . . . ."

"No argument. I am determined on the point. Your word."

"I give my word."

"Good. Your hand on the promise. Now come, let me show you the mechanism."

For the next half hour Seth practiced to achieve the delicate pressures needed on certain different woods that went to make up the mosaic in the center of the panel, marveling each time the door opened or closed. When it was in the latter position, it was impossible even with the keenest eyesight or most sensitive fingertips to determine the line of demarcation.

A double wedding had been planned for early June in the following year of 1693. The months preceding were a whirl of frenzied preparation: the sewing of yards of brocade and of gold and silver tissue for the two brides; the refurbishing of a separate wing for Seth and Melissa; and a widespread hunt by Philip for a suitable property.

Hugh Russell left early in January to oversee a shipment of logwood from Honduras to England, but promised to return for the weddings.

Philip found what he wanted after what had seemed a hopeless search. He arrived back at Vane one evening toward the end of February, jubilant.

" 'Tis well night perfect, Rob. On a gentle eminence just this side of Oristan. No more than fifty to sixty acres. I'll to St. Jago tomorrow and complete the transaction. How long before I can build a house, Rob?"

"You'll have to resign yourself to living here after your marriage for a good many months . . . maybe a year or more. Before you can begin you'll need to get —*workers*. I'll have Seth travel with you tomorrow. He has some business of his own to transact in Port Royal, and he can buy what slaves you need. They can stay in the compound and rest after their voyage until you are ready for them. I hear that Port Royal is a-building again, despite the frequent tremors that lasted for months after the 'quake."

It was decided after much discussion to hold both weddings at Wells, as it would be an easier journey for the guests. As the day drew near, Wells Great-house was as packed with friends and relatives as Vane had been a few months earlier.

As Robert waited outside this beautifully decorated room, he remembered his own wedding so long ago and the doubts that had beset him . . . and how those doubts had grown into facts over the years. Then the memory of Ann came flooding back. He had trained himself not to dwell on her memory, but today she

277

would not be banished from his mind. He was to give Sarah away . . . Ann's daughter by another man . . . to give her to Philip, who would love and cherish her. But still it pained him to think that within a few months she would be gone from Vane, and all physical reminders of Ann would be gone from his daily life. . . . His thoughts were interrupted by Sarah herself as she took her place beside him, followed by young Sir Walter who, topping his sister by a full head, proudly acted the man of the family and led her down the center aisle, closely followed by Robert with Sarah's hand on his arm.

"I wonder if this is the shape of things to come in the island," muttered old Sir George Mullins of St. Catherine to his wife. "The mingling of the dark and the light skins. Don't seem right, goin' against nature. Still, handsome young feller, that boy of Vane's. Plucky of Vane too, to acknowledge him. Born wrong side of the blanket an' all that, y'know, thousands wouldn't. Lesson f'r us all. . . ." He stopped suddenly at the frown of mingled disapproval and suspicion his good lady bestowed on him and buried his nose in the scroll of parchment that gave the order of the service, convinced that he had been too explicit in his remarks, and was thankful when the double ceremony pursued its solemn yet joyous way.

To Charlotte the installation of Seth and his bride— her own half-sister—in a separate wing at Vane only heightened the conviction in her mind that her husband was overly partial to his natural son. Surely, she told herself again and again, Robert *cannot, could not, would not* pass over his legitimate son in favor of . . . of a bastard fathered in an unremembered moment of youthful lust . . . .

In desperation she sought out Matt, who was lazily playing at dice with a young Negro slave.

"Matt . . . send that boy away, I must talk to you."

He sulkily motioned the boy away but kept the dice in his hands, rattling them in an ostentatious way until Charlotte exclaimed sharply in a voice she very rarely used to him.

"Stop that fidgeting and sit up and pay attention. Your slothfulness around the house will not fit you to be a successful planter. From now on you will attend Master Oliver's classes each day and ride around the property with me each morning."

"But Mama, *why* . . . I will have overseers, book-keepers, and the like. What need is there for me to . . . ."

A ringing slap cut short his protest, and he gazed in startled amazement at Charlotte, who had never laid a finger on him in anger before. Her gray eyes were glinting steel and her normally pale face was flushed with anger.

"You little *fool* . . . do you want to lose Vane through indifference? Your father's indulgence and partiality to Seth grow daily, he delegates more and more authority, whilst you do nothing to win his good graces. You will lose Vane by your own stupidity and laziness . . . as Wells was lost through the machinations of my lady stepmother, and . . . Mother of God . . . Seth is now allied to her through her daughter, who demonstrates too well how like her mother she is become."

This added aspect filled her with even greater dismay, she felt as if there were a conspiracy compounded by Seth and Lady Wells to defraud her son . . . *again* . . . .

Matt's lazy bearing left him. "And that insufferable brat, Sir Walter, said to my face that Vane should go to Seth."

279

"He said *that?*" Charlotte's fingers dug into his shoulders until he winced with pain. "Don't you *see*, Matt, you've *got* to help me, you must do your part and help me *fight* for Vane."

Six

"Oh, Philip, my husband, God has granted my prayers and sent you safely back to me."

A French invasion had sent Philip, along with Robert and Seth, to serve in the militia. The fighting had been savage, and the task of restoring order after the depredations of the French had kept them months from home.

Even before he had dismounted and flung the reins to a waiting groom, Sarah was flying down the outer stairway and into his arms. He held her close, kissing the top of her head, then held her off and gazed down in wide-eyed amazement at the high forward thrust of her belly.

"Sarah?"

She laughed delightedly at his expression. "I neither knew nor suspected anything till you'd been gone a week—and then as the months passed, I feared our child would be born before you returned." Her smile went and she clutched him close. "These long months without you . . . sometimes I feared . . . ."

Philip stroked her bent head, then said in a gentle reproof: "You should not have run down the steps like that, nor yet be standing in the sun. Come." He kept his arm about her waist as they mounted the stairway. She touched his hand. "Look . . . a positive epidemic." He glanced down, where beside the mounting block

Melissa stood in Seth's arms, the former slightness of her body distorted by the child she carried in her womb. Seth's face above hers echoed Philip's in his expression of bewildered delight.

Charlotte stood at the top of the steps to greet them, her face white and taut. Philip loosed his hold about Sarah and bounded up the last few steps.

"Robert is safe, unharmed, and will be with us shortly."

"Oh . . . I . . . feared to ask . . ." she said weakly, but the relief didn't lessen her air of strain and worry.

He looked at her anxiously.

"Are you well, Charlotte?"

Even as he asked he knew: her previous thinness had lapsed to a gaunt haggardness; her eyes were sunken in a face where the bones stood out sharply; even her hair had turned completely white.

She brushed his inquiry aside: "Not seeing Robert, I was fearful for a moment. Apart from that, 'tis nothing more than that I am tired. I have worked from dawn to dark to keep the property running smoothly. Matt, come and welcome back our fighting men.'"

There was pride in her voice, not for them but for her son. Rather, there lay beneath that pride a mocking note, an undercurrent of criticism that they could have stayed away so long, probably needlessly, for the fighting had been far from Vane and only vague distorted rumors had trickled through. There was no way of conveying the horror and bloodshed of the battle, the utter inhumanity of the invaders and the vast tragedy of the ruined homes and plantations. These things touched not even the fringe of life at Vane. Philip sighed inwardly and turned to greet Matt. He was pleasantly surprised at the change a few months had wrought in the youth: he had grown, his muscles had hardened from their usual flabbiness; his formerly

282

flaccid face had a new firmness, a healthy tan. Yet with all this admirable change there seemed to be an air of covert debauchery about him and Philip's heart ached for Robert: how unlucky he had been in this son. His glance strayed to Seth, still bemused by the discovery of approaching fatherhood . . . and how *lucky* in that son. . . . He was brought back to the moment by Matt's somewhat patronizing tone.

"Good day, Sir Philip, I trust you have enjoyed your brief encounter with the French."

Philip's nostrils flared; but he said evenly: "One does not *enjoy* a fight, which I trust you will not have to learn by experience. But the 'brief encounter,' as you term it, has cost the life of many a good man—Dick Gough amongst those slain—and has made this island safe from the French for the time being. Perchance when they next attack you will be of age to join the militia and *enjoy* a campaign."

Matt's eyes flickered away from the scorn in Philip's, a little uncertain about this forthright friend of his father's, his brashness subdued for once.

That night at dinner the talk was exclusively of the war, and although they tried to play down the horrors, it was well nigh impossible to tell of those days without mentioning some of the terrible details. Philip could see that at last Charlotte was impressed by the enormity of the danger in which the whole island had been placed.

"But why couldn't Robert have returned with you?" she asked somewhat pettishly.

Philip hesitated. "There was talk that the French had landed first in the east—and that many properties . . . had been destroyed," he said carefully. "He felt it his bounden duty to see if there was aught he could do —to help—at Preston."

"But surely Preston must be safe? 'Tis many miles

from the coast, and I have not noticed Robert over-zealous of the plight of the Prestons in the past."

Philip compressed his lips. He had no qualms about shaking Charlotte's insufferable calm, but to alarm his young bride and the wide-eyed Melissa was another matter. "Robert will, I hope, reassure us all on his arrival," he answered ambiguously.

But when Robert did arrive some ten days later, there was another urgent matter which absorbed all their attention.

About eight days after Philip and Seth's return, Charlotte woke feeling listless and with a little fever. She forced herself from her bed and to her work about the plantation, although Seth had assured her that, now he was back, there was no need to tax herself. She had regarded him with the cold dislike which was her customary expression when she was forced to address him. "I have looked after my son's heritage these many months —*with his valuable help*—and can do so for a few days longer." But by mid-morning the fever had risen alarmingly, and she was forced to return to the house.

Bridget sought out Philip and said in a worried voice: "My mother is sick, the fever is consuming her . . . could you send a message to Lady Wells and ask her to send Leah?"

"Leah?"

"She is an old woman at Wells, well versed in medical lore. Mama had her over when the new slaves were sick, and although some died, others recovered and I fear—oh, Sir Philip—this seems to be the same sickness."

"Come, child, let us go and see your mother."

He went with Bridget to Charlotte's room and was appalled at her condition. Two female slaves were kept constantly busy removing the soiled linen as frequent attacks of diarrhea flowed from her bowels, leaving her in a state of exhaustion, and she moaned aloud as cramps attacked her legs and abdominal muscles. Even as Philip reached her side, her eyes mutely imploring him not to look upon her shameful state, a stream of vomit gushed unchecked from her mouth. He took a wet cloth and gently wiped her face, all his previous animosity toward her erased by pity at her state. He crooned meaningless words of comfort as he tried to aid her. Her skin was cold and clammy to his touch, though she seemed to be consumed by an inner fever.

"See that there are plenty of cool fluids for her," he whispered to Bridget. "She will have a great thirst with all this loss."

"But nothing stays down . . . It is heartbreaking to see her so."

He gestured toward the heap of soiled linen. "Burn every scrap of linen that comes from this bed," he ordered the frightened slaves. "And wash your hands well each time after you attend your mistress. Do you understand me?"

"Yes, sir. Yes, Mas' Philip."

"And you, Mistress Bridget." He turned to the girl. "Come no more near your mother. Go and wash from head to foot and burn all the clothing you wear."

"But Sir Philip, I must be with her."

"No, child—I saw a case like this once, a sailor come from the Far East—the fever is thought to be carried in the stool and vomit. Go child, I will attend her, with these good maids here, and let us pray that your father arrives soon—and the goodly Leah with her magic potions."

He stayed by Charlotte's bedside all that day and all the long night, tending her as ably as any woman well versed in the care of the sick, but toward dawn he noticed that although the purging flux and helpless wracking vomiting had almost ceased, a further alarming change had taken place in her: her eyes were deeply sunken, surrounded by dark bluish areolae; her cheek bones had become so prominent it seemed as if they would break through the fine, gray-tinged skin. Her hands were shriveled like those of a washerwoman and her voice when she attempted to speak was nothing more than a hoarse whisper. She lay inert in a state of complete prostration, and at times he feared that she had stopped breathing. He felt for her pulse but could find none, and even when he put an ear to her chest, the heartbeat was so slow and faint, he wondered that it had enough power to pump the blood through her body. Yet with all this she was conscious, and when she did manage to utter a few words she spoke rationally.

Within the Great-house there hung an unusual quiet, a brooding quiet of foreboding and the unspoken conviction that death hovered over that bright morning. And then this unnatural silence was broken by a flurry at the front entrance, and Philip craned his neck around the angle of the veranda and saw with unspeakable relief Robert dismounting from a lathered horse. Runners had been sent ahead to warn him of Charlotte's illness and urge all possible speed, for Philip had come to the unwelcome conclusion through his long night's vigil that Charlotte would not live to see another.

There came the sounds of muted, hurrying footsteps along the veranda, and Robert entered the room. He dropped on his knees by Charlotte's side and took one of her cold hands in both his warm ones. His eyes showed shock and grief at her appearance, but his voice was firm and gentle as he said:

"My poor Charlotte—to endure this and me not by your side. I hear that Leah is on her way. She will take care of you."

She managed a parody of a smile, and Philip's throat constricted: these two were closer now than they had been in all their years of life together. He made as if to leave, but Robert said quietly:

"No, stay, Phil. You stayed like the friend you are with her in her hour of need; now stay with me in mine. But send for Matt and Bridget, please. I think that they should be here. . . ."

He bent his head as she tried to speak, the hoarsely whispered words barely audible: "Robert . . . I tried to keep the plantation as you would wish . . . and as productive as our son will keep it. . . . I did well?"

"Very well, my love." Behind him the door opened and Matt slipped into the room. Robert heard the quick indrawn breath as the boy glimpsed his mother's ravaged face and wasted body. "Too well, for the hard work has weakened you, making it more difficult for you to fight the sickness. But think no more of the plantation now . . . think only of getting better."

"No . . . it is too late. . . . I should have . . . Leah wanted . . . wanted. . . ." She trailed off, then summoning strength from her frail body by force of will alone, she said: "Robert . . . our son . . . is a good boy . . . you will see. He has worked . . . like a man . . . these many . . . months. He *will* have . . . his . . . heritage? He will inherit Vane . . . won't he?"

He stroked her brow as Matt stepped forward and took one of his mother's cold hands.

"Think not on these things now, my dear," Robert said. "Do not worry. . . ."

"Robert?" The blue-tipped shriveled fingers clutched his hand. *"Promise* me. Promise me that Matt will one day be master of Vane.

"Robert?"

It was the barest whisper, but it held such a world of

pleading that he said in a broken voice: "Of course, my love, what else? Our son will inherit Vane."

She moved her hands slowly, as if they were of a great weight, until she had brought Matt's hand and Robert's together, then her fingers fell limply. A smile hovered for a moment on her bloodless lips, and the gray eyes that had been capable of flashing such wrath and derision, softened to a tranquil, limpid lucency before they closed forever.

Robert remained motionless on his knees for a long time, unwilling to believe that Charlotte had left him so abruptly, until Philip touched him gently on the shoulder and said softly: "Come Rob lad. 'Tis done."

"Yes." He got stiffly to his feet, then turned to Philip and asked dully: "What else could I have said? What else . . . to a dying woman?"

"Nothing, Rob. Nothing but that which you promised."

Robert took a tight hold on his feelings and put an arm around his son's shoulders. "Come, lad," he whispered. "Come, boy. We must learn to comfort each other, find joy in each other's company." He recoiled as Matt pulled away and turned to look at him, the dazed look replaced by one of sly triumph.

"I heard her words and I heard your promise. I want no comfort from you, Father, no joy . . . only what is rightfully mine."

Seven

The day after Charlotte was buried—the first lonely grave in the Vane cemetery—Leah presented herself to Robert, her former plumpness turned to a dropsical obesity.

"Mas' Robert," she wheezed. "Me try fe mek Miss Charlotte tek de iles, dem, me mek fe stop de sickness. But she laugh an' say it sickness fe slave. Let I give dose to all eena de house, or sure it sure de sickness spread."

Robert hesitated. He had the educated man's skepticism of these seemingly magical potions. Yet he had seen Leah work cures where none had seemed possible. "All right," he said at last. "How long before we can be sure that your preventive potions work?"

"Me no know 'bout p'ventive, Mas' Robert, me only know dat if you tek me iles you don't tek de sickness."

He laughed for the first time, it seemed, in months.

"All right, old lady, I shall give orders that every one in the household must drink your obnoxious oils."

He watched her gross form waddle away, and for the first time the realization was forced to the forefront of his mind that this old Negro woman, with her mysterious knowledge of sicknesses and ailments and equally mysterious cures, was the grandmother of his eldest son.

Whether because of or despite Leah's medication,

there were no more outbreaks of the illness, and life at Vane gradually resumed its daily routine. In his shock over Charlotte's death Robert had pushed to the depths of consciousness the horrors he had seen at Preston and in the town of Port Morant, and only to Philip did he later divulge the details.

"God, Rob, *no* one left alive?"

"No one. The house is a charred shell, the property ruined."

Lady Wells had sent word that Leah was to stay on at Vane until both Melissa Vane and Sarah Lonsdale were delivered of their children, both expected within a week or so of each other, and that she would be arriving at Vane in time for the double event.

Matt Vane had been stunned by his mother's death. He felt bereft and alone, not through any great love he had borne toward her, but because she had championed him against all odds, right or wrong, and now he felt naked and vulnerable before the combined might of his father, whom he resented in an obscure unformulated way; of Seth, whom he hated and feared; and of the arrogant newcomer, Sir Philip, who had married his bastard cousin and now wielded such sophisticated influence over the household. He might have turned for comfort to his sister, now fourteen and becoming more adult as each day passed, but Bridget, always closer to Robert than she had ever been to her mother, now drew even closer and had taken to accompanying him on his morning rounds of the plantation, much as Charlotte had accompanied her father at Wells.

Matt tried for a few days after Charlotte's burial to continue the work she had taught him in the running and management of Vane, but he was a boy of only thirteen, naturally mentally and physically lazy—and what the slaves called "cubbitch"—and with both his father and Seth to take over the reins and without

Charlotte's driving force, he soon slipped back into his old ways of sleeping late, eating too much, and playing at dice after dark with a few favored indentured bondsmen.

"I'm worried about Matt," Robert said at length as he and Seth rode out one morning in mid-September. Seth kept silent, his eyes downcast, and at length Robert asked sharply: "What is it, lad? Something I should know?"

"I . . . I'm worried about Melissa. . . ."

"Nonsense, she's right as rain . . . especially now that my lady Wells has taken charge. Out with it, Seth, it's something which concerns the boy, eh?"

"Father, I am loath to bear tales on the lad. If we were close, I'd speak to him myself, but he hates the very sight of me."

"Go on," said Robert grimly in a voice that brooked no denial.

"Well, sir, the rumor goes—no, not rumor, 'tis very fact—that young master Matt is overfree with the whip, he seems to take an indecent delight in using it for the flimsiest excuse, and also that he is overfree with any passable young slave girl who catches his eye."

"*What?* He's but thirteen summers."

"I know, father," Seth said unhappily, but having started, felt impelled to continue. "He's been heard to boast that come Christmas there'll be two new brats in the compound thanks to him, and he'll wager a dozen more before the next year is out."

Robert's nostrils flared in anger. "The young whelp! At this rate by the time he's twenty, he'll be as debauched as any middle-aged planter in the island—and this is the boy whom his mother made me . . .'." he stopped in mid-sentence. When at last Robert turned back to Seth, there was deep pain and a deep resolve in his eyes as he said in a fierce whisper: "I will not *allow* Vane to be ruined by neglect . . . I will *not* allow it."

When they returned at mid-morning for second breakfast, they found the house in an excited bustle. Young Mistress Vane was in labor and had been these four hours. Seth rushed to the wing where he and Melissa had set up housekeeping, but he was waved firmly away by Deborah.

"But I *must* see her," he pleaded.

"No, Seth, she is well but needs to concentrate all her thoughts and energy on the next few minutes. I will call you—as soon as the child is delivered."

They heard Leah call from within, followed by a sharp cry from Melissa, and Seth leaned his head against the veranda rail in answering silent agony. His gentle little Melissa: he vowed silently that he would never again subject her to such an ordeal. A hand gripped his shoulder: "Cheer up, Seth lad, and join me in a goblet of madeira," Philip drawled. "From one prospective father to another." He handed him a brimming goblet.

Seth relaxed and drank deeply, then asked: "How is Sarah?"

"From all the signs, my lady Deborah will not have much rest today. Seems like she will go from one delivery to the next."

For all Philip's lazy manner and casual words, there were lines deeply etched about his mouth, and his eyes were clouded with worry.

Robert joined them, and together they listened to the low murmurs and sudden movements from the room within. The morning wore on to late noon, and shadows began to lengthen across the lawns, the clefts and ridges on the mountains took on an evening glow, and swooping swallows sought the sanctuary of concealing palms before a high indignant wail cut across their low voices. Seth leaped to his feet, his eyes wide and blazing. Then Deborah opened the door and brought out a swaddled bundle. Her brown eyes were smudged with fatigue and her usual immaculate appearance disheveled. " 'Tis a boy," she announced in satisfaction as she put the bundle into Seth's arms.

He gazed down in awe at the wizened, dusky red face, the head covered by a thick ruff of soft black hair, and he thought: I will give this child all that I lacked in my early years. He will not grow up knowing the driver's whip or the stench of overcrowded bodies in the compound, the wretched food, the rough Osnaburg breeches, or the loneliness of never belonging to a family.

And this he will be spared.

He handed the child to Robert. "Your grandson, sir."

Robert felt a stir of envy of his son's pride and happiness and the beginnings of a fierce growing pride: his grandson.

Deborah took the child firmly from Robert's arms. "A few minutes, and you may come in."

"What will you call him, Seth?" Philip asked.

"Robert, sir. Melissa and I discussed it. Robert Walter."

Robert Walter Vane, thought Robert. How inextricably mixed are the fortunes of the Vanes and the Wells, and yet out of all the original Wells family from those far-off days when first my life became entwined with theirs, not one remains: Sir Walter; pale, pallid Mistress Bridget; young sickly Richard; my lovely Ann . . . and Charlotte . . . all gone, mere tombstones now in family cemeteries. He sighed, then met Philip's quizzical look and laughed.

"Permit a grandfather a few memories."

"A *grandfather*. S'life, Rob, we must drink a toast

to you and this new young Robert Vane. Seth, my boy, 'tis over now, you can lose your stunned expression and go to see your wife."

"Twins?" Philip repeated weakly some ten hours later.

Deborah sank exhaustedly onto a low rocker, her eyes ringed with dark shadows, but she wore an air of weary triumph. "Yes, a girl and a boy—the boy was born about twenty minutes before the girl. I don't feel like a grandmother," she added in surprise, remembering the earlier delivery.

Philip laughed: "I suddenly feel very much like a *father,*" he said, then went on quickly: "Poor Lady Deb, let me see you to your room and I'll have a hot posset sent to you, well laced . . . ."

"Thank you, Sir Philip."

Philip had taken to addressing her affectionately as Lady Deb, but she still addressed him in all formality by his title, for new-made father as he was, he was still some years older than herself. She sighed wearily: "It *has* been a long day, I would be grateful if you would send word to Susan for a posset. . . . But first, go and see your wife." She glanced around. "Robert?"

"I persuaded him to go to bed about an hour ago . . . he has a St. Jago trip tomorrow."

Philip looked down at Sarah, exhausted but happy in the big bed, then at the two little faces cradled in the crook of each arm.

"They are very *small,*" he said doubtfully.

"I am glad that they weren't any bigger," Sarah murmured. She smiled up at him, her huge gray eyes luminous. "Are you pleased with me, Philip?"

"Pleased? Oh, my darling, I would be pleased with you and proud of you whatever you did. Now let these little people be attended to so that you may get some sleep."

"You must be tired too. 'Tis almost dawn." Suddenly she giggled. "Vane will soon burst at the seams if Melissa and I go on at this rate: *three* babies in one day . . . ."

"You shameless little hussy . . . two should be enough for you, for a long time to come. . . ."

She flashed a look at him from beneath her lashes, then was abruptly asleep.

He stood by her side, looking down at her for a long time, his whole being suffused with love—to think that he had had to wait all this while to find such happiness, and then to find it with the daughter of the woman whom Robert had loved so deeply—God grant that he lived long to enjoy it. . . .

When the excitement engendered by the arrival of the three infants had abated and the two nurseries were accepted as part of the household and not places of wonder, Robert said to Deborah: "Cousin, you know how grateful I am for all your care these last weeks. I wonder if I could ask one more favor, a very big one?"

"*I* wonder that you doubt my granting it."

" 'Tis this: I am perturbed about Matt. He's wild and undisciplined—I accept much of the blame, I left him to his mother's care, thinking more of Seth's upbringing and developing the property. But 'tis not too late, I hope, to rectify that in some measure."

She pursed her mouth skeptically. " 'Twill need a stronger hand than mine, cousin."

"I'm not suggesting that you take him in hand, I would not contemplate asking you, but I would ask you to escort him to England, to London, and see him settled in St. Paul's School. I have written the dean, Dr. Guilfoyle, and have his reply here. Perhaps you would like to take Walter with you for company on the return journey, it would be good for him to travel and get a broader perspective than the confines of

Wells. I will, of course, furnish all monies necessary for both the journey and during your stay. And Seth and I will see that Wells is properly administered during your absence. What say you, cousin?"

She was silent for a while, then looked up with her slow smile:

"The favor is from you to me, Robert. To see England again . . . oh, cousin, I have dreamed so often of the chance. The soft green countryside, after the steaming heat . . . ."

"I imagined you were content with your lot."

"I was . . . especially this last year or so . . . but one may yet be content and still yearn for a sight of what was home. But let me take Bridget as well. 'Twill be good for her also to see a little of the world."

And so it was settled.

Philip declared that he would accept no payment for the four passages aboard his brand-new merchant ship the *Lady Sarah*, now in Savanna-la-Mar harbor after her maiden voyage, and it was planned that they would leave early in December.

Bridget was wildly excited about the proposed journey, but Matt was at first vehement in his protests:

"I'll not go . . . I'll not be sent away. . . ."

"It is not a matter of sending you away, lad," Robert explained patiently. "I want you to learn all that you may . . . to be worthy of Vane," he added.

"And when I am gone, Seth will have Vane," Matt burst out.

"Seth will be *here*, of course," Robert said. "He will be here working as he has always worked, it is his home as much as yours."

"He will take it from me," the boy said mutinously.

Robert folded his lips. "You will go to England and learn all that is possible, and I and Vane will welcome you home as a cultured, disciplined man and not the uncouth youth that you are today," he said coldly, and at length Matt subsided into a sulky acceptance of the inevitable. As the time for departure drew near his feeling gradually became one of tepid enthusiasm.

Long lists of goods to be purchased in London were given to the travelers, and at last they were gone amid a flurry of farewells.

"How goes your experiment with your freed men?" Robert asked as he stood with Philip one morning in the March of the following year and watched critically as a gang of men swarmed over the roof of the nearly finished house.

Philip sighed.

"Well enough, but 'tis difficult to get through to them that they *are* free. They accept their wages but know not the value nor what to do with them."

"They are free in name only," Robert stated flatly. "Free to do what? To leave here if they wish? Where would they go? Once they get beyond the bounds of your property, they'd be picked up soon enough and clapped in the pound at St. Jago."

"It will take time, I know. But I have plans . . . and patience. You will see, Rob, you will see."

There were murmurs throughout the island and sharp questions asked in the House of Assembly when Philip's policy became known, but few planters cared to tangle directly with the powerful Sir Philip Lonsdale, whose wealth was accumulating as his fleet of merchant ships grew. There were added murmurs when it was learned that he also refused to carry sugar in his ships. "Nothing that has been grown by slave labor will I transport," he declared, but he allowed the planters to import household goods and supplies and to travel back and forth as passengers. They would have liked to impose a boycott on the Lonsdale Line,

297

but his ships were faster than any other, the cabins more spacious, the food palatable, and at last the vagaries of "this mad Englishman" became accepted as part of the island pattern, for it was soon learned that, true to his initial statement, he was not in competition with the planters, and his workers hadn't yet accepted their free status and so did not "corrupt" the other planters' slaves.

Late in June the *Lady Sarah* arrived in port, laden with furniture, china, and silverware for Lonsdale House, and the travelers were greeted exuberantly.

"Oh, papa," Bridget threw her arms around Robert's neck as she stepped onto the jetty. "It is so *good* to see you."

"Well, well, what fashionable young lady do we have here?" Robert held her off admiringly. "A drab little Jamaican dilly went away, and a brilliant little London swan returns."

A tall young man came down the gangway leading Lady Wells by her elegantly gloved hand. Bridget became demure, a faint blush mantling her cheeks.

"Papa, may I present Dr. Jeremy Pierce? My father."

Robert grasped the outstretched hand and looked hard at the young doctor. He liked what he saw: a strong face with a firm jaw and frank hazel eyes, brown hair left unfashionably in its natural state, his clothes sober but of an excellent quality. Robert looked again at the downcast eyes and flushed face of his daughter which told their own tale and said warmly:

"Welcome to Vane, Dr. Pierce."

Later that day Deborah sat in Robert's study and answered his urgent query, "What is this, cousin? Bridget is but a child—and yet seems besotted of the man?" with a placid: "Patience, cousin, she is fifteen and mature enough for marriage . . ."

"Marriage?"

". . . and Jeremy will make a good, steady husband. He squired us round London and paid no address to the child before seeking my permission. He comes of an old Dorset family who can trace their ancestry back to the Normans. He is a qualified medical practitioner and has worked at St. Bartholomew's Hospital. He has ample private means and so can indulge his work as a hobby."

"He is somewhat old for Bridget," he said doubtfully, but she laughed that objection away, sure now of his consent to the match.

"Nonsense, he is but twenty-five or so. You didn't object to Sir Philip, who is nearly thirty years older than Sarah."

Robert knew he was beaten but took refuge in making more objections and provisos. "But will he want to stay and practice medicine in these solitary wilds after fashionable London?"

"He seems most anxious to do so."

"We will wait and see. If he be willing to remain after a year, when Bridget will be sixteen, then I will agree to the match." And with that Deborah had to be content. "Now tell me, what of Matt?"

She spread her hands.

"I find it hard to believe he is your son: a disagreeable boy. But Dr. Guilfoyle will be the one to instill some degree of sociability in him—if it is at all possible."

And so began a period of calm and ever-increasing prosperity at Vane and Wells plantations and at Philip's model farm at Lonsdale. The demand for sugar rose, and even after the war between France and England came to an end by the signing of the Treaty of Ryswick in September 1697, it continued to do so. Since so many mills and plantations had been destroyed by the

299

French invasion, the demand was heavy on those that had been unscathed, and both Vane and Wells expanded their acreage and increased their slave labor force.

Bridget and Jeremy were married in the summer of 1696, and a son was born the following year. As a wedding present Robert had purchased a small holding of about thirty acres adjoining the Vane property and built a medium-sized dower house, which became known at first as Little Vane and then over the course of many years as Pierce Piece. Jeremy had settled down quickly to island life and divided his time between the three properties, and the advantage of skilled medical care soon became apparent.

It was four years after the marriage that Matthew Vane, now aged twenty, after five years of rebellious school life, returned to Jamaica and to Vane.

Eight

Robert Vane sighed deeply as he finished his morning inspection and headed back to the Great-house. These two-and-a-half years since Matt had returned had been difficult ones; the harmony that had prevailed while the boy had been in England had turned to discord almost overnight. His arrogance had increased with his new learning and man's estate, though regrettably the arrogance was far in excess of the learning. Robert recalled the letter he had received from Dr. Guilfoyle: ". . . has a brain but declines to use it . . . plays truant frequently and keeps unsavory company . . . boasts of the size of the plantation he will inherit and the great wealth . . . there is some nebulous hope that he will settle down with the passage of years. . . ." Unsatisfactory to say the least; and far from settling down, Matt seemed to intensify his wild ways as time went by. He had taken to going to Kingston—previously he had gone to Port Royal until that unfortunate city had been razed by fire in 1702—and spending long hours in gaming, wenching, and drinking. He wasn't all bad, Robert thought, searching for exculpating points in the boy's character; there had been a time last year when he had taken a whim to help Jeremy, dispensing drugs and applying dressings. But when Jeremy chided him for his rough handling of his patients, he had retorted brutally: "The blacks know no difference between the sense of pain or the lack of it, they don't have feelings like us." After that he had lost interest and gone his own way. The disappointment that Robert felt over this son of his gnawed incessantly at his waking thoughts and intruded into his dreams.

He tossed the reins to a waiting groom and was half way up the stairs when the pain clutched at his chest; he gasped and felt blindly for the railing, then slowly slid to a sitting position while sweat trickled into his eyes and his breath came with difficulty.

It was there that Seth found him some half an hour later. He bounded up the steps and bent over Robert:

"Father . . . what is it? You're ill . . . let me help you to bed, then I'll fetch Jeremy."

Robert motioned him weakly to wait, unable to speak, in a state of collapse. Then, as the pain subsided, he murmured: "Just a touch . . . of indigestion . . . no need to call Jeremy."

"Jasper," Seth called down to a passing groom, "Send someone quick for the doctor. Then come help me with Master Robert."

Seth gazed down at him as he lay on the big four-poster bed. Why, he looks an old man, he thought in surprise, yet he's still this side of sixty. This sudden collapse unnerved Seth. He had never known his father to have a day's illness; he had always been fit and trim muscled—apart from that time before Philip's arrival, when he'd been drinking steadily—but since that time his drinking had decreased to a modest glass or two of madeira at the dinner table.

Seth touched his hand.

"Have you had an attack like this before, Father?"

The lids fluttered open.

"Why . . . just a twinge a month or so back . . . nothing . . . nothing to worry about."

Seth left him as he heard Jeremy at the door.

"He swears it's indigestion . . . but I don't like the look of him."

"You must rest," Jeremy ordered his father-in-law a few minutes later, after he had gently palpated his chest and listened to his heart. "No more riding round the plantation, no more heavy meals in the evening."

"Nonsense." Robert was still weak, but his voice had strengthened. "I'm fit as a fiddle. Too much roast suckling pig last night . . . ."

"No, sir. I . . . don't like your heart sounds, nor yet your breathing and your pulse rate. I beg you sir, take my advice."

Then Jeremy insisted on cupping him, despite Robert's protests that the practice still further weakened him.

"Allow me to know what is best in this matter," Jeremy said firmly.

The house was strangely quiet for the rest of that day. Young Robert Vane, banned from his usual play hour with his beloved indulgent grandfather, was fretful. And with Priscilla, aged six, and Michael, aged four, he was sent to the nursery with the baby, Deborah, aged eighteen months. Seth and Melissa now had four children and a fifth soon to be born—so much for Seth's resolve when Robert was born—beautiful golden-skinned children, but only Michael had inherited the brilliant blue Vane eyes. The others had large liquid black eyes, sparkling or meltingly soft as the occasion dictated.

Robert lay listening to the faint sounds of the Greathouse and musing over the past years and the prospects of the future. In March of this year Dutch William had died and Anne—the last of the House of Stuart—sat on the throne of England. Within two months of her accession, England was at war against her old enemies,

France and Spain—a formidable alliance. Robert shifted uneasily in the big bed: this war, 'twould mean an increase in the demand for sugar. He'd best buy more acres, more slaves—the plantation was a hard master, ever demanding more land, more workers, more hours from him . . . this cursed pain . . . .

All right, he'd obey Jeremy's commands for the moment, but at the first opportunity he'd journey to St. Jago. There was something he *had* to do, something he had put off too long, God trust he had not put it off really too long. Jeremy must be wrong . . . nothing serious . . . and yet . . . .

Charlotte's pale face swam before him, her silver-gray eyes accusing and infinitely sad, and he shut his own to blot the vision out, but she still hung in his mental view, reproachful and pleading, until at last Jeremy's medications took effect and he fell into a deep sleep.

Two days later he rose and dressed just before dawn and made his way quietly to his study, from where he emerged a few minutes later and went stealthily, like a guilty schoolboy, down the inner stairwell, managing to get out of the house and to the stables without anyone in the house being aware of the fact.

"And how is Master Robert today, Venus?" Melissa inquired as she took her morning chocolate from her body slave.

"La, Miss Melissa ma'am, Isaiah cyan' say 'Im say Mas' Robert not in 'im bed when 'im tek up she brekfus."

"Oh no. Seth . . . did you hear?" Melissa pushed aside the chocolate tray and ran to the veranda in her night shift. "Seth, Venus says that Papa Robert has left his room—and Jeremy said—Seth, you must find him and make him rest."

"All right, my love, but back to bed with you. Jeremy also said that *you* need more rest."

He kissed her quietly and was gone, but in half an hour he was back, his face creased into worry lines. "He took a groom with him and left a message that he'd gone to St. Jago. Oh God, *why?* If it was some urgent business I could have gone for him . . . ."

Jeremy looked grave when summoned and told the facts.

"Five days' hard riding to St. Jago, he'll. . . ." He checked his tongue as he caught the anguished looks of Bridget and Melissa. "Seth, can you go after him? You may catch up with him, he's had about six hours' lead, and if he has any sense at all he'll go slowly— if you can't persuade him to return, then for God's sake make him rest frequently, preferably put up for a night or two at Wells, and *insist* that he rests for a few days at St. Jago before attempting the return trip. I'll give you some physic that may help him."

The days dragged slowly by, and from the end of the tenth day Melissa and Bridget kept a constant watch from the landing over the main stairway, from where they could glimpse the beginning of the driveway. But it was not until the evening of the fourteenth day that the three awaited horsemen came into sight. They paced slowly up the long drive, and Seth helped his father from his saddle.

"Papa." Bridget was ready to weep at his safe return. "How are you? We've been so worried . . . ."

He smiled tiredly, "I'm fine . . . a little tired, but Seth took good care of me." Jeremy and Seth made to help him up the steps, but he shook them off. "There is no need, I can manage," he protested, but Jeremy said firmly: "Sir, as your physician, I *insist* on our help and that you immediately go to rest."

"All right . . . but later . . . ."

305

There came the scamper of feet, and eight-year-old Robert came tearing up to his grandfather.

"I'm so glad you're back, Grandpapa . . . it's been so *dull* without you."

"Don't worry Grandpapa, Robert," Melissa chided in her soft voice. "He has to rest after the journey."

Robert gazed down at the earnest, alive face of this child whom he loved above all else in the world, a strange expression in his eyes.

"I'm never too tired for my grandson. Come to my room in about an hour, young Robert, and I'll tell you a story."

Robert waited until Seth and Jeremy had settled him in his room and Melissa and Bridget had fussed about him, taking off his riding boots and plumping up the pillows; he waited until they had all gone and all was quiet, then he took a roll of parchment from his jacket pocket and padded on stockinged feet to his study. His fingers were strangely stiff and he fumbled a little as he probed the intricate carving that released the panel in the wall, but at last it swung smoothly open, and with a sigh of relief he thrust the document into the dark recess. As he pushed the panel into place the pain struck again. . . .

. . . it seemed a hundred times worse than before and he sank helplessly to the floor, clutching feebly at his chest as the agony heightened beyond belief. . . .

"Papa, papa, come quickly . . . oh, quickly. . . ." Young Robert's frightened cries echoed through the Great-house as he hurtled onto his parents' veranda.

"*Robert* . . . control yourself. What is it?"

"Grandpapa . . . he's on the floor and . . . ." The child burst into passionate weeping as Seth and Melissa hurried away.

"Fetch the doctor," Seth called as the house slaves stopped their work to gape.

306

They got Robert to bed, and Jeremy's face was grave as he straightened up.

Robert's lips moved.

"Don't talk, sir, I beg you."

But he tried again, and Seth bent over him to catch the mumbled slurred words.

"Get . . . Philip . . . hurry . . . ."

His head fell back against the pillows, his face contorted in agony. Jeremy held a small goblet to his lips.

"Try to drink this. 'Twill ease the pain."

Gradually, as the physic took effect, the searing pain lessened to a dull ache, his mind grew hazy, he began to have mental visions of incidents from the past. They were so vivid that he seemed physically reliving his life: the dark face of Maria when he first saw her, laughing at his inept attempt to cook. Ann . . . Ann as he had first seen her as a child, as she clung to him when told that he was to marry Charlotte, and her cry of "One day you'll love *me*." And he had, oh gloriously . . . she seemed so close, he breathed the perfume of her hair and felt her soft warm hand on his cheek, her falling tears on his brow. . . . He opened drowsy eyes, and there was Ann by his side, her silver-gray eyes filled with tears and compassion.

"*Ann*—oh my darling, you have come back to me."

"No, 'tis I . . . Sarah."

Ann's face melted and dissolved into Sarah's lovely dark one, her tears falling unchecked. Before he could feel disappointment, he drifted off again and was once more a boy in the vast green expanse of the cane field, the noon sun merciless above, and Jez Davies' whip was about his back . . . what was he saying?

"Weep in the sun, boy, weep for what you were and what you are."

He swirled out of the past and muttered. "Aye, I wept in the sun, many times, but I laughed too, laughed

307

and loved and life was good. . . ." He opened his eyes and slowly focused on Philip by his side, and suddenly the mists of the past swept away.

"Philip . . . dear friend . . . ."

"Don't talk, Rob."

The pain seemed to have gone now, but he was overcome by a feeling of weightlessness, as if his body were drifting on air. He was having difficulty in getting enough breath, though his blue eyes were serene as he said quite clearly: "Seth, get the roll of parchment from the safe. Give it to Philip as soon . . . as . . . *soon.*" He stopped, struggling for breath to continue. Seth put out a restraining hand, but Jeremy said quietly:

"Let him talk, it seems that he has something to say, and it will distress him still further if we try to stop him. There is nothing I can do to save him now."

Seth left his father's side, then returned on silent feet, the parchment in his hands.

Robert nodded weakly.

"Philip . . . read parchment . . . ."

"Yes, Rob, yes."

"Read to *all* . . . as *soon* as I . . . ." The ragged breathing faltered . . . one last gasping attempt, then stopped . . . completely.

Seth handed the parchment to Philip as the sound of weeping grew in the big room, and from outside, as if the news had been conveyed by supernatural means, the high keening wail rose from the waiting slaves.

Philip took the parchment and brushed a hand across his eyes.

"You all heard? . . . He wanted me to read this to you . . . at once."

He looked down at the roll with its big unbroken seal, then up at those grouped about the bed: Melissa, big with child, held fast by Seth's strong arms. Bridget,

308